MW01133587

# Aaron Michael Ritchey

# Machine-Gun Girls

# The Juniper Wars Book Two

Aaron Michael Ritchey

# Copyright

# Dedication

*For Scott. That's my brother, dammit.*

Aaron Michael Ritchey

# Magnificat

*Part of the federal government's responsibility is to secure our borders and provide a stable environment for our citizens to pursue life, liberty, and happiness. The region known as the Juniper is foreign soil. Her grand cities, Denver, Cheyenne, Taos, Salt Lake, Billings, are no more. At best, they are ghost towns from another time. At worst, they are breeding grounds for terrorists and outlaws.*
—President Amanda Swain
50th President of the United States
February 8, 2054, on signing the Security, Identity, and Special Borders Injunction (SISBI)

HOLY MARY, MOTHER OF GOD, HELP ME WITH THIS NEXT part 'cause the truths I had to swallow choked me like a magpie wrestling with carrion too big for her craw.

I'd been plucked from my cozy life in Cleveland, Ohio and thrown back into the Juniper, a place where electricity didn't work and life was cruel. In the U.S., my days had been filled with ease and comfort. Eterna batteries provided perfect energy and science provided a cure for most diseases, including cancer. America was almost a paradise—gun laws and legal systems, peace and happiness. But for the states-turned-territories—

5

Colorado, New Mexico, Utah, Wyoming, and Montana—they'd become a lawless wilderness thrown back two hundred years; the most dangerous place on Earth.

And I'd grown up there. Twelve years of violence and struggle until Mama sent me away to boarding school to learn electrical engineering. She was certain the power would come back on, and she'd need me.

I hadn't wanted to leave. I'd wanted to stay with Mama and my oldest sister, Sharlotte, on the ranch, working cattle and riding horses and carrying guns, 'cause of the Outlaw Warlords.

I can still remember that cold morning I first left home. We stood on the Burlington platform before first light, waiting for the train, a thruway that would take me to Sterling and then on to Cleveland. You couldn't see the sagebrush around us, but you could smell it sleeping.

Mama hugged me for a long time and then let me go. Sharlotte stood cross-armed beside us, she didn't hug me, only gave me a nod and a murmured, "Good luck." Wren didn't even do that. My middle sister, four years older than me and knocking on seventeen, hadn't come home the night before. She wasn't there to say goodbye to me. Not surprising, and kind of a relief.

The train wheezed in, leaking steam and smoke, and chugged off, taking me with it. I only went back once, two years later for Christmas. Wren had already run away, so I didn't see her again, not until she came to get me in Ohio after Mama died of a heart attack, when I was sixteen. By then I was happy in the World, programming apps on my electric slate, watching internet videos, and hanging out with Yankee girls who hadn't grown up loading clips for their mother's M16.

Then Wren came to collect me. Mama was dead and the ranch in trouble. Like it or not I had to go home, and I didn't like it, not one bit.

Wren and I left the westbound train in McCook, in what used to be Nebraska, and we walked the train platform before dawn. It felt like an echo, only this time my home was back in Ohio and the Juniper had become foreign soil.

American laws and Yankee comforts lay behind me, far away and long gone.

Wren and I had to fight our way back to Burlington for my poor mother's funeral. Tore me up to know I'd never hear her sing again. Scared me to death to walk once more on Juniper dirt.

Father Pilate, our close family friend and a Sino-American War vet, buried Mama. We could bury her body, but we couldn't bury her debts. Before she died, Mama went deep into debt, borrowed money to pay for my education all the while waiting for the power to come back. Mama then made a deal with a food distribution company executive who'd pay top dollar for Juniper beef, only she wanted our family to drive the cattle west, across the entire length of the Juniper, from Burlington, Colorado to Wendover, Nevada. What a story it would be. And great stories can bring in even greater profits.

We drove those cattle nearly halfway to Nevada, through outlaws, a blizzard, and a gun battle that left many of us wounded. Along the way we picked up a mysterious boy who I loved and who loved me, but secretly, 'cause wouldn't you know it, but Sharlotte had romantic feelings for him, too. We made up a love triangle of sharp points and sharper edges.

Boys were rare back then, 'cause of the Sterility Epidemic. Wren had wanted to sell him, though of course, we wouldn't let her. If she had known who he really was, well, we wouldn't have been able to stop her.

His real name was only the first truth I learned. Others would follow, like the nature of the army sniffing his trail and why they would do anything to find him.

He wouldn't tell me his whole story, not for a long time, but that mysterious boy carried the future of the world in his pocket like so much spare change.

Yet that's how life is. It's the small things that give it meaning. Or kills us dead. Big dollar bills of tragedy we can handle, but not the pennies and nickels of our daily suffering and doubt.

# Chapter One

*Certainly the Juniper is a dangerous place, but not because of outlaws, rustlers or stray bullets. No, the real dangers are the wind, solitude, and a drifting mind. When in doubt, I stay in my house and count my money. I never get lonely that way.*

—Robert "Dob" Howerter
*Colorado Courier* Interview
August 3, 2057

## (i)

THE CUIUS REGIOS WERE COMING. I DIDN'T KNOW it then, but the Regios were on their way and we didn't have the guns to stop them.

The pain from my gunshot wounds barked like a dog on a distant neighbor's porch. I sat on the floor of the strange room, my back against the bed. I couldn't move. The Christmas issue of *Modern Society* magazine lay on my lap. The perfume of a cologne sample wafted from the glossy pages. Micaiah, cleaned and groomed, smiled at me on the cover.

But his real name wasn't Micaiah. It was Micah Hoyt, son of the richest man on Earth. His father, Tiberius "Tibbs" Hoyt, was CEO and general jackerdan-in-charge of the American Reproduction Knowledge

Initiative, otherwise known as the ARK. Tibbs Hoyt had hired an army to find his son, and we had the bullet wounds to prove it.

The foot soldiers were known as the Cuius Regios, and their commanders were the Vixx sisters, who could heal almost any wound, which sounded suspiciously like genetic engineering, however unlikely. I'd kept an eye on the popular science websites and hadn't seen anything close to creating actual people with enhanced biology.

The idea scared me, scared me deep. How could we fight such a soulless army?

But why would Daddy Hoyt send in troops to retrieve a son who didn't want to be found? Then again, if you give a rich man a cause, he can turn a family feud into a world war.

Before I'd gone unconscious, Micaiah had wanted to run away to protect us. Was he gone? That opened a floodgate of questions. Was Pilate still alive? Had Wren run away for good 'cause of what I'd done to her? And did my oldest sister Sharlotte still have us bound for Wendover, Nevada with our herd of nearly three thousand cattle?

First things first, I slid the magazine underneath the mattress, not sure what I would do with the information, but it felt dangerous in me.

I stood, moved to the window, and used my right arm to pull open the yellow curtains. My left arm throbbed as I held it to my belly. From the second story of the house, I saw our tents below—our chuckwagon dominated the front yard. Mama and I had fixed up the Chevy Workhouse II with an attachable ASI steam engine, and then found a long trailer for it to pull. We called the whole thing our chuckwagon. Next to it sat the old Ford Excelsior that had saved our lives. Cattle and horses meandered around outbuildings, barns, and hay sheds. I recognized a few of our horses—Elvis, Taylor Quick, and Bob D. Two of our best cows, Charles Goodnight and Betty Butter, stood in the strange yard, chewing cud. To my right rose a ridge of pine trees and craggy rock.

I searched the skies for the *Moby Dick*, the zeppelin that we'd hired to re-supply us and scout. There was no sign of it, but then Sketchy, Tech, and Peeperz might still be trying to find us after the blizzard.

Green grass pushed up from wet soil, which meant I'd been unconscious long enough for the snow to melt. Might've been a day. Might've been a week. Someone must've dribbled water into my mouth and then cleaned me up afterwards. Dang, but I hoped it was family that had done the work to keep me alive.

Out of the corner of my eye, something flashed in the distance—sunlight off a cast-off hunk of metal, or some bit of chrome, or a mirror, something, southeast of the house. The blinking stopped. Something didn't feel right about it, but I had other things to worry about.

Like where I was and who owned the house.

### (ii)

Getting to the door took most of the energy out of me. My legs were weak, like frayed rubber bands. My head filled with woozy.

I creaked the door open. Light from my yellow room splashed onto the floor. Shadows clung to the corners of the hallway while the floors gleamed, swept and polished. The wallpaper also didn't have the dust I'd have expected. It had been washed recently, and I could smell the disinfectant. A set of stairs led down. Another set led up. Doors lined both sides of the hall.

"Hello?" I asked.

The door across from me opened.

Backlit, the outline of a tall woman in pants stood in the doorway. For a moment, my eyes played tricks on me. I could've sworn it was my own mother. Could Mama have somehow tricked everyone by faking her own death? If anyone could, it would've been her.

"Mama?" I whispered the question to keep alive my impossible hope.

"Good morning, Cavatica," the woman said. Wasn't Mama. She didn't have Mama's voice nor her walk. When the woman drew nearer, the sunlight showed me both their similarities and their differences. This woman was the same age, same shape, and she had Mama's brown hair going grey. Crow's feet clustered around her eyes like Mama. But instead of the gray shapelessness of a New Morality dress, this woman wore a maroon cowgirl shirt tucked into jeans. A smile brightened her face. She had a musical way of walking, light and joyful. Mama had stomped around, always busy.

"Cavatica, what are you doing up? You need to rest." The woman took me by the arm and helped me back into the bed orbited by medical supplies: pill bottles, bandages, tape, antibiotic cream, and a pair of scissors.

The woman seemed familiar, but how could I know her? How could I know anyone so far west? Unless we'd turned east.

She shined a grin on me. "You don't remember me, do you?"

"I'm sorry, but I don't remember a thing." My voice croaked. I swallowed to get it working.

The woman's smile deepened her wrinkles. "No, I don't mean from just now, I mean from a long time ago. I was friends with your mom. I'm Jenny Bell Scheutz."

My mouth dropped open. Dim, toddler memories filled my head, memories of a tall woman, hard and lean on the outside, but soft in spirit. Jenny Bell. Her and Mama laughing and talking about the old times. Jenny Bell had run cattle with Mama in the early days and then took off into the wilds. We figured she'd been killed.

"Are we in Sterling?" I asked. Sharlotte had threatened to sell our headcount to Mavis Meetchum. That would've been foolish, though, since Mavis couldn't give us a fair market price, not with Dob Howerter breathing down her neck. Even if Mavis could pay us reasonable prices, the three-million-dollar loan to Howerter would still put us in the poor house, and we'd lose the ranch.

And I couldn't allow that. Never. Our ranch was hallowed ground.

Before Ms. Scheutz could respond, I answered my own question. "No, couldn't be. We're too close to the Rocky Mountains. Where am I, Ms. Scheutz?"

"Call me Jenny Bell," she said. "Ms. Scheutz was my mother, only everyone called her Mrs. back in the day." Jenny Bell sat on the bed. "You're in my house— on my ranch—just north of Fort Collins. Officially, we are in June Mai Angel's back yard, but there's not like a state line or anything."

I leaned over and picked up a glass of water, drained half in a blink. The water cooled my throat and got better with every swallow.

Jenny Bell eased the glass out of my hands. She smelled clean and nice, like American deodorant, but how could that be?

"Easy, Cavatica. You were hurt bad. We heard about the stampede and the attack, and how you saved the day with the old Ford out front. It's all a shame, but I guess June Mai was bound to give you some trouble."

Jenny Bell hadn't mentioned the Vixxes nor the Regios. Sharlotte prolly blamed my gunshots on June Mai Angel, and I wondered what my sister had told our people—most likely the same story, or else it might've caused morale problems.

Jenny Bell also hadn't talked about Micaiah, so I'd keep him a secret. I wasn't sure yet if knowing about him would keep her safe or put her in more danger. All along, Micaiah said his true identity was like the apple in the Garden of Eden—one bite would damn us all forever. And I'd eaten the whole thing. Yeah, it did upset my stomach.

"How did I get to be here, Jenny Bell?" I asked, though I couldn't help but feel funny calling her by her first name. Such informality wasn't New Morality, but then her jeans proved neither was she.

"Sharlotte and your people stumbled upon our ranch, and she remembered me, but then she's what, ten years older than you?"

"Eight." I said. Then asked, "What day is it?"

"April 24."

Dang. I'd been unconscious for four days.

"Is Pilate here? Is he dead?" I wanted him to still be alive, so I could yell at him. Yeah, he wore a priest's collar, but he wasn't a priest. He and Petal had come to run security for the cattle drive. But Petal turned out not only to be a sniper, but a doctor, and a drug addict as well. And it was Pilate who had been giving her the Skye6.

"He's here and alive," Jenny Bell said. "He's still unconscious in the room next to yours. Bullets aren't going to stop Pilate. Mark my words, he'll die of old age in a bed surrounded by women weeping over him."

"So you know him?"

"Oh, yeah. Who doesn't know Pilate?"

I felt relieved. Still no mention of Micaiah or Wren, but then Wren was probably gone for good after what I'd done.

"Cavatica, you need to rest." She uncapped a medicine bottle and shook a pill out into my hand. "Let me give you a Vicodin. We have new meds, so don't worry."

I did feel terrible, but I didn't want to break the spell of the moment. Here was a woman who had known my mother, and being so near to her felt like I was connected to the past.

I held the pill, but didn't take it.

Jenny Bell put a soothing hand on my arm. "I'm sorry to hear about your mama, Cavatica. She was the best of women, but stubborn. I tried to get her to come out here with me, but she wanted to stay in Burlington. She thought once the electricity came back on, it would be the gateway to the new Juniper. She could be a hard woman. I never once saw her cry."

I had, but only once. When Daddy died, Mama cried like rainclouds stormed inside her, the agony like lightning, her despair the worst of thunder.

I thought about where Jenny Bell lived. If we were north of Fort Collins, the Wyoming border was only about eighty kilometers away. We'd come a long way, but true halfway remained out of reach.

"Why did you move all the way out here?" I asked.

"No competition, Cavatica. Profits don't go up for small operations, only down. Sooner or later, Howerter or Mavis or even your mother was going to monopolize the whole cattle industry. And to be honest, I wanted to be as far from the World as I could get. The Juniper is special. I saw the opportunity to travel back in time, and I took it. Why not? Probably the last time anyone will ever get to live like it's the nineteenth century. Yeah, life out here isn't easy, but there's a joy in the work and survival."

She didn't try and stuff the words into my ears, but spoke in a comforting, even voice, inviting me into her life.

Suddenly, I loved Jenny Bell Scheutz. "What about June Mai Angel?" I asked.

Her grin turned mischievous. "Well, the Juniper can create friendships out of rainstorms. Or so the saying goes. We can talk more about that later. First, we have to go tell everyone you're awake. Sharlotte will be relieved."

She held out a glass of water, a prompt for me to take the pain pill. I did. My mouth soured at the chalky coating.

"Your mother was funny. She was so sure the electricity would start up again in the Juniper," Jenny Bell said. "From what I understand, that's not going to happen any time soon."

"Prolly not," I said.

Near the start of the Sino-American War, the Chinese nuked Yellowstone. We didn't need to worry much about radiation since the Chinese used a hydrogen bomb and most of the particles were consumed in the blast. The attack, however, caused a flood basalt and an electromagnetic field. Ionized molten iron coming out of the Yellowstone throat disrupted all electrical current and wiped clean hard drives. No one knew how long it would last, only that the Deccan Traps in India, another example of a flood basalt, had erupted for a million years.

We sat quietly, and I spoke to fill the silence. "You know, GE even looked into the problem, and they thought they could create suitable shielding, but they haven't yet. Maggie Jankowksi even looked at it."

Ms. Jankowksi had invented the Eterna battery, and I had a little of the hero worship for her.

"Well, like I said, it's like living in the nineteenth century out here." Jenny Bell stood, stopped, and cocked her head to listen.

At first I didn't hear anything, and then internal combustion engines, a lot of them, and something bigger, roaring closer.

"Do you hear that?" she asked, wonder in her voice.

I nodded even as my throat went dry as dust.

"Those are engines." Her eyes went wide. "Like old-school engines, diesel, not gas, but who on earth has that kind of money?"

I knew, but didn't say.

"Stay here," Jenny Bell said sharply. Her simple, easy style was gone, and what was left was hard. Had to be hard as stone to live way out here.

"Yes, ma'am," I wheezed, trying to suck in breath through my fear.

She left without another word.

The Regios had found us. No Wren. No Pilate. And who knew if Petal was in any shape to shoot?

And where was Micaiah? They were coming for him.

### (iii)

I got out of bed, too full of adrenaline and Vicodin to feel my gunshot wounds. At the window, I watched as dozens of black ATVs rolled into the front yard of Scheutz ranch. Four black Humvees followed, and dozens of troops piled out. All the women carried AZ3 rifles. All wore sagebrush camouflage uniforms. All looked furious and focused.

At least fifty soldiers closed ranks in the yard. Jenny Bell and Sharlotte rushed over to talk to them, but those soldiers weren't there to chat. A blink later, my sister and our host had their hands zip-tied behind their backs.

Floorboards creaked outside the door, which sent my heart rate spiking and stole the air from my lungs.

I expected one of the three remaining Vixx sisters to come barreling in, but no, Micaiah, pale and sweaty, stepped into the room. I covered my chest, feeling naked, and with how thin the nightgown was, well, that wasn't much of a stretch.

He rushed over. "The guns. The ammunition. You have to help me hide Pilate's quad cannon and Petal's Mauser. They are going to search the place, and those weapons might implicate us in the battle that destroyed those other units. Sharlotte is going to hide the AZ3s, or at least try."

"What about you?" I asked.

"And yeah, I have to hide, too. I can't run, not yet. They'd find me, and I can't … can't …" he blinked sweat out of his eyes. His boy smell, fueled by fear and running, came off him strong.

The truth was easy to see. If he gave himself up, they'd leave us alone. But he couldn't. Why, I didn't know. But I'd chosen to believe him. He was on some kind of quest, and I was going to help him, though a stupidly rich boy like that shouldn't need anyone's help.

No time for me to tell him I knew he was Tibbs Hoyt's son.

"Follow me," I said. We hurried out of my yellow room and into the gloomy room next door. It took a minute for my eyes to adjust. A shape lay in the bed, tall and lean. Pilate. Next to the bed, Petal slept in an overstuffed lazy boy filling the corner. She was a wispy, ghostly woman, pale, with frizzy, mousy-brown hair and a face like a teenage girl, though the years and the Sino had cut wrinkles across her skin.

She didn't wake up, even though Micaiah and I weren't being quiet. We knew why. Her drug, Skye6, kept her under.

Micaiah opened the closet and grabbed Petal's sniper rifle and a Mossberg & Sons G203 quad cannon, otherwise known as a Beijing Homewrecker. Pilate's gun—part shotgun and part grenade launcher.

I took the sniper rifle from him while he shouldered on Pilate's bandolier of ammunition. We sped out into the hallway.

I was back in the thick of it, fighting, running, trying to breathe. My heartbeat thudded in my ears. The Vicodin dizzied my head a little, but mostly the pill squelched the pain.

"Basement or attic," Micaiah whispered.

"Attic," I said. Going down the steps seemed like tempting fate.

We climbed the stairs to the very top of the house, into the attic, which overflowed with furniture, boxes, antique this and that. A hutch and mirror set towered over the very back of the room. A mothball stench fogged up the dusty air that tickled my nose. There seemed to be a hundred places to hide and none at all. Once the Regios busted into the house, they'd search and search well for their quarry.

Then I saw it. A string dangled down from a trapdoor in the ceiling. It would be cramped up in the crawlspace, but better than nothing. And if we could move the hutch under the trapdoor, they might not notice.

He watched where my eyes went. He ran for the string, pulled it down, and a ladder unfolded itself down to the floor. He clambered up, and I handed him up the rifle, the Beijing Homewrecker, and the bandolier. I folded the ladder halfway and let it ease up a little. Micaiah kept it open to watch me.

I took hold of the hutch—it was big, and I was hurt, but I had to move it.

I threw my weight against it. Nothing happened.

"Hurry, Cavvy."

I tried again, and the huge piece of furniture scratched across the floor, but came to a halt. The thing teetered.

If it crashed, the whole house would hear it. I struggled to keep it upright.

"Careful," Micaiah hissed from the attic.

Panic fueled me. I mustered every bit of *shakti* I had and shoved it again. Screeching, scratching, the hutch moved under the ladder. It would have to be good enough.

But what if someone saw the ripped-up floor? I stacked boxes to cover the scratches and said a prayer.

"Go, Cavvy. Get back to your room."

The spring-loaded ladder folded the rest of the way into the ceiling.

I was out of time, but Micaiah's hiding place didn't seem secure. If they found him, what would happen to him? To us?

*Please, God, please help us.*

I tiptoed down the steps and back into the yellow room.

Nausea struck me all at once. I seriously came close to barfing up my guts on the floor.

Back in bed, I wanted to check my wounds, to see if I was bleeding again, but I didn't have the chance.

Three Regios threw open the door and stormed into my room, AZ3s lowered.

"Anyone else in the house?" one roared the question.

"Next door," I squeaked. Sweat dripped down my face. I knew I looked flushed, but I hoped they'd blame it on a fever.

Another Regio spun. "Stay here."

I wasn't sure if she was talking to me or the other two, but all three of us stayed while she bashed into the room next door.

The house shook from tromping boots and slamming doors. Heavy footfalls sounded in the room above me in the attic. Furniture or boxes scraped across the floor. I prayed with all my might that they didn't see the scratches in the floor or the trapdoor above the hutch.

"What do y'all want?" I asked the two soldiers. Shaved heads, dead eyes, they held rifles across their chests and stood stiffly by the door. They stared straight ahead. Might as well have been statues.

Time ticked by. I couldn't stop sweating. The house shook from yells and stomping, but so far, there hadn't been any gunfire.

A Regio stuck her head in the room. "Two suspects in the room next door. We couldn't wake the man. We have the woman. The Praetor wants you to bring this girl downstairs." She motioned at me.

The two guards took me, none too gently, out of the room. My nightgown ripped treacherously. I was driven down the steps and into the parlor with my sister, the rest of our team, Jenny Bell, and her many daughters.

Jenny Bell's ranch house had become a prison, complete with armed guards and a warden.

# Chapter Two

*We take security at the ARK very seriously. How could we not? The financial ramifications of our work are nothing compared to our work preserving the genetic diversity necessary for humanity to continue to evolve.*

—Tiberius "Tibbs" Hoyt
President and CEO of the
American Reproduction Knowledge Initiative
January 1, 2058

## (i)

IN THE SCHEUTZ'S PARLOR, SOFAS LINED ONE WALL and dining room chairs lined the other, leaving an open aisle between the two sides. The Regios shoved me into one of the chairs.

Across from me, Sharlotte gave me a long stare, and I returned it. She had my same straw-colored hair, a round face like our mother, but with Wren's exotic dark eyes, which they both got from Daddy. All of Sharlotte's pretty languished in her dark-lashed, nighttime eyes.

We didn't dare speak. Regios and their guns surrounded us. They watched their leader as she paced back and forth in an angry silence. Dark-skinned, shaved head, the woman walked on thick legs, sturdy and strong. Eyes the color of wet pine searched our faces—the twelve of us from the Weller party and the eight of the Scheutz family.

Nikki Breeze and Tenisha Keys, two of our employees, sat close together, hands brushing. I'd learned they were *gillian*, as in same sex love. They took comfort being close to one another, but subtly 'cause of the New Morality. Sweat painted their dark faces.

Not sure how I felt about them and that *gillian* love. I'd heard enough sermons on that kind of sinfulness to make me wonder.

The Regios had left Pilate in his bed, but Petal sat crumpled on a couch. Her eyes were sunken blue jewels lost in the ink around her eyes. She looked pale and as fragile as ever, though she was our last warrior still standing.

Finally, the woman in charge spoke. "I am Praetor Gianna Edger. I am looking for a boy."

That word, praetor, seemed familiar. I couldn't place it though, and I couldn't Google it either. My tablet was long gone and would've been destroyed by the Yellowstone electromagnetic field anyway.

"We told you," Sharlotte said. "Not a lot of boys out here on account of the Sterility Epidemic. We ain't seen none. Any males this far into the Juniper are either killed by the Psycho Princess or sold by June Mai Angel."

All of that was true. The medical community couldn't figure out the problem, but only one out of ten births resulted in a boy. Of those males born, ninety percent were sterile. Worldwide. The first cases of the Sterility Epidemic were reported after the Yellowstone Knockout, but both geophysicists and geneticists agreed that the one hadn't caused the other.

Edger shifted her gaze to Jenny Bell. Jenny Bell echoed my sister, "We told you, the closest boys are in Sterling."

"This boy." Edger thrust a picture into Jenny Bell's face.

"We've not seen him. We've not seen any boys out here."

"Pass the picture around," Edger said. "I will interview you all alone, youngest to oldest. Who here is the youngest?"

A couple of Jenny Bell's daughters raised their hands, trembling. One was single digits; one was middle school age. Who was the next oldest?

Maybe Crete, otherwise known as Lucretia Macaby, who sat trembling. Tears stained her face. From my conversation with Jenny Bell, I figured the Scheutz's were in the dark about Micaiah. But Crete knew. And she looked about to crack right there and spill her guts all over her shoes.

If she did that, I knew what would happen, they'd torture us until I told them about the crawl space above the attic, half hidden by the hutch.

"I'm fifteen," one of the Scheutz girls said.

"I'm seventeen," another said. She glanced over at the oldest sister, who looked remarkably like Pilate. Couldn't say I was surprised.

"I'm sixteen," Crete said. She started sobbing, eyes closed, shoulders shuddering.

"Me, too," I threw in. Dang, but I couldn't remember Crete's birthday.

Edger's dark eyes reached into me. I didn't know if it would be better to bow before that gaze or to meet it.

I met it and didn't look away. Maybe it was the Vicodin, or maybe I channeled Wren, but I was going to show her we had nothing to hide.

Only we did. We had everything to hide. And somehow, she knew it.

"Legate Baxter, get birthdays," Edger said, turned, and stalked up the stairs.

Baxter marched over to Crete. "When were you born?"

I ripped Crete apart with my eyes. I needed to talk to Edger first. She needed to know we were going to keep Micaiah a secret.

"November 17, 2041," Crete whispered.

No, Crete had a summer birthday. I never remembered eating a cupcake in her honor during our time in elementary school. Good, I was glad she was lying 'cause she'd have to do a lot more of it.

Baxter pounded over to me. *Legate. Praetor.* Both words itched at my brain.

"You?"

"October 7, 2041," I said. The truth.

That settled it. I'd be the first of the Wellers to be interrogated. Aunt Bea would go last. She was a large Mexican woman, not like Aunt Bea in that old black and white video, but big and wide, smiling with gaps in her teeth. She served as our cook, and I'd grown up eating her homemade tortillas and green chili.

She gave a laugh when she said her birthday. "Do you also want to know how much I weigh?"

A few of us let out a whispery snicker. Baxter frowned like she was close to hauling poor Aunt Bea out to a firing squad. They had the guns for it.

"Are you really fifty-five, Bea? I thought you were my age," Dolly Day Cornpone chirped. She was forty, but life had aged her cruelly. She'd been running cattle for a decade or more, and you could see every bad night on her wrinkled face. She liked to drink and didn't much care for baths, so she was stinky and boozy and had a big mouth.

Crete might cave, but I also had my doubts about Dolly Day. She'd given us trouble before.

"Don't worry," I said. "This'll go quick. We don't know a thing." The picture of Micaiah came to me, and I gave it a long look, and it was Micah Hoyt all right, a color photograph of him in a city somewhere. I lifted up the picture. "If we did see someone as good-looking as this guy, I'm sure we'd have remembered it."

More nervous chuckles.

"No talking," Baxter snapped. "Absolutely no talking."

"Will you shoot us?" I asked. "I've already been shot, you know. June Mai Angel and her soldiers attacked us to get our cattle, and I took two bullets getting away from them. So did Pilate upstairs. And how come you're only interrogating us girls? You sexist?" Wren wasn't around, so someone needed to be a smart aleck.

Baxter slapped me. She did a good job of it. My head rocked back; my cheek stung, but prolly didn't sting as much as it would've 'cause of the Vicodin in my belly.

"No. Talking." She emphasized each word.

"Good thing we ain't seen the boy," I said back. "Seems to me you wouldn't leave anyone alive here if we had."

She slapped me again, harder. Stars exploded, shaking my vision. Then she hit me a third time.

I leaned forward and forced tears out of my eyes. I let them fall on the picture.

*I'll give you my tears, Micaiah. I'll give you my blood if it comes to that. For your quest. For you. No matter what.*

I handed the picture on down the line. Sharlotte caught my eye, and we both nodded, but only slightly, secretively. I'd given us all a basic story. June Mai shot us up. We didn't know about any boy. And even if we did, we had to keep him a secret or we'd be killed.

My sister and I were risking our lives to protect the boy we both loved. It filled me with an odd combination of pride and guilt. We were going to save him, but then what?

How could I tell Sharlotte that Micaiah wanted me and not her? Then again, I'd made it clear if he couldn't be completely honest with me, I couldn't be with him. Not romantically. But that was going to be a hard promise to keep.

I did love him. Loved him deep.

The first three Scheutz girls were interviewed first. Then came my turn.

### (ii)

The Regios herded me up the stairs to the attic. They'd cleared a space, found a desk, and put me in front of it in an old folding chair. The trapdoor looked horribly exposed under the hutch. So far, they hadn't moved the boxes, or they'd have seen the scratches. Dang.

Two soldiers stood by the top of the staircase with their rifles over their chests. Edger sat behind the desk on an office chair. On the top of the desk rested a black-handled Betty knife and 9 mm Smith & Wesson full automatic pistol with an extended clip. Lots of bullets in there.

Edger had the sleeves of her shirt rolled up to reveal a strip of EMAT on her left arm. Emergency Medical Adhesive Tape. What kind of drug was she giving herself? Had she been wounded?

A terrible thought struck me. What if she'd been at the office building fight? What if she knew all about us and this was some kind of tricky piece of horrific theater?

No. Couldn't be. I'd stick with the story I'd told the crew downstairs.

"Sit." She barked.

I sat.

She turned the gun so the barrel pointed at me. Theatrics. I thought of how Wren had tried to intimidate my principal back in Cleveland. If only Wren had been there, but she was gone.

More guilt. Another rock for me to swallow.

"Talk." A single word from Edger. Renee Vixx hadn't been chatty either, but at least Edger seemed human enough—harsh and sharp, but human. The one Vixx sister we'd fought had been a snake wearing a human suit.

"What's a Praetor?" I asked. Still couldn't remember where I'd heard that before. Knew I wouldn't get an answer, but I had to try.

"Have you seen the boy in the picture?"

"No."

"We discovered the remains of a gun battle in an office complex in what used to be Broomfield. Many of our soldiers were killed. Do you know anything about that?"

I knew everything about it. I'd been there.

"Look," I said, "we ran into June Mai Angel's girls in Denver. We got shot up and ran away north. I passed out in a mall, prolly in Boulder, and I woke up here. That's all I know."

"You are Cavatica Weller. You are on a cattle drive to Nevada to save your ranch in Burlington. Is that correct?"

I nodded. The stink of my own sweat assaulted my senses.

"The boy we are looking for was shot down in a zeppelin by Strasburg, in the Colorado territory. Your cattle drive went through Strasburg, is that correct?"

"Along I-70, yeah, but we didn't see any boy or see any zeppelin crash."

She stared, unblinking. "In Strasburg we found empty shell casings. We found .45 caliber shells. We found .338 Ostrobothnia magnums. We found twelve-gauge shotgun shells, and we found the remnants of twenty-millimeter grenades. Similar ammunition was used in Broomfield, at the office complex. The evidence is clear. Your team used your guns in Strasburg, and you used them in Broomfield. Where is the boy?"

Every word she said pounded a steel spike into my spine. She was close to sniffing us out, and she knew it. I kept myself steady. Everything depended on it.

"Where are the guns?" I asked. "If we have .45s, shotguns, and whatever that other thing you said, well, you'd find us packing them. But I don't think we have any of those. We have MG21s, sure. It was standard issue in the Sino, so there are a ton of those around. And my sister has an old M16 that might fire twenty-millimeter grenades, but I'm not sure. I don't know much about guns."

If I was going to lie, might as well lie big.

Edger got really quiet. My body vibrated in the silence. Thank God Micaiah had thought for us to hide the guns. He was there, only a few meters above me, listening. Or maybe he'd found a way out and run off. That was hard to think on.

I closed my eyes. "I ain't feeling too well," I murmured. "I don't know about a boy or any kind of gun battle with you people. We're just on our way to Nevada. We stopped over at the Scheutz's since they knew our Mama. That's all I know. I guess if you're gonna beat on me, you better get to it."

Silence.

I waited.

Edger spoke. "It seems convenient that we find you and the man, both injured from a gun battle, and recently."

I shrugged. "Welcome to the Juniper. It's a hard place."

More silence. I thought I heard something shift in the attic above us, but it might've been my imagination. I prayed it was.

"We will continue to question you," Edger said. "We do not believe you are innocent."

Soldiers took me toward the steps.

Before I could stop myself, I glanced over at the hutch. Long scratches marred the floor, only partially covered by a cardboard box. They looked fresh. We were in trouble.

Back in the yellow room, I lay on the bed, facing the wall, wondering what Crete was telling Edger. Or Dolly Day. Some of our people, like Tenisha Keys and Nikki Breeze were family, but others we'd hired. Would they give up Micaiah out of fear? Or what if Edger started offering huge sums of money?

Or what if Edger noticed the marks on the floor? One glance up, she'd see the trapdoor, and all of our lies would be exposed.

My worried mind fought my exhausted body until, finally, my brain gave in and I slept. I woke up hours later.

The guard was gone. The light dimmed in the window, getting ready for dark. Cooking noises drifted up from downstairs, the tap of spoons on pans, shuffling sounds of dishes, and the slam of cupboard doors. Those familiar sounds made me ache for when I'd listen to Aunt Bea or Mama cooking on our ranch in Burlington. But my childhood was gone, gone forever.

I sat up in bed.

"Good," a voice said. "You're awake."

My sister Sharlotte rocked herself in the chair in the corner. "You and me have to talk," she said quietly.

We had plenty to talk about, but I knew we'd circle around until we landed on one topic in particular.

Micaiah.

I wasn't going to talk with Sharlotte about Micaiah, not about who he was, where he was, and not about his feelings for me. Sharlotte had been hurt enough.

The highways through the Juniper are paved with good intentions. All of them lead straight to hell.

### (iii)

Sharlotte leaned forward in the rocking chair. Afternoon light lit up the dust in the air, but her cowgirl hat shadowed her eyes.

"Where's Edger and the other Regios?" I asked from my bed.

"Outside. They've created a perimeter. We are all confined to the house while they wait for the Vixxes to come. So far, I think everyone told them the same story."

I let out a long breath. "I was worried about Crete and Dolly Day."

"So far, so good," Sharlotte said. "But we're not out of this yet. We're going to be taken in for questioning again and again even before the Vixxes get here. Only a matter of time before one of us starts singing like a spring robin."

Yeah, it was. And when the Vixxes came? Edger might not have the stomach to torture us, but I'd stared into the rattlesnake eyes of Micaiah's aunts, and I knew they'd have no problem chopping off our fingers to get us to talk.

"What about our headcount?" I asked.

"We let them loose on the open range. Jenny Bell says there's still enough barbed wire left in the country so they can't get far. And since it's spring, and after that snowstorm, there's enough for them to drink. Our cattle are fine. Wish we could say the same for ourselves."

"Do our people know about the Vixxes?" I asked.

Sharlotte shook her head. "I got the full story from Petal, but we both agreed … it's best that our people think it was June Mai's girls that shot y'all up."

"Good."

My sister went on. "We had three AZ3s, but I had Nikki and Tenisha bury them. Along with the extra ammo Petal and Pilate had for their guns. Wren kept her own stash with her, and we don't have any other .45s with us. Thank God. Our boy knew exactly how to keep it all a secret."

Of course he did.

We sat in a heavy quiet for a long time.

She finally spoke. "I need to know about you and Micaiah."

My insides twisted. What could I say?

Sharlotte took off her hat and held it in her hands. "I need to know where he is and how much you know."

I was going to play dumb on that. The less anyone knew about Micaiah the better.

My mind raced to find words, but my head was full of cotton from the long sleep and the medication.

"I know you have feelings for him," Sharlotte said. "Wren told me she found you and him kissing in the mini-van during that first attack. And then after you found us at the mall, he was real distant toward me. While you were unconscious, he barely said two words to me. Something changed, and it has everything to do with your time alone together." Her next words came out like a whip crack. "That's fine."

No, it wasn't. Not by the tone of her voice.

She paused, then said forcefully, "But now is not the time for romance. He came in to get Petal and Pilate's guns. Did he come in here?"

I shook my head. The lie strangled me. I wondered if Micaiah felt like that when he played around with the truth. "I don't know where he is," I said softly.

"He's gone then," Sharlotte said.

"I'm sorry. I know how you felt about him as well. I saw it."

Sharlotte had to unclamp her jaws to speak "You saw it, and still, first thing you did was run off with him. But then you're used to always getting what you want."

"Not now." I couldn't get a deep breath. "We can't fight about him now. He's gone."

Sharlotte's grip on her hat turned into a white-knuckled vise. "Of course he's gone. We were both stupid, so stupid to think a rich boy would ever let himself love girls like us; Juniper girls, not worth a dime. Now he's gone, and we're in a mess."

"I didn't run off with him." An oily anger was wanting to slide down into me, but I fought it. "There was the attack and the stampede, and I didn't plan any of it. I was going to let you have him."

"You were going to," my sister said, "but you didn't. 'Cause you're selfish. Tell me the truth. It don't matter now, but you kissed him, didn't you? Even after you saw how much he liked me, you kissed him, and you loved him, didn't you? And he loved you back."

"No. He was yours." My own words surprised me, but when you start lying, stopping can be a problem.

"Don't lie to me!" Sharlotte snapped like a bear trap. "He told you this big story about being on some kind of quest, about getting him to Nevada so he can tell us the truth and give us six million dollars. And you believed every word."

"That's right," I hissed, the anger taking over. "You did, too, or else you'd have told Edger about him. So don't be a hypocrite. And don't you call me a liar. Let's just drop it. It's done. He's gone, and we have to figure a way out of this."

Sharlotte's own rage forced her to her feet. "There is no way out. We were doomed to fail from the start. All 'cause Mama died at the worst possible time. And here we are, paying for her mistakes. All her many mistakes. Power coming back on in the Juniper. Stupid. Mistake one. Borrowing money from Howerter. Another stupid mistake. Then she sends you to that expensive school, and then she signed paper for us to get our headcount to Nevada when it can't be done. All mistakes. So let the Vixxes come and murder us all. It don't matter. When I'm dead, I'll really tell Mama how stupid she was."

The optimism she'd had in the Boulder mall was gone, and she paraded her despair around like she was proud of it.

I huffed in fury, but I kept my voice low. "You take that back. Mama wasn't stupid. It wasn't her fault she died."

Sharlotte came over and leaned into my face. "Tell me the truth. We might die, but I want to know it for sure. I want the truth about you and Micaiah."

I looked her full in the eyes, and all my promises to spare her went right out the window. I wanted to hurt her. I wanted the truth to cut her throat for what she'd said about our dead mother. "Micaiah and I kissed, and he loves me, and he's just playing you 'cause you're in charge and he was afraid you'd let Wren sell him, or that you'd send him away to die. But all that changed, didn't it? Now, you don't care about the Regios, our cattle drive, or anything. All you want is revenge for not getting him."

Sharlotte raised a fist. If I hadn't been lying in a bed, she would've clocked me. Instead, she whirled around and made for the door.

"That's right," I said, "that's what you do, right? You turn your back on me and run 'cause you can't deal with things."

Sharlotte stopped and talked to me over her shoulder, in a voice dangerously quiet. "I can't deal with things? *I* can't?"

Uh oh, I'd said the wrong thing.

Rage trembled through her body. "Who dealt with Mama while you and Wren were gone? Who got us on the road? Who has had to make the hard decisions, over and over? Me. Over and over. Even now. Everyone is looking at me to get us out of this mess, and I ain't got a clue."

I was speechless.

Sharlotte turned to face me full on. Her face was stony—eyes, cheeks, mouth rock hard. "We were fools to think Micaiah cared about either one of us. He played us both, and now he's run off. Well, good. A liar-boy like that isn't worth our love."

An awful lump filled my throat. Micaiah did play fast and easy with the truth. All along, I hadn't known if he was the apple, promising forbidden knowledge, or the snake in the garden, full of evil lies. When I was with him, I believed him. When he was gone, I had my doubts. Which is how it all works when the truth has been stomped under foot and lays like a worm in the dirt.

She saw my confusion. "Yeah, that's right. I'm sure his kisses were sweet, but he's gone and his six-million-dollar reward is gone with him. Good. Prolly just another lie, anyway."

Sharlotte's mouth twisted smaller. "And maybe we won't be able to escape, but maybe dying here wouldn't be so bad." Her anger was leaving now, but the sorrow that remained hurt my heart.

Her hand snaked into the pocket of her New Morality dress, fiddling with what was inside. I heard paper rustle.

"What do you have in your pocket, Shar?"

Instead of answering, she hit me with a non sequitur. "Jenny Bell's daughters … the older ones look like Pilate. Like her oldest, Zenobia, she looks exactly like Pilate."

"Is ignoring my questions like a hobby for you?" I asked it lightly, as a joke.

"It doesn't matter," Sharlotte said. "What I have doesn't matter, not in the long run, I don't think."

Instead of leaving, she sat down. Surprised me.

We sat for a long time, not talking. Why hadn't she left?

Sharlotte took in a deep breath and asked, "Do you know why you care so much about the ranch?"

"Why?"

"You got to leave it," she said, "and leaving things makes them special. Whenever I think about our ranch, I feel cold and hollow, hateful. We need to pay off our loans to Howerter, and it makes financial sense to keep the land, but I don't think I'll ever be able to live there again. I'm sorry I got mean. You're right. Fighting about Micaiah doesn't make sense now."

"I'm sorry too, Shar. About everything." About all my lies of omission and commission. Of what I had done and what I'd failed to do. Me purposefully trying to hurt her. Not telling her about Micaiah in the attic.

Sharlotte sniffled and took a handkerchief out of the pocket of her New Morality dress and blew her nose. "Here we are, trapped in this house, and I'm coming down with a cold. Doesn't feel fair."

She smiled at me. Kind of shy and embarrassed.

I smiled back, glad she could forgive me. She took my hand. Another surprise. Who was this new girl? What was happening to my sister?

"So, Cavvy, what are we going to do?"

"Wait, Shar, and pray for a miracle."

"I can wait," she said. "Don't have much of a choice there. But I'm too empty to pray. Losing Mama made me lose myself, I think. I feel so empty inside. Empty. Lost. So hollow that when the wind blows, it blows right through me, and I'm left cold." She patted my leg, then got up and left the room. Her pretty, tragic words stayed.

I wondered about Micaiah. We'd have to do something to save him. And then what? How would Sharlotte and I deal with having the boy back with us?

I didn't know.

We ate a silent meal in the parlor that night, all twenty of us, barely talking. We could see the fires of the Regios outside. Every window showed the guards around us, waiting for the Vixxes to come.

Then the real interrogations would start. And the torture.

We had to get out of there. I didn't have a plan, but I was hoping that Micaiah did. I planned on asking him later that night.

If he was still in the attic.

If I could move the hutch without waking up the entire house.

# Chapter Three

*The Juniper tests us, but God didn't create the Juniper to find our weaknesses. God did it so we could find our strengths.*

—Mavis Meetchum
*Colorado Courier* Interview
August 4, 2032

## (i)

BEFORE I WENT TO BED, I GUZZLED A TON OF water with my pain medication. Drinking water before bedtime was an old trick to make sure I woke up in the middle of the night. Sure, enough, a little after two in the morning, I got out of bed and used the toilet. Then I tiptoed down the hallway to the steps.

A murmur came from one of the rooms, but it wasn't talking, too low and muffled. I froze. Waited.

The murmuring stopped. Prolly a Scheutz girl, stressed out and talking in her sleep.

Poor Jenny Bell, it felt like I was betraying her, but what would happen if she knew about Micaiah? What would she say? What could she do?

It was a variable I didn't want to consider in my already messy equations. In the parlor downstairs, Dolly Day snored like a Cargador with a boiler about to blow.

I moved up the stairs to the attic room, walking on the edges 'cause everyone knows the center of stairs squeak.

A board squealed under my foot nonetheless. Made me stop and listen. Every noise seemed like it would bring all of Jenny Bell's daughters, if not the woman herself, barreling out to search for who was walking around. After a while, though, when nothing happened, I thought it might be safe and kept on creeping upward.

In the attic, the windows glowed from moonlight, creating dragons and ghosts out of the furniture. The room was how Edger had left it—the desk, the chairs, the whole interrogation chamber. I moved on the pads of my feet, soft as a mouse, 'cause the Scheutzes were asleep directly below. That mothball smell reminded me of cleaning out closets with Mama. She'd pull out an old box, and then always said the same thing. "Why do I keep this stuff? Well, salvage monkeys make great pack rats."

I'd always laughed. Monkeys and rats and Mama.

The windows showed the Regios fires silhouetting the soldiers on guard. The ranch was a prison, all right, and there wasn't any kind of escape I could see.

First things first, moving the hutch. I silently cleared boxes away. Four long scratches marked up the floor. I couldn't shove the hutch again, too loud. Then, abruptly, another memory rose up in me, from when I was little—nine or ten years old at most.

Mama had run our house not as a general, but as a president. Sharlotte was her general, and I'd grown up following her orders. Wren, though, Wren loved to be treasonous. Sisters trying to raise sisters was a bad setup, but Mama was busy running the ranch and doing a million other things, so Shar took up the slack.

When Mama told Sharlotte it was time for spring cleaning, Sharlotte handed down the orders. I got to work. Wren went off on a horse to raise hell out on the plains, which left me alone, which wasn't so bad, 'cause I liked to work and Wren would only complicate things. However, I was left to move our big china cabinet by myself. I remembered standing in front of the massive piece of furniture, wondering how I'd ever be able to push it back from the wall so I could clean it.

Aunt Bea found me like that, staring at the china cabinet, pondering. It was Bea who showed me how to slide an old fleece blanket under the legs, so we could slide it across the floor.

When Sharlotte came down to check on my progress, she'd nodded in approval. The china cabinet had been moved, I was cleaning behind it, and all was right with the world. Until Wren came in, muddy boots leaving tracks on the floor I'd cleaned. Which led to yelling and fighting.

And Mama, gone most of the time, not able or not wanting to referee the fighting and quiet the yelling.

All those old thoughts and feelings made me miss the ranch, and once more, I couldn't imagine losing it. Yes, it hadn't been easy growing up there, but it was home, good or bad, and the nostalgia for it felt both rich and right.

But first, we had to get out of our current predicament before we could continue the task of saving our home by selling the cattle in Nevada.

In the Scheutz attic, I found two thick blankets, one for the back legs and one for the front.

My breathing shallowed; scared I'd make noise and scared of the pain. My wounds stiffened and throbbed, but I managed to get the blankets under the feet of the hutch. It slid easily, noiselessly across the floor. If only I'd used the blankets the first time.

A pull on the string brought the collapsible ladder down, and I carefully, silently, rested the bottom feet on the floor. I climbed up the rungs, wincing at the pain.

Micaiah didn't whisper or warn. Nothing.

My heart turned to wood in my chest. If he was gone, it would make things simpler in a lot of ways, but I didn't want a simple life. I wanted him.

I pulled myself up into the crawl space by one of the struts holding up the ceiling. Not sure how wide the space was, 'cause my eyes strained in the blackness. A little light glowed down the way. I crawled off the ladder and onto dusty, grimy wood. Something brushed me, and at first I thought it was a spider, but then I reached out and touched plastic. It seemed like bedding, maybe winter blankets, wrapped in plastic for storage. The musty smell of ancient insulation filled the dusty air.

"Cavatica?" Micaiah whispered.

"Yeah, it's me." A little spark of joy lit me up.

On my hands and knees, I eased over to him, reaching out until I could feel his jeans. Light spilled in from a square of screen where the attic fan had been. Of course it'd been removed, since after the Yellowstone Knockout it wouldn't have worked.

I got closer. He'd made a little bed of blankets, taken from the plastic. Petal's sniper rifle and Pilate's Beijing Homewrecker lay next to him against the wall. I drew up close, right next to the screen, so we could see each other in a silvery light.

"You okay?" I asked.

"Yeah, but I'm not sure for how much longer. God, it's so good to see you." He bent forward to kiss me, and I pressed him gently back.

"Sorry, Micaiah, I can't. Not now." I thought back to my conversation with Sharlotte and how hurt she'd been. And I'd wanted to hurt her more. Shame on me.

Sharlotte aside, I'd made it clear, I needed him to be truthful before I could be with him. I believed in his quest, but that didn't mean we needed to get all kissy and sweaty.

Still, even in the nothing bit of light, such love filled his eyes. Like always, his dirty blond hair was just long enough to be perfect. A few wisps hung over his eyes. His lips swelled so full, red, and kissable.

No, once we reached Nevada, and once he could tell me everything, then I could kiss him again. Until then, he'd have to be okay holding my hand. But his touch was dangerous. It had melted my resolve before.

"I should've left," Micaiah said with a sigh so strong I felt his breath on my cheek. "I listened to Praetor Edger, interrogating you all, talking about the shell casings they found in Strasburg and Broomfield, and it killed me. Dolly Day got mean and nasty, and Crete cried until she couldn't talk, and they were all so scared. And it's all because of me. I'm so sorry. I'm so, so sorry."

I felt my forehead crinkle at the sound of his guilt and sorrow. "It's okay. We'll make it okay. But what's a Praetor?"

"The ARK armies use the old Roman military system … praetors, legates, that sort of thing."

"That's right," I whispered. "I'd forgotten. History class feels like a long time ago."

He dropped his head. "I was going to take off after we met up with Sharlotte at the mall, but I couldn't leave without knowing you'd be okay. And to be honest, I'm afraid I won't be able to get to Nevada without help."

I couldn't stop myself. I took his hand in mine. "We want to help you. I believe in you."

Another long sigh. "After everything that's happened? Really?"

"Yeah," I said. "We'll figure this all out. Not sure what we'll do, but we'll get through this together."

He raised his eyes to take me in. "I'm just thankful you don't know anything about me, not really."

I'd lied to my sister. No way was I going to lie to Micaiah. "But I do. I know who you are, now, Micah Hoyt."

Everything, and I mean everything, changed in a second. He jerked his hand away, his lips tightened, and I could hear his sharp gasp. "No. You can't know. How? *How?*"

He didn't raise his voice, but those last two words came out harsh.

My mouth went dry. "Under the bed, I found a *Modern Society* magazine. You were on the cover."

He clenched both hands into fists and his eyes squeezed shut. "No. Now you're dead. You're all dead. I've killed you."

His words scared me, but I missed his hand in mine. I missed how we were before. It was gone. What would remain?

I generally talk when I don't know what else to do. Not sure where I picked up that particular genetic trait since Wren and Sharlotte and Mama wouldn't say two words if they didn't have to. "Okay, I know who you are, now. What does this change? How is that going to kill me?"

"No one can know," he whispered. His eyes were open, but he was looking past me into some kind of horrible place. "If they think you know who I am, they'll kill you to keep you quiet. Because you might know other things."

I shivered. I'd been right about the Regios murdering us to keep us quiet.

"I won't tell anyone, especially not Edger. And I won't treat you any differently."

"You will." Micaiah slapped a hand across his eyes. "How can you not? Now I'm not just some mysterious rich boy. I'm *the* mysterious rich boy. And I know you, Cavatica, you'll start making connections. I'm the son of Tibbs Hoyt. That, right there, is the secret of me. The son. You can't …" His voice failed him. "You can't think too much about this … about me, or why my father wants me. Okay?"

It all came down to that. Why would his father send in a squadron of highly trained soldiers using a fortune in diesel to retrieve his son? Especially when that son didn't want to be retrieved. The Vixxes and the Regios certainly didn't seem like they were on a rescue mission.

It was like he could hear me thinking. "Don't, Cavatica. Don't."

"The apple again," I said, sighing. "But, Micaiah, I already know so much."

"But not everything," he said firmly. "You're still in Eden, whether you know it or not."

"I don't think there are soldiers and interrogation rooms in Eden," I said quietly.

"Still." He wasn't reaching for my hand. He'd tried to kiss me before, but now seemed distant. Maybe I wasn't the problem. Maybe he couldn't handle me knowing the truth.

"So should I call you Micah or Micaiah?" I asked.

"Micaiah," he answered immediately. "You don't want to know Micah Hoyt. He was bad, limited, damaged. Who I am in the Juniper? Micaiah? He's okay. Not perfect, but far better."

Before I could say another word, he reached out and touched my cheek. "I love having you here, but you need to leave. It's too dangerous. For you. For everyone in this house."

"You'll need food and water," I said softly. "And a jar for, you know, stuff." A blush warmed my cheeks.

"Eventually," he said, "but I should be okay for a bit. Water is the main problem. I'll go and get a drink now, with you, and then I'll come back. I should be good until tomorrow night."

"Edger is going to stay until the Vixxes get here."

"I know." He swallowed hard. "People will die, Cavvy, if we don't figure a way out. The Vixxes will do anything to get the truth. They aren't above torture. They aren't … human."

That little bit of truth wasn't hyperbole. I'd watched Renee Vixx get shot through the heart then the throat and keep on fighting. They weren't human, but then what were they? Micaiah wasn't going to tell me, not if he thought it would put me in danger. Made me love him and hate him at the same time.

"Well, we'll just have to outwit them. I'll come up with a plan." Ha, that was a laugh. My head was empty.

"We probably have until the day after tomorrow," Micaiah said. "I would imagine it would take a day for a Regio scout to reach them, and a day for them to reach us."

And just like that, he started up a doomsday clock. Thirty-six hours until the end of the world.

*Think, Cavatica Weller, think.*

### (ii)

We snuck down through the house. Micaiah used the bathroom, drank a bunch of water, and returned to his hiding place at the top of the house. I slid the hutch back into place, thinking about Anne Frank and the Nazis. We'd read her diary in school, and here I was, living out the book.

I hoped our story had a better ending.

After the hutch was in place, I slid the blankets out from under the hutch and folded them. I stacked the boxes back around the hutch. This time, I made sure all the scratch marks were covered.

I crept back to the yellow room and got back in bed.

My gunshot wounds ached, so I took another pain pill, as prescribed by Petal, who knew all about drugs and pain. I tossed around in the bed, got too hot, got too cold, my head running like a demon on fire. I'd given up all hope of finding sleep, but somehow, sleep found me.

I woke up with sunshine making that yellow room glow.

My mind immediately came to life again, the fire demon clawing and chewing on the problem of the Regios and the doomsday countdown. Guards surrounded us. Micaiah lay trapped up in the attic. Pilate was out of commission. Wren was gone. Petal? She couldn't go up against those hard soldier girls alone, and besides, she'd started to crack from only half-doses of the Skye6.

The only plan I had required suicide. If one or more of us went up into the attic and used the guns there, we might create enough of a distraction for everyone else to run.

But whoever did the shooting would certainly die, and Jenny Bell's house might be blown to bits. No, there had to be another way. I had to come up with a better plan.

I thought and thought until it felt like my head might pop right off my shoulders.

Staying in bed wasn't going to help me. Normally, I would've taken off on a pony and ridden until my head came up with a solution, but Edger wasn't about to let me leave.

Well, no matter what I did, I couldn't do it dressed in a nightgown. I got up and went to the closet. There I found clothes—a silver-buttoned red cowgirl shirt and a pair of jeans. A shelf unit held several pairs of Nferno socks still in the wrapper and even some underwear and brassieres, also new by the look of them. How could Jenny Bell have new underwear lying around? I recalled the smell of her deodorant, quite fancy, way out west.

My old New Morality dress also hung there in the closet on a wire hanger. It had been washed, stitched.

Jeans or the dress?

Who did I want to be?

I held up the jeans. Should I put them on? What kind of person would that make me? I knew the girl who wore the dress. That girl had been young, in some ways innocent, in a lot of ways naïve.

I'd liked her all right, but I wasn't her anymore.

Then I laughed. The jeans, the dress, were only clothes. Jenny Bell wore jeans, and she was a good, kind woman.

Still, putting on the denim felt like risking hellfire. I put them on. They didn't cling flirty like the tight jeans Wren had forced me into back in Cleveland when we were running from the cops. Nope. The jeans fit nicely. The brassiere was a little snug but new and not frayed like my old one.

I gazed at myself in the mirror on the back of the door. Did it for a long time. The cattle drive had thinned out my face. My brown eyes stared back at me, big and watering. It wasn't that I thought I was pretty; it went deeper than that. I felt powerful, smart, and looked gunslinger cool. I had survived things other people hadn't, and I had a boy who liked kissing me. Well, at least I thought he did. He sure did get all moany.

I felt powerful, not from the clothes, not from the boy, but from who I was and who I was becoming.

I knew, right then, even in jeans, Mama would've been proud of me. I knew she had been with me during the hard parts, and she'd continue to guide me. Sharlotte was horribly wrong, hating Mama like she did.

I checked the right pocket of the New Morality dress and searched for the .45 caliber bullet, the one I'd retrieved after I'd pointed our family's M16 at Wren to keep her from beating the truth out of Micaiah. She'd been drunk. That didn't make me feel any less guilty.

The bullet was gone. Not surprising. It could've fallen out in the wash, or maybe it had tumbled out when I was unconscious. I didn't think much of it.

I did feel bad, though—losing such a memento. If anything was symbolic of my sister, it was a bullet.

The smell of coffee drifted up from downstairs.

From a room next door, Pilate's voice rang out. "Hey, if there's coffee, can someone get this old ex-drunk a cup of Joe before he dies?"

Pilate, awake, alive, it felt like Christmas for a minute. Then I remembered Petal, the drugs, and the part Pilate played in keeping her addicted. Yeah, it felt like Christmas, but I wanted to kill Santa Claus.

### (iii)

I waited in my room while Jenny Bell, her daughters, and some of our people made a big fuss over Pilate. They loudly congratulated him on being alive, then murmured about the Regios outside. No doubt they mentioned the shell casings Edger found and her theories.

When he was alone, I went out into the hall and threw open the door. Petal was sleeping in a chair—not sleeping, drugged, now that I knew the truth.

I barged in and got right to it. "Okay, before we talk about the Regios outside and how we're gonna deal with 'em, you and I need to have it out. You kept Petal hooked on Skye6. Don't even try denying it."

Pilate sat on the bed in a white t-shirt with a blanket over his lap. His regular clothes lay patched, laundered, and folded on top of the dresser. Guess Jenny Bell didn't have extra men's clothes lying around.

Pilate smiled up at me. His thick dark hair was long, like always, but I could see the line in his scalp where Renee Vixx's bullet had nearly lobotomized him. Dark whiskers crept up his cheeks. I'd never seen him with such a full beard. I didn't like it, and I didn't like him, not anymore.

"Oh, Cavvy," he said, "it's so good to see you. It's so good to still be alive and breathing."

I didn't say a word.

He finally answered my initial question with a smirk, "Yes, Skye6, that's her medicine. There's a great deal of synthetic morphine going through the Juniper. It's the drug of choice for your typical outlaw skank, to quote Wren. You didn't tell Petal what the medicine was, did you?"

"No, she figured it out, but I think she must've known all along. How can you keep giving it to her like it's okay? Like drugs ain't evil?" I stood there trying to glare him to death.

His smart aleck smile left him all at once. He sighed. "How can I? How can I not? You think you're free once you fight your way out of hell? Well, it doesn't work that way. When Satan claws his way into your heart, sometimes you can't get him out, no matter what you do." Another sigh that ended in a horrible, wheezing cough. Wet. Deep.

Took him awhile to get his breath so he could finish. "Hell is in Petal. It crawled in during the Battle of the Hutongs, and it's taken root. We've tried the church. We've tried twelve-step programs, talk therapy, electroshock therapy. We've tried stews of psychotropic drugs, soups of anti-psychotics, teas and broths and compresses of every root, herb, and chemical known to science and superstition. And the only thing that helps, the only thing, is the Skye6. Go ahead and hate me for doing it, but I would hate me more if I didn't. For some people, there is no other side to their pain. There is only hell."

Before I knew it, my voice had become a vicious hiss. "According to who? You? I bet you told her there was no other side for her. How can you take away hope from people? And I saw Wren going into your tent, and I know about Betsy and all those other women. I know you ain't no real priest, the way you tricked that soldier girl in Strasburg into running by quoting scripture. And you ruined Mama's funeral with your atheism. Where's your goddamn faith?" I cursed and didn't apologize. I was wiping away tears as fast as I could cry them. If we hadn't been surrounded by the enemy, I'd have screamed at him.

Pilate sat on his bed, face in his hands, not saying a word. And this was Pilate, who loved talking like he loved cigars and coffee.

"Well, say something," I said.

He looked up at me. He was so gaunt now. The light had gone out in his eyes. Like a dog, whipped for no reason by a cruel master.

"Say something, dammit," I said again.

He swallowed and rattled off another deep cough.

"I'm sorry," he whispered. "Sorrier than most." He shut his eyes, then clenched his teeth and growled, "But you have no idea what you're talking about. You're young and stupid, and you think life is all going to come together like a paint-by-numbers picture of rainbows and unicorns."

"I don't think that," I said, but I didn't sound very convincing. I wanted to hate on him some more, but he looked brutalized.

"And here we are, once again," he said. "The enemy is at the gate, and we are outnumbered and outgunned, and it's all turned to crapjack. And the only thing that might save us would be how well we can shoot. All of us. Petal included. But in order to shoot, she'll need her medicine."

"I can't." When Petal talked, we both jumped.

"Sorry," she whispered, "but I can't wait until we reach Nevada to stop. Before the Regios came, Micaiah put me on a schedule to wean me off slowly." She paused, took in a deep breath, and went on. "First, do no harm. I'm not going to harm myself anymore. And I'm not going to harm anyone else. No more shooting. No more drugs. No more rhymes."

Once again, even if Micaiah and the truth had trouble getting along, my boy showed me how wonderful he could be by helping Petal get clean.

However, I didn't want her to give up killing until after we figured out a way through Edger. I knew it was selfish, but Pilate was right. We needed every gun we could get.

Petal got up and crawled onto the bed so Pilate could hold her. He did, gripping her hard. His jaw muscles tightened.

Petal whispered, "I'm gonna find my other side, Pilate. I'm gonna find it even though you don't think I can."

He didn't say anything else 'cause Petal had said the truth about him. Though his shirt folded on the rocking chair had a priest's collar, he was a man who had lost his faith.

I should've pitied him. I couldn't.

The tromp and clatter of troops entering the house ended our conversation. Edger appeared in the door.

"You." She pointed a finger at me. She held out her hand. The .45-caliber bullet I'd had in my pocket sat like Judas Iscariot's corpse in her palm.

I must've turned white as death 'cause she smiled at me.

"Bring them all outside," Edger said.

Regios poured into the room.

# Chapter Four

*I wouldn't call the women who keep the ARK safe mercenaries or soldiers. I prefer the term security advisors.*

—Tiberius "Tibbs" Hoyt
President and CEO of the ARK
January 1, 2058

## (i)

REGIOS USHERED US OUT OF THE RANCH HOUSE. My mind squirmed. How could I explain the bullet?

Edger had made it clear, the .45-caliber ammunition matched the make and model of the other shells she'd found in Strasburg and Broomfield. In the police dramas my friend Anjushri Rawat had loved, they were always matching bullets.

Pilate stumbled and sank to his knees in the yard. The blanket and T–shirt covered his top half, but his bare legs showed pale white in the bright sunshine. He'd just come out of a sick bed and his muscles were still weak. I knew the feeling.

Pilate squinted up at Edger. "I'm sure the fine people at Winchester would be honored you think so highly of their ammunition. Perhaps, instead of torturing us, you could write them a kind letter."

"Explain this!" Edger barked. She wasn't looking at Pilate. She was looking at me. Petal stood by my side, but she had retreated into herself, a mouse standing on two booted feet.

"It's a Winchester .45 caliber bullet." When in doubt, play dumb. "I'm sure there are lots around."

"We found it in your dress."

Dumb wasn't working. I had no other answers. All my cunning was nowhere to be found.

Pilate laughed. "So you're going to kill us over one bullet? Come on. Kind of thin, don't you think? Do you know how many bullets Winchester has made over the years? Enough to finance that creepy house in California."

"Shut up!" Edger kept her eyes on me.

"I don't shut up well." Pilate laughed. "Just ask God. He thought making me a priest might keep me quiet, but that didn't work too well. Now I'm always in His ear, but let me tell you, that Johnson can ignore me like nobody's business."

"Shut him up," Edger said.

Two Regios rushed forward. One slammed a foot into Pilate, driving him onto his belly. The other stepped on the back of his neck and pressed her rifle into the back of his head.

Like that was going to stop Pilate from joking. "Oh, you mean I should shut up. Okay, no more, not a peep out of me. Shut up, shutting up."

"Stop." Both Petal and I said it at the same time.

It was time for either the truth or tears. I wasn't going to give them skanks a thing, so I burst into well-timed tears.

Edger wasn't impressed. "Explain the bullet. Now. Or we kill Pilate."

Of course they knew his name. Everyone knew Pilate, in one way or another.

I couldn't. No lie seemed good enough.

"Hey, there, ladies!"

All heads turned. Wren Weller came striding out from behind the house, leading Christina Pink by her reins. Wren walked steadily, almost jauntily, boots, jeans, vest, and long dark hair that hung dirty and limp across her back. A dark-green wool poncho covered her from her shoulders down to her hips, hiding her pistols. She pushed her cowgirl hat back to reveal a face deeply tanned where it wasn't bruised blue from her encounter with Renee Vixx. Wren's eyes were as dark as ever, full thick lashes, and perfect, though her face had thinned some. Even bruised, hungry-looking, and sun-roasted, she was gorgeous.

Instinctively, the dozens of Regios pointed their guns at her. They were right to. They were just lucky Wren was talking and not shooting.

But why wasn't she? And if they searched her, they would find a lot more Winchester .45 caliber bullets and her twin Colt Terminators.

"Who are you?" Edger asked.

"Prodigal daughter," Wren said, then spit into the dust. "But no fatted calf for me. Can't eat too much beef and keep trim. But you don't care about that. Or me."

"Who are you?" Edger shouted.

I sniffled at my tears and muttered, "She's my sister. She's been out scouting," Fear scrambled my stomach. We weren't out of danger just yet. If only we'd been able to get word to Wren about her guns.

"That's right," Wren said amiably. "Three Weller sisters. The good, the bad, and the ugly. I'm the bad one."

Well, dang, that meant Sharlotte and I would be drawing straws for ugly.

Wren went on. "About twenty klicks from here, there are a whole lot of your girls shot to crapperjack. You think we done it. Makes sense, since my little sister over there and Father Pilate both got holes in 'em. But if you check the bodies of your posse, you'll know they were hit yesterday or the day before, and me and my family have been here for days."

"Search her."

Wren threw back her poncho. She wasn't wearing her twin .45 Colt Terminators with the cherrywood grips. Her hips were bare of anything but swell and denim.

They also went through Christina Pink's saddlebags and came up empty. They found a couple MG21 assault rifles we'd pulled off June Mai Angel's outlaws. But no pistols.

"Where are the bodies?" Edger asked. "Tell me exactly."

Wren did.

"Have you seen a blond boy in a blue silk shirt, jeans, boots?" Edger asked.

"No," Wren said. "Ain't no boys out here."

Edger frowned. Then addressed me. "Where did you get this bullet?"

"From me," Wren said. "It was my lucky bullet. What's the big deal?"

Edger explained her theories.

Wren laughed. "Good luck finding out who shot up your troops. If you think one bullet is the answer, then I feel sorry for you."

Edger wasn't laughing. In a quick flash she was up in Wren's face. "What about you and your people? Maybe you killed them."

"Me? Alone? Do you really think I'd stand a chance against a unit of your soldiers? I counted twelve bodies. Tracks led south to Denver. You want revenge, your best bet is June Mai Angel." Wren didn't back off a bit. I knew she'd done it. I knew that while I'd been unconscious, she'd tracked those last Regios on their ATVs and killed them all. Her alone.

Edger threw the cursed bullet at my sister who caught it easily. Wren grinned, as if she didn't have a thing to hide.

The Regio officers and Edger all conferred while we were shoved back into the house.

Pilate sank heavily into a chair, coughing like it would kill him. Petal couldn't do much but hold him while his lungs convulsed.

Wren stood at the door, looking out through the window.

I sidled up next to her. "Thank God you came when you did."

"God don't care about me, Cavvy," Wren said. "And you don't either. So don't get friendly."

Her words cut me.

Sharlotte joined us. Three Weller sisters. I would let Sharlotte be the good one, and I'd take ugly. Sure, just as long as we were alive and together.

"Do you think they bought your story?" Sharlotte asked.

"Prolly," Wren muttered. "They don't have a clue about me or what I can do. Stupid skanks. They're tough. I'll give 'em that. I'd have gone up against that Edger *kutia* and her girls, but there were a whole bunch of them, and they had you chicken-cooped up in here. I didn't want to see any of you shot up." She paused. Frowned. "First time I ever tried to talk my way out of a fight. Don't like it."

We watched as Edger gathered up her troops. They packed up, piled back into the Humvees, and sped off, the trucks, the ATVs, the whole contingent. They didn't tell us why they left, and they didn't leave anyone behind. That we could see.

I glanced over at Wren, my eyes full of questions.

"Either that's really good news," she said, "or it's really bad."

I had a memory of running from the police in Cleveland. Wren had gotten us out of the fix, at first, until the policewomen came back with a vengeance.

Jenny Bell let out a long sigh. We could hear it across the room. "Thank God. They're gone. Wren, thank you for saving us."

My sister shrugged. "Saved us for a minute. Maybe. They could've left people behind, or they might be back. It's not like we can outrun them, not with three thousand cows." She turned her eyes on me. She wanted to know what had happened to Micaiah.

I shrugged.

"What about the Vixx sisters?" Sharlotte asked. "If Edger is right, they'll be coming tomorrow sometime."

No one had an answer to that. But like Wren had said, how fast could we run with three thousand cows?

"I hid my pistols," Wren said after a bit. "I figured they were piecing together what happened along the way. Now, I have to go fetch 'em. Feel naked without my holsters."

She pushed out of the front door and strode down the steps and into the sunlight. She rode off on Christina Pink.

I slumped against the door. My wounds, the pain, the stress, all hit me at once.

"We should leave," Sharlotte said. Her nose was red from her cold, and I knew she was drinking hot toddies to keep it at bay. That wasn't really drinking, not really. Doctors might as well write a prescription for it— tea, a little liquor, and some honey; take as needed.

Pilate started up another round of coughing and before I knew it, I was on the floor. We were too busted up to be going anywhere.

## (ii)

Wren didn't come back. I didn't think she'd try and go after Edger and the fifty of her soldiers, but with my sister, it was hard to tell.

I found myself in the yellow room again, bored out of my skull. Jenny Bell had plenty of books, but most were westerns or romances. She did have a few of the Gertrude Goodpenny novels, but everyone had at least one of the *Wayward Wizardess* series even in the Juniper.

I wasn't much for fiction, but I did find an ASI 3.0.3 manual and a thick overview of the modern train. Everyone frowned me back into bed. I was to rest while they all recovered from being prisoners. And of course, our animals needed to be managed. While the miles of barbed wire still strung across the plains might keep them relatively clustered together, cows had a way of wandering far. I knew Breeze and Keys would be out on ponies to check on them.

Sure, they get to ride out under a bright blue sky, and I was stuck inside, reading over the old ASI 3.0.3 manual, going over schematics. It was more funny than technical. I laughed every time the writers tried to tell me how wonderful the technology was when I knew for a fact the 3.0.3 was real buggy. I'd been lucky to get the Ford Excelsior running after our fight at the office complex.

The modern train book was both fascinating and fun. I'd studied the mechanisms before and how to convert the engine from using steam to using Eterna batteries.

The books kept me distracted some, but my mind would always go back to churning over Micaiah, the Regios, and the Vixxes. We didn't know for sure they'd come for us. Maybe once they found the bodies of the unit Wren had killed, they'd head south and tangle with June Mai Angel's troops. I prayed for that to happen, but we just didn't know, and even if we left, they'd catch us easily.

I got tired of worrying about the Vixxes coming, so I switched to obsessing about the long kilometers ahead of us. Sharlotte might not care about the ranch, but I did, and I was going to get us to Nevada, all of us,

Micaiah included. We had to save the ranch. My daddy, Mama, and my dead baby sisters were buried there. It was sacred ground.

And if we couldn't get our cows to Nevada, we'd need the reward money Micaiah promised.

I snuck him jerky, biscuits, an old Gas 'n' Sip travel mug of water and an empty mason jar. We didn't talk. I stuck it up in the attic and retreated back to bed before anyone caught me. More thoughts of Anne Frank filled my head.

Downstairs everyone was planning, thinking, wondering what we should do. Let them talk. I needed to get on a horse, clear my head, and come up with a plan.

By mid-afternoon, I was feeling better, but I had to get out of the house. What started out as nice yellow accents to the room eventually would drive me insane if I had to stay one more minute looking at them.

I dressed in the jeans and cowgirl shirt, then carried my boots out into the hall and down the steps. Had to sneak or everyone would've raised a fit.

I made it outside, stayed hidden, and strapped a saddle on Bob D. I was a little worried about leaving alone, but I promised myself I wouldn't go far. Even without the Regios sniffing around, the territory wasn't safe. I was in the Juniper. Safety was a gamble, and if you lived in fear, you might as well live in a hole.

That wasn't how my mama raised me, God rest her soul.

In the end, though, I prolly should've taken a gun with me.

**(iii)**

I managed to get my horse out of the corral without anyone seeing. The heavy scent of Bob D brought back a million memories, most good. I loved horses, everything about them, including their smell. I thought about trying to get Micaiah out of the house, but what if the Regios were watching? Better to wait until after dark.

Thinking about him made me consider his secrets. He was the son of Tibbs Hoyt. I tried not to draw connections, but I couldn't help myself.

Micaiah had run away. Why would Hoyt kill to get his son back? No, something else was going on. But what?

I found an off switch to my thoughts. I'd done enough thinking trapped inside. I rejoiced in the wide blue sky above me, the endless horizon, and the strong horse next to me. I couldn't wait to ride off across the plains, spring green and bees buzzing.

I led Bob D away by his reins, and he kept hurrying up to nuzzle me, to whicker softly, to let me know how much he loved me. Tears sprang to my eyes. If only Micaiah could've been like a horse, open and forthcoming, but he wasn't. Thank God for animals. I swear, they were so much easier than dealing with people, even cantankerous horses like Puff Daddy and Christina Pink.

When I was a fair distance away, I shoved a boot into the stirrup and saddled up, wincing at the stiffness of my gunshot wounds. But moving helped ease the healing itch. I got Bob D going, charging across the plain, leaping over tangles of brush, swooshing through the greening grasses, streaking across the gray dirt. The sun baked my shoulders, warm and nice, and I took in a huge breath of fresh air, perfumed by the sage. I felt like I'd been released from prison. Our guards were gone, and I had a horse under me, feeling the strain of his muscles, the rough hide, the leather tack creaking. For a minute, I was glad to be in the Juniper. Easy to be happy right then 'cause no one was shooting at me.

I rode Bob D until Jenny's Bell's house was only a small red box behind me, and then I stopped to let my pony catch his breath. I'd gone far enough. Around me stretched the plains, so familiar—the sage, the house, even the few clumps of Herefords I saw in the distance. While Herefords are known for their red bodies and white faces, from a distance they look black.

Sitting astride my horse, I breathed in the leather of the saddle and watched cattle amble across the wide plains in front of a house rising like a citadel above the scrub. Every part of me felt at home for a second. This was what I was made to do. This was my destiny.

A great peace settled into my spirit. I knew we'd make it to Nevada, and I knew we'd return to our ranch house in Burlington, rich and victorious, and with the resources to gather up another herd and maybe do it all again.

Bob D tossed his mane and nickered. He wanted to run more, and so we did, until we found a little creek in a gulley below the edge of the plain—a good place to lie low for a minute. The path down to the water had been trampled into a tangle of muddy hoofprints. Most likely our own cows had come here to drink. Dead cottonwood skeletons, trunks thick and gray, surrounded us. I sat on the old wood while Bob D drank. I lifted my face to the sunshine and sighed.

A stick snapped behind me. I wasn't alone.

## (iv)

I whirled to my feet.

Wren stood on a broken limb. Christina Pink meandered behind her. The pony nosed at some grass as if we humans didn't matter a bit.

Wren and I spent several long moments looking at each other, not saying a word. Was she glad to see me? I couldn't tell. As ever, Wren's face showed no feeling except for a shallow little smirk which could mean anything. None of it prolly any good. She slouched a little, her right hand resting on the Colt Terminator holstered at her hip. Bullets filled both belts, the one for her right holster and the one for the left. I wasn't sure where she had hidden her guns, but they were back on her, tied around her thighs.

What should I say to her? Thank her for saving us? Apologize for pointing a gun at her? Maybe. Prolly. But seeing her, I remembered who she was and how violence trailed her like a bad stink. I couldn't have watched her beat the truth out of Micaiah, though it did make a certain amount of sense.

She bent, picked up the bone-white cottonwood branch, and threw it at me. I ducked.

Wren's smirk grew cruel. "If I'd been an unfriendly, you'd be on the ground right now with my Betty knife in your throat. You bring a gun on your little trip, Princess?"

I shook my head slowly. Her being there, throwing stuff and reminding me of my stupidity, completely unnerved me.

"You glad to see me again?" she asked. She kept her lips together when she talked, to hide the teeth she'd lost when she fought the Vixx. I'd seen Wren cry twice. Once when Pilate hugged her. And once over her vanity.

Was I glad to see her again? Not sure.

"Surprised to see me?" she asked.

"Definitely," I whispered.

"Wondering why I came back after what you did?"

I nodded slowly.

Wren spit into the dust. "There are two rules in life. I learned them from a bad man I fell in love with during my time in the circus. You wanna hear 'em, Princess?"

"Don't call me that," I said. I'd already been fighting with everyone—Sharlotte, Pilate, Edger—if Wren wanted a battle, I'd give her one. She'd beat me, but I was feeling tired enough and hopeless enough to go up against her one more time.

Wren talked on like I'd never said a word. "He told me to never let your heart get in the way of a paycheck, and always, always, always, hit 'em right between the eyes. I ain't never been a part of this goddamn family, not really, and I never will. That's fine. But at the end of the road is a big paycheck. Ten million dollars for our headcount and another six if your boy ain't too much of a liar. Where is he?"

"Not sure," I said.

"Uh huh," Wren said, clearly unconvinced. "Anyway, my heart wants me to put as much distance between me and you as I can, but I will not let it get in the way of a sixteen-million-dollar paycheck. Not never."

"That's a double-negative," I said. I couldn't hit Wren with my fists, and I didn't have a gun, but I could hurt her in other ways. "If you'd stayed in school, you might not sound like such a hillbilly."

She frowned and spit again. "It wasn't my goddamn grammar that saved your asses time and again. It was my guns and my fight, which I learned by bleeding. Like I said on the *Moby Dick*, you got your education, and I got mine. Maybe both are just what this cattle drive needs to get us through." She paused. "You hurt me, pointing that gun at me. Don't do it again."

"Or what?" I asked.

She stepped closer to me, eyeing me. I eyed her back. What did I have to lose?

"Or maybe I won't be able to forgive you next time. Maybe I'll let my heart decide such a paycheck ain't worth it. You need me. You need what I can do. So don't be stupid. Besides, I thought you were a Christian."

"You've never cared about that." Getting Wren to church on Sundays had been one of the forgotten labors of Hercules. Still, she'd admitted I'd hurt her, which was one of the forgotten miracles of Jesus.

"Good to see Pilate ain't dead," Wren said. "I was worried. I was around even before the Regios got here, but I couldn't get a bead on Pilate in Jenny Bell's house. Didn't see no fresh graves neither."

"That's a triple negative," I said in a whisper.

"Whatever," Wren said. "I watched your boy until he went into the house and didn't come out. That was the day you woke up and the Regios came. I hung out, watching, trying to figure out what I should do. Them pulling Pilate out forced my hand. Oh, well."

"Why'd you stay away so long?" I asked harshly.

She answered me just as rough. "For being smart you sure are stupid. You know anything about strategy? If I'd been there from the start, I couldn't have shown up to help provide you an alibi. Jesus, Cavvy, think."

"You could've checked in with us and then left."

"Why? You hate me. So quit pretending you don't. All you hypocrites. You hate me until it's gun time, then you're all real grateful. Like how I just got you out of this last jam. After the blizzard, I found that unit of Regios chasing us. I found 'em. I got 'em. They kept coming after me, and I kept shooting, while the bodies piled around me. It was a party ..." her eyes went away in the memories. "Such a party. A good fight, maybe my best ever." She talked about it like it was a date and the boy she loved had taken her dancing. Wren didn't want love out of this world, she wanted mayhem, and she got it. Which was the only reason she came back to us. She was far more interested in shooting people right between the eyes than she'd ever be in a paycheck.

She leveled her gaze at me. "They're tough skanks, Cavvy, and if they get us all together, we won't survive it. I didn't like spying on you, and I don't like being out here, sleeping hard, but it's better I'm out here alone watching over you."

She waited for me to reply, but I couldn't find the words. My anger had faded, and I was feeling bad. I needed to tell her I was glad she was alive, that she'd found us, and that I appreciated her watching over us, but I couldn't.

"That boy tell you anything more about the Vixxes?" Wren asked.

I shook my head.

71

"His whole talk about the Vixxes being his aunties is a load of crapperjack. I know you and Sharlotte love him, but that boy is bad business, and if it weren't for the money he's promising, I'd grab him and sell him off. Get two hundred thousand dollars, easy."

She could do it, sell another human being like he was a prize bull, collect the money, and not look back. Even though I'd known her my entire life, Wren had always been such a stranger. I swallowed hard. Tears crept into my eyes. Seeing Wren again was sad. She made everything so difficult. Right then, I wanted her gone. God forgive me, but she was too hard to handle.

"He still in the house?" Wren asked.

I gave her a long shrug and nothing else.

She didn't press me. What she knew or didn't, I couldn't tell, but once again, only me knowing the truth felt like I was keeping her safe. I wonder if Micaiah felt that way when he kept his own secrets to himself.

"I should be getting back," I whispered. "I'm not feeling well. They said I should've stayed in bed, but I got bored."

"Yeah, we got shot up back at that office complex, but we heal," Wren said. "We Wellers always heal real good." Her eyes went to the ground, and she stood aloof, awkward it seemed.

Guilt stung me. I was being mean, and I needed to be kind. What would Jesus do with someone like Wren? Not sit sullenly or say mean things. I needed to reach out, but with Wren, too often when you reached out, she bit you.

Could I take her bite? I could. I'd spent the first part of my life with her teeth in me.

It was all so exhausting. Why was family so much work?

I wanted to be back in bed, eating chicken noodle soup, and reading about modern trains, but I couldn't give in to my selfishness. I had to invite Wren back into the fold. She'd questioned my Catholicism, and surely, I needed to do the Christian thing. "Wren, come to the house and be with us for a bit. Just for dinner. Then you can come back out here and do what you do so well."

Wren dropped her head. Her cowgirl hat covered her face, and her raven-dark hair hung stringy and filthy over the muted colors of the wool poncho.

I remembered what Pilate had said a lifetime ago in our bathroom after the funeral when I'd spent the night throwing up. He'd said that Wren was afraid of being a part of our family 'cause no matter how hard she tried, she always brought chaos with her.

"Maybe this time will be different." I approached her like a spooked horse and slowly slid my hand into hers. Both our hands were hard, calloused to leather, but hers were softer, to my surprise.

I expected her to strike me or cuss me or march off to streak across the plain on Christina Pink.

She didn't. She raised her head but didn't catch my eyes. She looked off across the grass, mussed by the wind. The shake of the sagebrush brought the sweet smell of home to us both. Only for her, it didn't seem sweet.

"Different? No, it'll be the same." Wren cleared her throat. "They have showers in the house?"

"Yeah."

Wren patted my hand with her other. "You did real fine with the truck, Cavvy. Real fine. I'm even glad you went to that fancy school, and I never thought I'd say such a thing." She sighed then pulled away.

"I'm sorry for pointing the gun at you," I whispered.

"I accept your apology, Cavvy, but you be careful with that boy. He's pulled us all into trouble deep."

I nodded. She was right.

Wren fished out of her jeans the .45 caliber bullet that had almost got us caught. "You keep this, Cavvy. In memory of me."

I didn't like how she said it, as if she were quoting Jesus from the Last Supper.

Before I could say a thing, my sister grabbed ahold of Christina Pink roughly, finding her role to play again, always so tough. "You know I stepped on that stick on purpose, right?" she asked.

"Hadn't really considered it."

"Jesus, Cavvy, you have to be more careful and a lot smarter." She grinned at herself, showing her ruined teeth. "And maybe I'll work on my grammar."

I had to smile, too. "You don't have to. Your education has saved us again and again." Yes, Wren was a horror show, a wreck of a woman, and yet she played the gunslinging hero so well.

Wren saddled up. "Remember that when you talk crapperjack about me behind my back." She dug her heels into Christina Pink, and instead of going up the slow steady rise, she went right up the ridge, straight up, with her mare squealing, fighting, afraid she'd stumble.

She didn't. Wren wouldn't have allowed it. She knew all about taking the hard way out.

She cleared the top of the ridge, and Christina Pink's hooves pounded the ground back toward Jenny

Bell's ranch. A dozen of our Herefords took to running away from her, spooked by her speed and the vibrations on the ground.

I closed my eyes and let out a long breath. Wren might save her worst sins for her family, but more and more, I was seeing I did, too.

### (v)

Back in the yellow room, the bed looked like a prison cot, so I sat by the window. I drew back the lace curtains and watched our cattle, our horses, our people. I felt such love for them, and I was glad Wren was with us. With Petal done shooting, we'd need every bit of Wren's awful education to see us through.

Kitchen noises from below relaxed me again. They were so familiar, so much like home, like when Mama was still alive.

I was dozing when a knock came at the door.

"Come in," I said.

Pilate stood in the doorway, a little sheepish. We hadn't said two words to each other since our fight. "I heard you went MIA even though the Regios are dying to find us in a lie and kill us all. Not very bright, but I won't try to parent you. That ship has sailed." He colored some, cleared his throat, and went on. "Not sure if you've heard the news, but Wren finally returned with her pistols and her sweet disposition."

"Yeah, I know."

The light from the window had grown soft with evening. I'd slept all afternoon in the chair, and I was feeling lazy enough to want more.

From downstairs a voice shouted up at us. "Cavvy! Pilate! Dinnertime!" It was Sharlotte, yelling. She sounded drunk. That couldn't be though. Yeah, she'd been sipping on hot toddies, but Sharlotte drunk? Might as well call Sally Browne Burke a *besharam besiya*.

"Sounds like a party," he murmured.

"Sounds like trouble," I said.

We were both right, but I was righter.

# Chapter Five

*Ladies in Waiting—that's what we call the brave women who were stranded in China, but we have all been waiting, waiting for the nightmare of the Sino to be over. Waiting to see our mothers, sisters, daughters, aunts, and cousins again. History books say the Treaty of Honolulu ended the Sino-American War on Easter Sunday, 2045. I say the Sino ends today with the return of these American heroes. Finally, both the waiting and the war are over.*

—President Amanda Swain,
49th President of the United States
April 14, 2055
San Diego, California, on the landing of the *U.S.S. Exodus*

## (i)

THE PARLOR DOWNSTAIRS OVERFLOWED WITH tables and chairs 'cause it was too cold to eat outside. Spring had tripped, and winter had stumbled over her. The packed house was hot, but I was happy to drown in the heat. The Regios were gone, and we were together again, all of us except for Micaiah.

Though it was good to see Wren with us again, she worried me. She was throwing back brown bottles of homemade beer as fast as Jenny Bell could bring them to her.

Wren stood near Pilate, a cigar drooping from his mouth. Jenny Bell must have found some for him. He wasn't smoking it, but just having the cigar in his mouth seemed like he was courting further sickness. Yet, with the cigar and his Starbucks mug from Rome in his fist, he seemed like his old self, only he couldn't look me in the eye, and a machine-gun cough kept rattling him. Petal was asleep in their room on a quarter dose of the Skye6. Pilate had taken over Petal's new schedule. He also gave me a pill for my gunshot wounds, and it was working well.

We ate a huge meal until we couldn't eat any more—beef ribs, beans, coleslaw, potato salad, corn bread, and rhubarb cobbler with more crust and whipped cream than rhubarb, which made it good.

We were all lounging around, letting our food digest in the light of the hissing sapropel lamps, when Pilate asked, "Well, Jenny Bell, I'm not complaining, but I am curious. Where did you get the coffee and cigars?"

And dang me if Jenny Bell didn't say it outright. "Where do you think? June Mai Angel."

You could've heard an ant's breath in the quiet. Wren's bottle froze at her lips. Pilate's cigar nearly dropped into his lap.

And Sharlotte cursed. "Jacker me down tight."

If I hadn't heard it with my own ears, I wouldn't have believed it. Upright Sharlotte had just cussed. Then I saw the mug in her hand—her hot toddy—the only liquor Sharlotte ever drank. Oh boy.

Before my sisters could say a thing, I spoke first. "We fought June Mai Angel three times, and she almost killed us all twice. How can you deal with that Outlaw Warlord?"

Jenny Bell tossed back a shooter full of rye and made a face. "You know why June Mai Angel and her girls are out here? Ever wonder why the Psycho Princess is psycho?"

"'Cause their mamas didn't love 'em?" Wren asked. She'd passed through her fighting drunk to her mellow drunk. I wondered what kind of drunk Sharlotte was going to have.

Jenny Bell discussed the conspiracy like she was talking about her alfalfa crop. "President Swain knows her history. She knows what happens when soldiers come home; especially soldiers who have been away from home for too long. She sent the veterans to the Juniper by the trainload. Gave them a hundred dollars, which buys you exactly nothing out here, then waved goodbye. I must say, though, I've read her speech about the landing of the *U.S.S Exodus*. It was moving."

"Ladies in Waiting," Pilate whispered. It was what we called soldier girls who got stuck in China and couldn't get home 'cause the world had run out of fuel. Vietnam had MIAs. The Sino had the Ladies in Waiting. Some were stranded for a decade until GE perfected their Eterna batteries. The U.S. used them to power the ships and planes to bring the veterans home.

Jenny Bell rolled her shot glass back and forth across the table. "Did you know President Swain could've brought the troops home sooner? But first she had to pass the SISBI laws."

I'd only been in Cleveland a short time when I first heard about the Security, Identity, and Special Borders Injunction, or SISBI. The news had focused on the privacy issues, since it required all U.S. citizens to register eye-scans with the government. The law also gave the U.S. government permission to build a militarized border around the Juniper, though no one cared too much about that since the permanent EM field seemed border enough.

My heart trembled 'cause I could guess where Jenny Bell was headed.

"June Mai herself told us all about it. The rest of the U.S. either doesn't know or doesn't care." Jenny Bell set her shot glass on the table. "Once the SISBI laws were in place, President Swain made a big show of bringing our troops home, and when they started causing trouble, she sent the Ladies in Waiting out here. That way, the U.S. government wouldn't have to pay for their PTSD therapy, and the good Christian women of the New Morality wouldn't have to worry about homeless vets filling the streets because of their mental illness, drug addiction, and alcoholism. Just send them all to the Juniper along with the worst of the criminals. That's why the U.S. has been closing so many prisons. They've found the perfect place to send all their problems. Here. With us. Cheap and convenient. And they've been doing it for years."

I felt my throat close up. I remembered the fence I'd seen outside of the Buzzkill. Wren said the U.S. border guards didn't care about people going into the Juniper, only about people leaving.

My home was a 1.5 million square kilometer prison, a penal colony. Feeling choked, I pulled at the collar of my shirt and wished everyone would stop talking for a minute so I could digest what Jenny Bell had said. But that wasn't going to happen.

Pilate shook his head. "June Mai Angel rounded the veterans up, gave them a purpose, gave them an illegal economy, and now probably wants to set herself up as the Juniper's queen."

"Something like that," Jenny Bell said. "We trade with June Mai, beef for various supplies. And if she had been around when that Edger woman showed up, well, things would've played out far differently."

Ironic that one of our enemies might have saved us from another. I knew June Mai also dealt in illegal contraband, so I asked, "What about Skye6? Do you have any?" It would help to have a surplus, if Petal needed more time to get clean. Or if we got shot up again.

"Some," Jenny Bell said. "But mostly we use pain pills or spools of EMAT for broken bones and such. Most of the time, we trade for luxury goods like sugar, soap, shampoo, new clothes from the World. Yankee stuff."

Now I knew where my new outfit had come from. And Jenny Bell's deodorant.

She continued. "June Mai doesn't take just anyone, though. You have to be well trained, and you have to be stable. The sicker girls go north, to join up with the Psycho Princess. We can't trade with her or her people because they're too crazy. I'm sure you've heard the rumors about her killing boys and nailing them to trees. All true. The Psycho Princess knows if she got out of line with us, June Mai would come calling. And the Psycho Princess keeps the Wind River folk from crossing the Wyoming border, so it all balances out. We have a good life here. Most people wouldn't understand. I figure you may or may not."

The Wind River people were what we called the Native Americans who'd reclaimed the Montana and Wyoming territories. God help whoever tried to trespass on their land.

I lost it before I could rein myself in. "June Mai took her armies and marched them into Burlington. She's laying siege to our hometown."

Jenny Bell frowned. "I knew something was up, though I thought she'd go after Lamar first. She wants the world to know what Swain did with the veterans. She wants justice or money, or maybe even, like Pilate said, to be governor of the territory. The only way she thinks to do it is by the gun, but way out here, we can't get involved in politics. I'm just glad Edger and those women are gone."

Wren wobbled up. She talked with her bottle in front of her mouth to hide her missing teeth. "Aw, no more of this boring talk. I say we have our Irish girl sing. Let's make this a party. Come on, Red, sing one pretty."

Others asked as well, so Allie finally stood. "All the talk of the Sino, I know a war song. It's not a jolly song, but I know it through."

"Sing anything!" Wren yelled.

Allie opened her mouth, and her voice came out strong and heartbreaking. She hadn't sung a dozen words before most of us were in tears. It was called *Another Waltz for Matilda*, based on an Australian song about Gallipoli and the horrors of World War I. Like the Sino, that war had also left a generation crushed and disillusioned.

> *Another waltz for Matilda*
> *Another song for the dead*
> *We prayed for a blue sky, got a black*

*one instead*
*And a little girl weeps*
*For her sister Matilda gone.*

*The song is stuck on repeat again*
*The storms sicken the ground with rain*
*In darkness we cling to hope, slipping*
*into pain*
*The parades for our daughters have all*
*been in vain*

*Another waltz for Matilda*
*Another war to end wars*
*Until it happens again on some distant*
*shore*
*And another mother weeps*
*For another Matilda gone.*

As I listened, I felt pity for June Mai Angel. Yes, she'd tried to kill us, but that tragic song made me pity her and Petal and all the broken-souled veterans who had been tortured by war so we could be free. I even felt sorry for Pilate.

He sat in his chair motionless. Not sipping his coffee. Not chewing on his cigar. Just sat there until he choked out the words. "If you sing any more, Allie Chambers, I do believe it will kill me."

"Good!" Sharlotte shrieked. She jumped up. Her face flushed a fiery red, her pretty eyes slitted. From her pocket, she took the piece of paper she'd worried near to pieces. "Good. I wish you dead, you miserable jackerdan. I wish you worse than dead. I wish you hell bound for what you've done to me and my family."

## (ii)

Sharlotte swayed on her feet. Zenobia, Jenny Bell's oldest daughter, tried to help her from falling, but Sharlotte shoved her away. "Get off me. You're his seed." Sharlotte shot a finger at Pilate. "I prayed you'd die. When I saw you lying there, I prayed you'd die, and I would burn this paper and never say a word. Mama didn't. And I'm as good as she was."

Wren's smile was so sharp I thought she'd decapitate herself with it. Sharlotte was finally taking her turn as the troubled Weller girl, making a cow-patty-wet mess of things.

"Sharlotte, sit down," Pilate whispered.

I wanted to say something, do something, but I was paralyzed. Pilate and Sharlotte seemed like forces of nature right then, and getting between them would've been like running out into a street with a hurricane on one side and a tornado on the other.

"You know what this paper says?" Sharlotte asked. Foamy spit wet her lips. Her eyes spun crazily.

"I have an idea," Pilate said.

"It's a medical report I found going through Mama's papers after she died. Says Daddy wasn't viable."

I felt all the blood drain out of my face. The world tilted, and I knew the tilt would never go away. I'd have to walk leaning for the rest of my life. My daddy wasn't my daddy anymore. Charles Weller had been a thin, laughing kind of man, Colorado born and bred, who never left, not even after the Yellowstone Knockout. All the memories stormed through my head—us together, him holding me, and wrestling me, and sips from his beer, and then what he became, in the bed. Sick getting sicker. Dying and getting deader. Mama crying like it would break her.

So who was my father? I could guess, but I needed it said aloud.

Pilate sighed. "I figured this would happen. I prayed it wouldn't, but I'm coming to understand the Lord resents every one of my prayers. And yet I beseech Him so ardently."

Sharlotte took a swaying step toward him. I hoped she'd fall down, pass out, and we could burn the paper and forget all about it. Nope. She launched into a speech full of acid and agony. "And if Daddy was sterile, only one other man in Mama's life, and that was you, famous Father Pilate, wearing a collar and a gun, and hopping from one bed to another and laughing at his vows like they don't mean nothin'. Laughing at the church and God like they don't mean nothin'. If you weren't so good at killing people, I never would've allowed you to come with us on this goddamn cattle drive. You bastard. You miserable, jackering bastard. I got your blood in me, and it makes me want to cut my own throat."

Pilate? My father? I gripped the arms of my chair, praying to get off the wild ride we were on—a rollercoaster plunging down into an abyss.

"Sharlotte, please—" Pilate tried.

Sharlotte, vicious, cut him off. "I've seen you and Wren together. She'd come into camp, thinking no one could see. But I saw. Your own daughter. You're going to hell, Pilate, and I'd gladly shun heaven to spend all of eternity watching you burn."

Wren burst out with a raw, jagged laugh. Not quite a scream, but close enough. She stood to join in the fight. Here we go, Wren and Sharlotte, the next battle in a never-ending war.

Jenny Bell stood as well. "We should clear the dishes. It's pretty clear the party is over."

Sharlotte turned her finger on Jenny Bell. "And you. Pilate fathered at least Zenobia. How could you let him touch you when we all know what kind of filth he is? He pretends to be a priest, just so he can go sniffing around, like a dog lookin' for a *kutia* in heat."

"That's enough, Sharlotte!" I shouted. Whatever we thought about Jenny Bell's ethics, it wasn't right to attack her in front of her daughters. And I heard myself in Sharlotte's snarling. I'd spent a lot of time judging Pilate and the women he'd given children to. I shouldn't have. Like Pilate had said, the world wasn't a paint-by-numbers picture of rainbows and unicorns. Life was messy.

I left my chair to stop the madness, and it was a tableau of the Weller sisters, like an outtake from an all-female version of the *Lord of the Flies*.

"That's enough," I said. "We're embarrassing ourselves. We can talk about all this later." No way were we going to stop, though. Might as well try stopping a bad storm from hailing.

Jenny Bell and her family shuffled away even as our employees and hires ducked out the door. Even Aunt Bea. She was right to run. With the Regios gone, our people could sleep in their tents again.

Pilate, of course, stayed.

Jenny Bell was headed for the kitchen when Sharlotte called to her. "You didn't answer my question, Jenny Bell. You like getting all sweaty with Pilate?"

That lean, hard Juniper cowgirl turned. In a low voice, strong and sure, she said, "I wanted a big family, and I needed hands for the ranch. If you weren't drunk, you'd know that. But you are drunk. And it's a shame. I want you off my property in the morning. Out of respect for your mama, I'll let you stay the night." It was what our own mother would've done with a guest who turned nasty.

Jenny Bell and her daughters cleared out.

Wren grabbed someone's half-finished drink. Drained it in a second. "I tried to kiss Pilate when I turned eighteen. Did kiss him." She downed another glass. Had plenty to choose from—the Scheutzes sure weren't going to come back to clean up. "It wasn't Pilate's fault. It was back in his drinking days, and I went for him. 'Cause I'm wrong in places that'll never be right. Like you are, Sharlotte. Only Cavvy is good and clean. Only my baby, Cavvy."

Pilate lowered his face. Couldn't tell what he was feeling, but then it dawned on me. Pilate got sober right around the time Wren turned eighteen three years ago. Call it intuition, but I knew why he'd quit drinking. Wren's kiss bottomed him out.

I thought he might be crying, but then he laughed, and the sound of it made us all jump. It was manly, deep, very Pilate. It surprised us so much that Sharlotte fell back into a chair. Wren tripped and suddenly we were all sitting down.

Pilate stood—laundered shirt, priest's collar, scratchy beard, and long hair, more rock star than priest.

"Are you sure you want the truth, Sharlotte? Because the truth just might get in the way of you hating me. And we wouldn't want that, would we? I think with Abigail gone your hate for me is all you're sure of."

"You can't tell the truth," Sharlotte grumbled. "You're the father of lies."

"Tell me, what's the date on the report?"

Sharlotte snapped the paper in front of her face. "Why does that matter? Most likely Daddy went sterile before he even met Mama. First cases of the Sterility Epidemic were found in the early 2030s."

"The date, please," Pilate said patiently.

"February 2, 2039. But that don't mean nothin'."

"It means everything," Pilate said. "The report is dated after Wren was born. Charles Weller was her father. He was your father, too, Sharlotte. After Wren, when your Mama couldn't get pregnant, that's when they had him tested. The results were hard on them both, but we all know how tough Abigail was. Not just tough, focused. She was growing her cattle business, and she needed hands. Family works for free … that's what she said to me when she and I talked. We made the same deal I've made with a whole passel of women all over the Juniper. I do the bed part, someone else does the fathering part because that's the important work. What I do means nothing. Less than nothing. I'm only a body. A real father is heart, mind, and spirit. Your dad loved all three of you like he loved nothing else on this planet. He fought his cancer for years because he couldn't let go of you."

"Pilate," I whispered, "are you my daddy?"

He smiled at me. "Biologically, yes, and you're my little brown spider. Araneus Cavaticus. Named after literature's most famous arachnid and your mother's favorite book, *Charlotte's Web*. We were so happy when your mama carried you to term, after all your other sisters died." His voice failed him, and he had to close his eyes. "You were destined to live, Cavvy. You're one of the best things God ever gave to the Juniper. Someday, everyone will know your name."

My life kept on tilting, throwing me around some more. Pilate was my father. I felt that when he held me after Mama's funeral. Him looking at me when he thought I didn't notice, his eyes so full of love. Like Sharlotte, I wanted to hate Pilate 'cause of his sins, but my hate always faded, and I ended up loving him again. Sure, Pilate wasn't a saint, but deep down, he was kind, caring, and sad underneath the laughing and violence. Why else would he have taken Petal under his wing? Or agree to run security for us? Or try to rescue Micaiah when he knew it was suicide?

Wren spoke next in a slur. "You wanna know what Pilate and I did in the tent all those nights, Sharlotte?" The alcohol half-shut her eyes. "He held me and petted my hair and said people loved me in the world. Mama did, though she had trouble with me. And that you loved me, Shar. And Cavvy loved me. And he loved me and forgave me all my sins. He'd hold me and say I didn't have to kill myself 'cause someday, someday I'd have a family."

Sharlotte sat crumpled in her chair, leaning heavily on her arm. We all waited for her to talk now that the truth was out.

She started slow. "I guess I should feel relieved that Pilate isn't my daddy, but it was wrong for Mama to keep the truth from us. And I love Cavvy, always will.

However, let me make one thing perfectly clear." Sharlotte sat up real straight in her chair to look Wren in the eye. "You think I'm going to get all weepy 'cause you feel bad about yourself, Irene? You think you can ever change what you did to me, to Mama, to our family? You can't. You are a selfish child of chaos, evil to the core. You made our lives hell, and then left us and never came back. I hate you, Irene. I hate you, and I curse you." She staggered up. "I'm done with this goddamn cattle drive. Howerter can go jack himself. I'm gonna sell the headcount to Jenny Bell just enough to make payroll, and then I'm going to go live in the World. It's over."

She tottered out the door. Watching her go crushed my heart. Flattened it like a tin can. Sharlotte was through. Now what would happen? How could we save the ranch if we didn't pay Howerter back? Micaiah's promised reward money would do it, but then what?

Wren had to squint to pry open an eye. Sharlotte's words must've bounced right off her drunkenness. "Hell, Pilate, with how I am, I figured you were my daddy all along. I reckoned I was damned for certain on account of that kiss."

Pilate smiled and shook his head. "Wren Weller, you think hell would have you? Satan would spit you right back out like a rotten sunflower seed. Nope. Only Jesus has the patience to love you like you need."

"You gonna cheat Him with me once we're dead? Cheat that Jesus at poker with me, Pilate?"

Pilate nodded. "Yeah, Wren. You, me, and Petal."

"And me?" I asked, feeling left out.

Pilate got up and knelt down at my feet. "You won't have to cheat Jesus. He'll take you right to your mansion of glory, and you'll be safe and secure and loved forever. You're good, Cavvy. You're my little brown spider."

Tears shimmered in his eyes, and I had the idea that out of all the many kids he had fathered, I was the only one he'd ever held like his own. The only one he ever let himself get close to.

I cried as he hugged me. My hate was all gone, and it was blood on blood. I saw him now, for who he was and for what he did for women who needed children, for what he did for Wren. And I knew, if I asked, Pilate would help me get Micaiah to Nevada.

But maybe Sharlotte would change her mind when she sobered up. But what if she didn't?

While we hugged, Wren collapsed onto the floor. Out cold.

We both had us a little chuckle.

Then I said, "Pilate, alcohol sure makes a mess of things. I can see why you don't drink."

"Amen, to that. Amen to the third power."

"Pilate?"

"Yeah, Cavvy?"

"I just want to keep calling you Pilate. You're my daddy and all, but like you said, my real daddy died. You're more of my Pilate. Is that okay?"

"Sure, Cavvy. I'd like it better that way anyway."

"Pilate?"

"Yeah, Cavvy."

"You really think there isn't another side for people like us? For my sisters? Or for Petal? Do you really think we can't get to the other side of our pain?"

"I don't know. I just don't know." Pilate's weak lungs caught up with him, and he lapsed into a coughing spell.

We moved Wren to a sofa and covered her with a blanket. Then Pilate and I returned to our rooms upstairs.

I went to my window and looked out at the glowing tents in the dark yard. Most likely, all our hands were gossiping about how messed up the Weller girls were. Well, it wasn't gossip. It was the truth.

The cattle drive might be over. Pilate was my daddy. Sharlotte really did hate Wren. And Mama, well, Mama was still dead.

As for the boy? Yeah, my liar boy. Right then, I didn't care about his secrets. And to tell you the truth, I didn't care about the reward either.

It seemed like the end of the world, and I could do whatever I wanted.

Right then, I wanted to do it all.

### (iii)

I waited until the house settled, then I crept back up into the attic. I moved the hutch aside and unfolded the ladder.

My heart swelled like it was about to pop a valve. Every centimeter of my skin buzzed, like I'd been plugged into an Eterna battery. All my promises to stay true to myself had burned to coals, to ash, then blown away.

I climbed the ladder and crawled across the wood to where Micaiah was sleeping in his nest of blankets by the screen.

What was I doing? Who was I right then? I didn't know.

I was Cavatica, but I wasn't. She'd died the minute Pilate said he was my daddy. Now I was just a little brown spider, nameless, as I scuttled over to Micaiah, finding his mouth in the glow of the night, grabbing him between his legs.

He gasped and kissed me back, and I put his hand on my chest. This was what I wanted, wasn't it? Hard question to ask when you don't know who you are. He pulled back. "Cavvy, what the hell? What are you doing?"

Took me a bit, but I finally got enough breath to speak. "Back at the deserted house, you asked why I couldn't just enjoy myself with you. Well, I can now. It's the end of the world. Sharlotte cancelled the cattle drive, which means we'll just have to get you to Nevada so you can help us pay back Howerter. Oh, and Pilate is my daddy. And Jenny Bell is dealing with June Mai Angel, and she has Skye6 for Petal, if we need it. Not sure how much Jenny Bell has. You know, we could try using pain pills or maybe a strip of EMAT. Not sure if that would work on account of the differences in the chemical make-up. We don't know how she would react on a microcellular level."

Muted light from the screen shown on his face. His mouth gaped. His eyes widened.

"Cavvy, um, I need for you to tell me what happened slowly. Go slow. I was sound asleep when you, uh, attacked me."

That seemed reasonable to me. I would tell him a bunch of stuff, and then we could have the sex. However, talking slowly, the words etched themselves into my mind, like a river carving out a valley, and when I was done, I didn't feel sexy anymore.

I felt weepy. I felt lost. I felt alone. And it wasn't 'cause Pilate was my father, or that Mama had kept the truth from me, or that we failed to get the cattle to Nevada, or that we would lose the ranch, our sacred ground, where my parents and baby sisters were buried.

No. It was the way Sharlotte had acted. I needed her to be my rock. I needed her to be in control. Without Sharlotte, the world couldn't take care of itself. I couldn't take care of myself. God needed Sharlotte to run the universe 'cause He couldn't do it alone.

When Mama died, Sharlotte had taken over as the one person I felt I could depend on. When she got drunk and nasty, well, it was like losing another mother. Once again, I felt like an orphan.

So, like any confused girl who had her life unzipped and turned inside out, I cried. And Micaiah held me. He didn't kiss me or touch me inappropriately, he simply held me and promised me everything would be okay. In his arms, I didn't just feel comforted, I felt complete. Somehow, with his touches and his whispers, he glued the cracks inside me together.

Once my tears were dry and my sobs subsided, he slipped something around my wrist, on my right arm 'cause my wind-up Moto Moto watch was on my left. In the firelight, I saw the twisted wires and grasses of a homemade bracelet. I could just make out the colors, red and white and the dusty brown of dry winter grass.

"Keys taught me how to weave it," Micaiah whispered. "I saw her making one for Breeze, and I wanted you to have something."

I turned to him. Then kissed him. "I love it."

"I'm glad." He returned my kiss, but he felt distant, almost as if he wasn't all there. I'd been so wrapped up in my own drama that I hadn't noticed, but yes, something was different about him.

"You can't run off," I said. "I need you. We'll sneak you out of here tonight. I figure we'll take off in the morning. We can hide you."

He didn't say a word, but leaned in close and kissed me, softly, gently, and I knew it meant he didn't want to argue.

I couldn't let it go. "You'll stay, right? Promise me."

Staring into my eyes, not blinking, he didn't lie. He didn't respond, but he didn't lie. He went back to holding me, and he felt so good next to me, I couldn't help but fall asleep in his arms.

I woke up in the attic alone. Morning light swirled the dust. Micaiah was gone.

It took me a minute to realize what woke me—the *chugga, chugga, chugga* of an airship's steam engine hovering over us. Someone was yelling, I think it was Kasey Romero, one of our hired hands, who'd taken the morning watch.

Why was she yelling? I was pretty sure it was only Sketchy, Tech, and Peeperz in the *Moby Dick*, flying in to check on us.

I had to find Micaiah. He couldn't just leave. If Sharlotte was giving up on the cattle drive, I needed him to help us with our debts.

Fear of losing Micaiah and a desire to save the ranch took me back across the attic and down the ladder, though I did take a minute to move the hutch under the trapdoor. Micaiah might be gone, but our guns in the attic could still give us away. Might as well keep them hidden. I hurried down the steps, but I noticed the house seemed empty. But why? What was going on?

I came out of the house and all the Scheutzes, all of my people, were in the yard, looking up with mouths agape.

Four Johnny zeppelins filled the sky—the biggest blimps I'd ever seen. Battalions of uniformed Regios repelled down ropes dangling from the zeppelin like tentacles from an octopus.

I ran for my ponies, to grab Bob D, and make a run for it.

Not even a second later, my face struck the dirt. Someone had taken me down too fast for me to react. Strong hands wrenched my shoulders and zip tied my wrists together. I cried out.

Edger drove her knee into my back and hissed into my ear. "Remember this pain, Cavatica Weller. Reb and Ronnie Vixx will do far worse unless you tell them the truth."

# Chapter Six

*The pioneers who ventured into the Juniper after the Yellowstone Knockout were artists. On this blank canvas of plain, they painted new lives for themselves.*

—Mavis Meetchum
*Colorado Courier* Interview
September 7, 2046

## (i)

WHEN WE LEFT BURLINGTON, WE'D BEEN afraid of the wrong things—weather, deserts, June Mai Angel, the Psycho Princess, and the Wind River people. Never even heard of the Vixx sisters, but they had shot us up worse than anyone. And they would do anything to get to Micaiah.

I lay on the ground, hogtied. My bullet wounds yowled while my shoulders strained.

The adrenaline and agony made every detail stand out crisp. Pebbles lay on top of the hardscrabble. A few weeds, a few thin blades of grass, and a dandelion grew out of cracks in the ground. For some reason, that dandelion was the most beautiful thing I'd ever seen.

Sunlight warmed the air, melting away the shadow of cold from the night before. Morning dew dampened the sagebrush, and spring grasses made the

Great Plains smell green. For one brief moment, my senses gave me a little peace, but it was quickly taken from me.

Edger yanked me to my feet. I was determined not let out another cry and ground my teeth to keep quiet. She marched me into the Scheutz's corral. Sharlotte's dark eyes peered from a face as white as a toad's underbelly. All our people stood with their arms zip tied behind their backs, Pilate and Petal included. The Schuetzes, too.

We were surrounded by Regios in sagebrush camouflage. Grenades, knives, pistols, and little cylinders of pepper spray hung from their harnesses.

Knew it was pepper spray 'cause of the sharp, spicy odor mingling with the smell of wet dirt and old animal crap. They'd hit Wren with the spray, and she knelt in the filth. Tears and snot streamed down her red face.

I gazed at all the soldiers, more soldiers than even she could fight.

Two women came forward. Both had angled Scandinavian faces under hair buzzed down to the scalp. Sunglasses hid their eyes. They looked exactly the same as Renee Vixx.

"How can we help you?" Jenny Bell asked, still polite despite the terror trembling her voice.

"As you know, we're looking for a boy." Not quite sure which of the Vixx sisters said it. The voice was cold and mechanical, like a killer robot. Well, couldn't be a robot, no electricity in the Juniper.

"We haven't seen a boy in a long time," Jenny Bell said. "I'm sorry we can't help you."

Troops came out of the house. "All clear, ma'am," one said. Not sure when Micaiah had snuck away, but he was gone all right.

Edger held aloft the same picture she'd shown us before. The Vixxes shouted, "You have been asked this question already, but we will ask it once again. Have you seen the boy in this picture, seventeen, well-dressed, blond?"

Every eye went to Sharlotte. She was still in charge.

"We all told Edger the same thing. We ain't seen any boys out here." Sharlotte said. "Either the Psycho Princess kills them or June Mai Angel sells them."

"Reb." One of the Vixxes said.

"Yes, Ronnie." Then the one, Reb, drew her big Desert Messiah pistol and shot Jenny Bell in the chest.

I felt a howl rise in me. My soul cat-scratched.

All of Jenny Bell's daughters sucked in a breath, all at once, you could hear it. And then sobbing, shrieks, screams, and crying.

"Jenny Bell!" Sharlotte yelled it heartbroken, tried to pull herself out of the soldier girls' grip, but they held her tight. "I'm sorry!"

Jenny Bell staggered, holding her chest even as blood oozed between her fingers. "I know you are, Shar. I know. Being Abigail's daughter couldn't have been easy. Don't worry about me. Dying is easy. It's the living that's …"

Jenny Bell pitched forward and died right there.

I wrestled away from the Regio holding me and went for Reb Vixx.

She shoved the Desert Messiah's barrel into my face, pointing it right between my eyes. I fell to my knees, cross-eyed, staring death down.

"We're looking for this boy. I've proven my willingness to kill you all to get to him. It will make no difference to me. Talk now. Or die. You are nothing but dust."

She wasn't bluffing—dead eyes, dead voice, nothing human in it. Prolly had the human all trained out of her.

"No!" Both Wren and Sharlotte shouted. Both struggled against the Regios restraining them. Pilate took off for Reb, but he was tripped. On the ground, in the dirt, soldiers kicked him until he lay still. Petal let out a pathetic cry, powerless to stop them.

Wren lost it all to screaming. "Don't you touch her, skank. Kill me, if you got the balls to kill again. Kill me!" She stomped on the foot of one of the women holding her and head-bashed another one. Wren didn't take two steps before she was pepper sprayed again. She went down, puking into the dirt.

One of the girls drew her pistol and aimed it at Wren's head, standing well away from her. Smart. The Regio waited to get permission to shoot. Both Vixx sisters shook their heads.

Sharlotte disagreed with the decision. "Kill her. Kill me. Kill us all. We don't know nothing about a boy. We're just moving our headcount west."

Reb put her pistol to my forehead. Eyes on me, she talked to my sister. "You don't remember me, Sharlotte, but we remember you. Before your mother's funeral, you conversed with Robert Howerter in Burlington to ask for lenience. We were there at the zeppelin port. We watched you climb the ladder on the *Celebration Day*."

On our travels, Micaiah had mentioned the *Celebration Day*. That was the name of his zeppelin that had been shot down by June Mai Angel.

"Please," Sharlotte begged. "We're only ranchers on a cattle drive. We don't know nothin'."

All our people took Sharlotte's lead. She was in charge. It was her gamble, with my life on the table, and we were going to play it out. For some reason, it felt like the right thing to do.

Micaiah must've snuck away in the night. He hadn't promised to stay, and he'd left us. He did it 'cause he thought we would be safer. He did it out of love. What could he have done if he stayed? What could anyone do against the firepower and troops surrounding us?

Reb Vixx pulled the hammer back. Didn't need to. That hand-cannon was a double action revolver. If it didn't blow my head off, it would empty my brains out through the back of my skull. Knock my eyes out of their sockets in the process.

But cocking that hammer back was so very dramatic.

The sound triggered something in me. Might've been the pain in my arm and shoulder, might've been Wren's spirit filling me, but in a strong, growly voice I told her, "Go jack yourself, skank. We don't know crapjack about any boy."

Us Wellers are contrary, contrary to the very end.

I locked eyes with Reb Vixx and didn't glance away. I might die kneeling, but I was determined to die unbroken.

## (ii)

"Jesus," Pilate hissed the word. He was spitting blood, coughing, gagging. It wasn't a prayer. It was disbelief in what we were doing.

I didn't break eye contact with Reb Vixx. Not even when she eased down the hammer on her revolver.

In the end, I won. I beat her. I tricked her.

"We will be watching you," Reb Vixx said. "If you find the boy, keep him with you, and you will be paid handsomely. If you are lying to us, we will return and kill you all, like we killed Jennifer Scheutz."

The cold nothingness in her voice sent chilly fingers down my spine.

We watched as the Regios, Edger included, took hold of ropes and, hand over hand, climbed back up into the Johnnies. Tough enough to lift your own body weight, but when you added the gear and guns, it made what they did even more impressive. And terrifying.

The Johnnies chugged off, morning sunlight glinting off the buzzing titanium propellers. Black smoke trailed from the steam engine's exhaust. A fortune in manpower and equipment looking for Micah Hoyt.

Wren managed to get her Betty knife out, and she used it to cut the plastic ties off Pilate's wrist. They didn't stop until we were all freed.

Pilate held me tight. "Thank God, Cavvy, thank God you're alive." His lip was fat, his eye black, and his nose bleeding.

"I'm sorry, Pilate," I said. "I'm sorry they beat you."

He grinned. "Yeah, those girls tried to beat the hell out of me, but they couldn't." He touched his chest. "I can still feel some hell right here."

The sound of weeping pulled me away from Pilate.

Sharlotte was bent over Jenny Bell, along with her daughters.

"Y'all best be leaving," Zenobia said. "You've caused us enough trouble."

"I'm so sorry," Sharlotte said again. "We never meant—"

"Just go. No bad blood. But you best be leaving now, or there will be."

Sharlotte stood, her jaw set. "Okay, let's pack 'em up. Can't wait to see what the Psycho Princess is going to do to us. We've pissed off everyone else in the Juniper."

We packed. Fast.

I went inside, and I put the attic back the way we'd found it. Stuffed the blankets up at the very top of the house back into their plastic, discarded the mason jars and Micaiah's leftover water and food, then grabbed Pilate's and Petal's guns and ammo.

I moved the hutch back into place. Maybe they wouldn't notice the scratches. Maybe they'd never guess the boy had been in their attic all along.

Jenny Bell had died 'cause of Micaiah's secrets. The guilt blackened my heart, and I prayed with all my might that her sacrifice hadn't been in vain. That Micaiah's quest would make her death noble.

In the end, I'd like to think Jenny Bell watched us from heaven for the rest of our journey, and in God's perfect wisdom, forgave us.

Forgave me.

With the Scheutzes watching, heartbroke, we took off in record time. Zenobia was Christian enough to give me a bottle of pills for my pain. Ibuprofen mixed with Percocet. They tore up my stomach but kept the pain away.

Aunt Bea drove off in the Chevy Workhorse II, our chuck wagon. Wren was behind the wheel of the Ford Excelsior, puffing smoke.

The rest of us took to horses, pushing our cattle toward the Wyoming territory. No one said a word about Micaiah. We left the Scheutz's ranch behind like it was a graveyard now. They'd bury Jenny Bell, and forever more she'd sleep soundly in the dirt of the Juniper.

Petal left with a determination to kick the Skye6. Pilate left wanting to help her. I left behind my hatred for Pilate, and Sharlotte left any illusion of love she had for Wren.

No, Sharlotte left behind more than that. She left herself behind on the Scheutz ranch.

## (iii)

That afternoon, I rode through the herd, trying to find Sharlotte. I wanted to talk about her plans and why we were moving north. Not that I wasn't glad. I'd die before I lost the ranch, our sacred ground. We couldn't sell our beef in Buzzkill or to Mavis Meetchum, since she was being pressured by Howerter as well. Micaiah had disappeared and his reward money along with him. Our only hope lay in Nevada, on the deal Mama had made with Sysco.

It seemed we were free of June Mai Angel, and, yeah, the Vixxes might be watching, but we had nothing to hide, not anymore.

Yet if we continued north, we'd eventually run into the Psycho Princess. One more enemy to face and we were down a gun. Unlike Pilate and Wren, Petal hadn't put up a fight when the Vixxes grabbed us.

The longer I searched for my sister, the more afraid I got. Sharlotte was always easy to find, to answer questions and to tell you what to do and how to do it.

Everyone had talked to Sharlotte, but no one knew where she was. She'd told Dolly Day and our hired hands to go ahead of us to clip fences. No one had run cattle through this part of the world in centuries, and so the wire of former ranches still stretched across the land.

Then I saw Sharlotte walking Prince far behind the dusty cloud of our Herefords moving across the plain.

Couldn't figure out why Sharlotte wasn't in her saddle, unless Prince was foundering. Katy had recovered, or so I'd been told. Now it was prolly Prince's turn to have something go wrong with him. Horses' hooves could be fragile. Human hearts? Even more so.

I rode back to my big sister.

I thought she'd start talking right away—about what needed to be done, about why the Vixxes had let us go, where Sketchy and the *Moby Dick* might be, where Micaiah was—but instead she was wordless. Not a peep.

I didn't know what to say. Sharlotte always spoke first, and generally, it started with, "I need you to …"

I got off Bob D to walk next to her. "Sharlotte, why ain't you riding Prince?"

Her hat dangled from a string in her hand, so I could see her grin sheepishly. "The bounce from the horse is killing my head. Walking is horrible, too, but not as bad. Now I know why Wren is so surly in the morning. Hangovers. Ugh."

"Last night you said the cattle drive was over," I said shakily. "Why are we still going north?"

True to form, Sharlotte answered my question with a question. She was not what you would call a good listener. "You read *Macbeth* in school, Cavvy?"

Such an odd question from Sharlotte. School for Sharlotte had been an inconvenience—a cactus sticker in her thumb while she was trying to work the ranch with Mama.

"Yeah, I read *Macbeth*, Shar. They made us."

She nodded. "There's a line, and it's always haunted me. Don't know where I heard it. Maybe Pilate. He's likely to quote Shakespeare, isn't he?"

"Yeah." Talking about Pilate felt awkward now that the truth was out.

"Someone in that play, Lady Macbeth maybe, says she's swimming across a river of blood, and it's as easy to keep going forward as it is to go back. Not like that, you understand, but in that old Shakespeare language."

I didn't say that the Shakespeare language was actually English. I didn't want to shame her for not knowing.

Sharlotte stopped and sighed. We were in a little gully between two bumps of hills. All around us sprouted dandelions in a splash of yellow in the sunlight.

"I gambled you today, Cavvy."

"I know it. Nearly had to change my underwear."

Sharlotte smiled. Oh, she looked tired. "I'm a mystery to myself now. Getting drunk. Wanting to give up on the cattle drive. Basking in the love of that boy. Then risking your life to protect him and keep him hidden. He just seems important. More important than us somehow."

"I felt it, too. The Holy Spirit directed us, I think. Or maybe we're just contrary."

Sharlotte knelt down and brushed a hand over the dandelions. "If the Vixxes hadn't attacked us and killed Jenny Bell, I prolly would've stayed on with the Scheutz's. Sold her the headcount, made payroll, or we could've found a homestead near them, and set up selling beefsteak to the Outlaw Warlords, like Jenny Bell. Last night I said I'd go live in the World, but I can't. Not just 'cause of the SISBI laws, but more I'm Juniper born and bred. I don't reckon she'll let me leave." Sharlotte took in a deep breath. "And so, here we are, in the middle of a river of blood. As far to the other side as it is to go back. Halfway. We all wanted it, but now the halfway feels like hell."

We were in a mess all right, but I wanted to comfort her. "I'm okay with you gambling me, Sharlotte. I think all of us are okay keeping Micaiah a secret, or else someone would've come clean when Edger interrogated us. We made it this far. We can get there."

"I love dandelions, Cavvy."

That seemed an odd thing to say. Didn't know how to ask if she'd gone crazy, so I asked, "Ain't they just a weed, Shar?"

"Yeah, just a weed. But they can grow anywhere, and they're pretty, and they're tough. Like women in the Juniper. Like women everywhere. Tough, pretty, and we can bloom wherever we are. Don't need a home. Just need land and the sunlight of love."

I'd never heard Sharlotte talk like that, but here she was, emotion in her voice, saying such a pretty thing. It made me want to hug her, but Sharlotte wasn't one for hugs. She only ever pet her cows. Never even pet the dogs.

She stared at the weeds around us. "Sally Browne Burke talked about the quiet strength of women, and I liked that. I clung to the New Morality 'cause it seemed like the only sane thing in the world. But I don't know anymore. Breeze and Keys, their love is so pure. Watching them makes me feel alone. It made me doubt the New Morality even before Mama died. Now that's she's dead, I'm lost and gone."

"You knew about Breeze and Keys?" I asked, shocked.

She grinned. "Why do you think I put them in the same tent?"

I couldn't talk. How could Sharlotte accept their *gillian* love? And, in some ways, even encourage it? Both the Catholic Church and the New Morality saw any kind of homosexuality as the gravest of sins. Not venial, but mortal.

I was so surprised. Even more surprised when Sharlotte sat down in the dandelions. "When Micaiah was with me, I felt so good, like a dream come true, but I didn't really believe it. Felt more like a story than the real thing. And you know, it was like I was supposed to want his love. Girl meets boy and they fall in love, especially if he's handsome and viable. But it wasn't him I wanted. Really, I only wanted someone's affection. I wanted to be wanted. But that's over."

I suppose I should've been glad Micaiah was all mine, but seeing Sharlotte so hopeless, I didn't much care. Our love triangle had come undone, but then, so had Sharlotte.

"Mama's dead," she whispered. "I feel dead."

She lay back on the ground, yellow flowers around her ears. "I'm not going to cross to the other shore. I'm going to drown in this river of blood, right here. Dead, among dandelions."

I dropped to my knees, my heart tossing around beats that left me breathless. "Shar, don't talk like that. Please, I need you to be strong. If you aren't strong, who will be? Wren can't. She's crazy. For real. Mentally ill, prolly. And Pilate, he's uncertain. And the rest of them, they're okay, but they're not you, Sharlotte. I need you. Who else will lead?"

Sharlotte smiled at me. "What about you, Cavvy? You're the best of us. Mama was right to send you to school. I was jealous and hated you for it, but it was the right thing to do. I love you, Cavvy. Hate Wren, but love you."

"If you love me, be my big sister. Be the leader. 'Cause I can't. I'm too young and feeling it."

Sharlotte's long-lashed eyes fell kindly on me. "Pilate says us Weller girls were born old warriors."

"What does Pilate know, anyway?"

She sat up. "No, Cavvy, I don't want to be the leader anymore. I got Jenny Bell killed. We shouldn't have stayed as long as we did, and we should've told them about the boy."

"You can't blame yourself for that. If it's anyone's fault, it's mine. Please, Sharlotte."

The wind blew a strand of hair across her face. "Maybe you're right. Still, I need to leave, take off and be like Wren for a while. Y'all go on without me."

Just like that, I became the leader. Even though I was only in the spring of my sixteenth year, I had just been put in charge of the third largest cattle operation in the Colorado territory.

Our leader had quit. Our sniper took an oath to do no harm. We had hundreds and hundreds of kilometers in front of us. Deserts. The Psycho Princess. The Wind River people. The Vixx sisters.

Armageddon.

For a half-second, I thought about turning east, to follow through on Sharlotte's promise to end the drive right there. But no, Mama had built our cattle operation from nothing. She had bled to give us a house, a life, however hard. She'd killed Queenie, an Outlaw Warlord, to keep us safe in a home she loved. I would not be the one to give up on the dreams she'd built nor forsake the graves there. Never.

We might have been in the middle of a river of blood, but as long as I had breath, I was going to keep on swimming, so I could save our sacred ground.

*Holy Mary, Mother of God, help me.*

I got to my feet, quaking.

And 'cause I was a Weller to my bones, I got to work.

# Chapter Seven

*True leadership requires more than courage. It requires
an almost irrational determination to follow your vision.
Words like duty, honor, and responsibility turn to ash in
the fire of such a commitment. The Catholics believe I
will burn in hell for my research into the mysteries of
human DNA. I say by the time I die, I will have already
been completely consumed by my vision of a perfect
world.*
　　　　—Tiberius "Tibbs" Hoyt, Founder of the American
　　　　　　Reproduction Knowledge Initiative
　　　　　47th World Congress on Human Reproduction
　　　　　　　　　　　　　　　　　March 11, 2045

## (i)

B ACK AT THE CHUCK WAGON, I SECRETLY HELPED
Sharlotte gather supplies. I felt so overwhelmed
there wasn't any room in my head to be mad at
her.

Late afternoon sunshine made Prince's coat
gleam like he'd been oiled. Tina Machinegun bounced in
the holster on the saddle. Sharlotte only took two clips of
ammunition and one extra grenade.

Where would she go? What would she do?

I didn't know. She hugged me for a long time, her head on my shoulder, and I swear to God it was like being embraced by a stranger. This wasn't my sister. Sharlotte would never just up and leave us, but here she was, on her way.

I watched her ride off. My stomach hurt like I'd swallowed barbed wire.

But I pretended everything was normal. Any time someone asked me a question, I told them what Sharlotte wanted us to do, like she was just over the horizon and would be back at any moment.

Everyone accepted what I said easily. Our employees and hires knew how to run cattle. They'd been doing it their entire lives, and a leader doesn't need to be good when things are running smoothly. You only need a good leader when life starts throwing bullets into the campfire.

That evening we stopped on a big wide-open plain, thawed out from winter. Spring danced happily across fields full of wild flowers and honeybees.

Around a popping fire of sagebrush and cottonwood, we ate hash made from beans, re-hydrated sausage, and undercooked rice. Poor Allie Chambers and Kasey Romero, they missed such a questionable feast 'cause they were taking watch.

Petal stayed in her tent, Pilate sipped his coffee, and where Sharlotte should've been, there sat Wren, eyes still red from the gassing she'd taken that morning, face purple from new bruises, yellow from the old. A bottle of Pains whiskey glued itself to her hand. Distilled in the Juniper, the makers poured their hooch into any old bottle then slapped on a haphazard label. "Pains for the pain," that was the slogan, and the way Wren guzzled it, she must've been positively suffering.

With Allie and Kasey gone, it was nine of us, some sitting on folding Neofiber chairs, some squatting on their haunches, chewing and looking at the fire.

"Where do you think Micaiah is?" Leave it to Crete to ask such a question.

Dolly Day piped up. "Don't care. I hope that boy doesn't come back. Call me superstitious, but travelling with a boy is unlucky. Can't believe y'all were so willing to lay down your lives for him."

I should've argued with her, but I was too busy trying to figure out how I'd tell them I was in charge.

Dang Crete wouldn't shut up. "Where's Sharlotte?"

This time Dolly didn't answer, and the silence stretched out long and uncomfortable.

Aunt Bea sighed and left for her chuck wagon. Our dogs, Bella, Jacob, and Edward, tore after her, hoping for scraps.

Did Bea know what was going on?

Wren teetered up. Even drunk, she'd gotten good at talking with her mouth half-closed to hide her broken teeth. "Don't know about Sharlotte. She prolly left 'cause she hates me so much. As for Micaiah, that goddamn boy is a jackin' genius. Ran away and left us knowing nothing. I was stupid to try and beat the truth out of him. Glad I don't know who he was. Glad I killed as many of those goddamn Regios as I could. Skanks."

"Why did they let us go?" Dolly asked in a nasty tone.

Wren cackled. "They didn't let us go. They killed Jenny Bell to show how hard they were, then packed it up, and took off. But not all of them. Left behind a unit to watch us. They know we know something. They're watching our every move, and I gotta say, it kinda makes me feel all comfy."

A splinter of dread stabbed my heart. Most likely, I'd never see my boy ever again. No way would he'd come back if the Regios were spying on us. I had to shake away those thoughts and say something. "We're still going to Nevada. Even if the Vixx sisters are watching, it doesn't change our day to day."

Dolly Day ignored me, glared at Wren. "Is that why you're with us around the fire? I was wondering. If I had my druthers, you'd be ten kilometers that way." She pointed to the line of sunset glow spread across the Rocky Mountains. "Out there, where you normally are, skulking around."

Wren's laughter sounded choked. "Skulking around and keeping you safe. Buncha hypocrites."

That shut us up for a minute. The fire popped sparks into the darkness.

"What about Sharlotte?" Crete asked again.

I knew I had to tell them the truth, but I couldn't do it. I prayed for forgiveness, then did my best to pull a Micaiah. I stood and lied my butt off. "Sharlotte's doing some scouting for us for the next few days or so. She'll contact me, and I'll tell you what she says to do. We'll go slow, take our time. No use hurrying until the *Moby* finds us again. It's real dry from here on out."

Dolly Day squared with me. Distrust fried her piggy little eyes. "So we do what you say, Cavvy?"

"No." I made sure I kept my words slow and strong. "You'll be doing what Sharlotte says through me. Business as usual."

I could see the uproar bubbling, about to burst.

Aunt Bea came back with her pot to ladle out the dregs of dinner. "Yeah, I talked with Sharlotte. It's okay."

Aunt Bea and I exchanged glances. She knew I was lying. She also knew if Dolly Day guessed that, there'd be a mutiny.

Breeze added to the lie. "That's right. Sharlotte's done this before on other drives. She likes to get a scope on the land. We've been so crazy lately, what with the attacks, the blizzard and all, she didn't have time. Usually, she talks through me, but with Cavvy here, well, Cavvy is family." Breeze and Keys were sitting next to each other, closer now. Might even been holding hands in the darkness.

Breeze's words sealed the deal.

"Well," Dolly Day said, "who am I to question the bosses? I'll do as I'm told. Too far to go back. Too dangerous, and with June Mai all over Burlington, we're better off out here. But we have a long way to go. Got the Rockies and the Great Salt Flats. Whole lake of salt, the way I hear it. And we ain't got no French fries."

We chuckled uneasily. The joke wasn't funny, but we needed a little laughing right then. We divided up watches, and most folks went to bed. Well, I didn't. And Aunt Bea didn't. She had dishes to do.

Aunt Bea stopped me on my way to check on the remuda.

"Do you think Sharlotte will come back, *mija*?" she asked. "I've known this family all my life, and I can piece together what happened. Considerate, hardworking Sharlotte Weller finally snapped and pulled a Wren. Gotta say, not too surprised, but her timing is awful."

I smiled. Bea had us all figured out. "Sharlotte's just feeling bad about last night, this morning, everything. You know she's been having trouble since Mama died. They were so close." I paused. "Thanks, Bea, for covering for me. And thank Nikki, too. I won't let you down."

When Bea nodded, her chin disappeared into the fat on her neck. "Aw, *mija*, we'll do this together. You ain't alone out here. Remember, there is only one leader, and that's the Lord God in heaven."

"Amen to that, Bea, but we both know He needs someone here on Earth to make the difficult decisions." I hugged her and got a little girly 'strogen teary.

I then went to check on the horses. Since I was leading now, Crete would have to take over the remuda. She wasn't going to like that, and I wasn't either. I cared for those animals and loved the time I got to spend with them.

On the way to my ponies, I crossed paths with Wren. "Sharlotte took off, didn't she?"

"Scoutin'," I muttered.

"Uh huh." Wren grinned. "Don't worry, she'll come back. She ain't got the stomach to really leave. Leavin' is harder than it looks. Lonelier."

I needed to make peace with Wren, and part of me wanted to offer her some comfort, so I said words I didn't really believe. "Look, Wren, I'm sorry we've not been so close. I really do love—"

"Don't." She spit into the dirt. "You don't love me, Cavvy, despite what Pilate says. Shame on you for such a lie, but then you've learned a lot from that boy. What else has he been teaching you?" She answered her own question before I could defend myself. "Miss Prissy

Cavatica Weller, getting all hot and bothered with a guy before marriage. Another hypocrite, just like Sally Browne Burke. I bet she likes a diddle, though she'd deny it to the end. I just hope the diddlin' didn't get you pregnant. Last jackerin' thing this world needs is another Weller girl, and it'll be harder for you to lead if you're pregnant."

Before I could say another word, she wandered off.

"I'm sorry." Those words I meant. Sorry Wren struggled in the world, and there wasn't a thing I could do to help her.

The horses nuzzled me, and I petted their noses and brushed their flanks and smelled their strong smell. The night was chilly, but being surrounded by the bodies made it feel just right. My family was trouble, and I couldn't imagine we'd ever get over all the pain we'd caused one another, but at least I could find solace in my horses.

I left them, looking forward to sleep, but my night wasn't over. Pilate sat at the fire, a cigar in his mouth. If he lit up I would strike it off his lips. He fixed his eyes on me. "You and I need to talk. There's a few things I need to get off my chest since it appears you are now our fearless leader."

My heart took off thudding in my chest.

What did Pilate want to talk to me about?

## (ii)

This was Pilate, so he didn't get to the point right away. He lounged back in his Neofiber chair, cigar in his mouth, coffee mug in his fist. "Did you read Stephen King in high school, Cavvy?"

I shook my head. I was sitting in a folding chair near him, but not too close, so the smoke from the fire could pass between us. Normally, I would've asked for the truth quick, but I wasn't in a hurry to hear how young and stupid I was.

"No, of course not," he said. "We've all gone back two hundred years, to simpler times. You're reading Dickens and Jane Austen and those long Henry James novels. Like if we read enough nineteenth century literature, we can pretend the Sino never happened and that the Juniper is the set of a John Ford or Sergio Leone western. It's sweet. With the New Morality dresses and the cute way of talking, I sometimes feel like I'm trapped in a *Little House on the Prairie* episode. But we can't go back. Only way through is forward. For us. For America. For all of our troubled civilization."

Okay, he was going on and on, so I got impatient. "Pilate, are you going to preach me to sleep or are we going to talk, really talk?"

He smiled. "I was thinking about fate, that's all. You've never read any Stephen King, but the Dark Tower series is about obsession, fate, and destiny. Given my nature, I've been obsessing. I think it's our destiny to bring these cows to Wendover, Nevada. But Micaiah is more important. Somehow. He's a part of our destiny, and we're a part of his. I can't say how I know. I just know. Fate."

"If he's out there alone, should we track him?" I asked. "Should we try to bring him back and hide him?"

"No," Pilate said. "If we look for him, the watching Regios will follow us right to him. It's better that he's out there alone. He's smart. Really smart. Whoever he is, and whatever he has, it's important. Obviously. Why else would the Vixx sisters be hunting him with an army?"

I knew part of the answer—he was the son of the richest man on earth—but did that explain four zeppelins and hundreds of soldiers?

"They shot Jenny Bell for nothing." I had to swallow hard to get the lump down and the words out.

"Yeah, I know. I held Zenobia while she cried. I touched Jenny Bell's cold face. I offered to do the funeral, but Zenobia wanted us all gone." His voice dropped. "Before we left, I got more Skye6 for Petal, just in case. She wants to quit. She's in our tent now, asleep or delirious enough to not realize I left her alone. She'll beg. She'll plead. She'll scratch the skin off her bones. And those are the good times."

"How can we help her?" I asked.

He chewed on his cigar. "I don't know. I've never seen her like this. You have to know that Petal is done shooting." It was his turn to swallow hard. "And Wren is going to get worse. What Sharlotte said was Wren's worst fears coming true—that her own family hates her."

"How come Petal hates Wren so much?" I knew it didn't really follow anything in our conversation, but I didn't want to talk about me leading. Not yet.

"The truth?" He sighed long and hard. "Petal thinks I'm in love with Wren. Petal knows all about the women I help. It hurts her because she wants me to be faithful and I can't. With Wren, though, it's a different type of thing. I do love Wren. Not in a sexual way, more like *agape* love, unconditional love, because we're such

119

kindred spirits. Me and Wren. So alike. Troubled. Contrary."

He removed his cigar to sip his coffee and then pushed the cigar back into the corner of his mouth. Coughs wheezed out of him, but he suppressed them with a grimace.

I gritted my teeth and got to the heart of our conversation. "Most folks know it already, but Sharlotte took off. I'm in charge. What I said to Crete and Dolly Day were lies."

Pilate nodded. He spit tobacco flakes into the fire, burned down to embers now, creaking in the heat. The coals gave off a hot, dry smell.

"I'm your security, Cavatica," Pilate said. "I watched you sneak Sharlotte in, watched you gather supplies, then watched her go. Made me smile. It's her turn to leave and be the wild one." Pilate fixed his eyes on the coals. "You were able to leave. Wren got to be wild. And all Sharlotte ever got was more work. So, she's taking her turn doing both, leaving and going wild. You have to respect that. Most people want to rebel, but they don't have the courage. I didn't think Sharlotte did. But, here she is, leaving at the worst possible time."

"Mama never would've left us." I couldn't help but be petulant about it.

Pilate laughed. "What? She did leave! She left her family right when they needed her the most. During the Sino, after the Knockout, the economy was going to hell, people were dying like mosquitoes in a frost, and her family needed every hand to keep their business afloat in Cleveland, and that's right when Abigail Weller gave them the big 'go jack yourselves' and ran off to the

Juniper to salvage. And where did she get her salvaging skills? From the family business."

I frowned at his cursing.

Pilate tried to soothe me some. "Don't worry. Sharlotte will come back. She loves you, she loves her cows, and deep down she enjoys how much she hates me and Wren. Like Catullus, she loves and she hates, and it tortures her, but she likes the torture. People can be funny like that."

"Until she gets back …" My heart turned jittery in my chest as I asked in a breathy, broken voice. "Do you think I can lead?"

It all came down to that one question.

# Chapter Eight

*War, in reality, is prohibitively expensive. The cost in natural resources, in armament, in loss of productivity, is cheap, so cheap, compared to the price we pay in the shattered minds and ruined lives of those who return. The expense of taking care of our veterans in body, mind, and spirit is more than this country can afford. War is far too costly, always has been, always will be.*

—Dr. Anna M. Colton, PhD
Professor of Sociology, Princeton University
*60 Minutes* Interview
February 27, 2056

## (i)

PILATE THREW ON A COTTONWOOD LOG AND SAID what he said every time he stoked the fire. "Flame on, Johnny Storm."

I never asked him what it meant. Trying to figure out everything Pilate said was like spelunking into prairie dog tunnels. He went every which way—the Bible, old video, fantasy novels, comic books, English translations of outdated Latin theologies.

The piece of cottonwood smoked for a bit, then caught flame. Cottonwood burns with a sharp, almost bitter smell, but it was one of my favorite odors in the world. It was home.

"I went hunting with my dad when I was thirteen." Pilate settled in to talk a long time.

"We drove all the way out from New York to Colorado. It took days and days, but back then, I had my Tendo XVS, and we had tons of movies in the car, and I was reading *The Lord of the Rings*, so the ride went quick. Even though I was just a kid, I laughed when we drove into Denver. I mean, I was used to New York City and Washington, DC and Boston and Philadelphia. Denver seemed like a cow town with skyscrapers. Then we hit the Rocky Mountains, and it was another world. I loved the trees, the peaks, and the wildlife. It was gorgeous. Loved it all until it was time for the hunting part.

"We were looking for deer over near Steamboat—me, my dad, a few of his friends. I had my own rifle. I had practiced shooting, and I was pretty proud of my aim. Hubris, of course, but a teenager's pride can change the world if they can hang on to it.

"I'll never forget it, Cavvy." His voice dropped, and he sat with the cigar in his fingers, inches from his mouth, the campfire gnawing at the cottonwood log. "I had a doe in my sights. But I was worried about the recoil. I was worried what my dad would say if I missed. And then I really looked at the doe, so pretty, so scared, eyes with long lashes. Gentle. I couldn't do it. It was murder, and I couldn't murder her."

He put the cigar in his mouth and chewed on it. Pilate rarely told stories about his past. This was a first, but I couldn't quite imagine him gun-shy. I'd shot a deer before. It was hard, but I'd done it. And here he was,

Pilate, this great warrior, too soft to pull the trigger on a doe.

"Thou shall not kill," Pilate continued. "It's a full one-tenth of God's holy commandments, and people could go to church, week after week, and still go off and kill. Oh, how I loved Mass. The grandness of it all. The spectacle, the ancient history, the otherworldliness. *Holy, Holy, Holy Lord, God of power and might.* And every Sunday, we got to witness a miracle, bread and wine changed into flesh and blood. A holy sacrifice. Magic."

"Is that why you became a priest?" I asked. Couldn't help it. I needed to know if he thought I could lead the cattle drive, but he was drawing me into his story.

"Partly. Partly to avoid the war. I was fifteen when China invaded Taiwan, to restore their great empire. Chinese history is cyclical. Lose land during the bad times and gain land in the good. The Yangtze and Yellow Rivers flood, and it all starts over again. The Chinese were just following history's script. And the U.S. has a script of her own ... when natural resources grow lean, go into countries with armies preaching freedom, democracy, and blue jeans while companies fill their pockets with oil, tax dollars, and gold."

I did the math in my head in a minute. "So you were my age when they nuked Yellowstone."

He nodded. "I was a thousand miles away in upstate New York, in my little town, and we all watched the smoke, felt the chill as the sun went away. The great Sino-American War didn't pause a bit, and I knew if I didn't figure out how to get out of the draft, I'd find myself in Shanghai with a gun in my hand."

What he said sounded cowardly, but this was Pilate. How could he have changed so much?

Pilate smiled wanly. "My dad encouraged me to become a priest. He knew I was different. He knew the church was the perfect place for me, especially the Jesuits."

I interrupted again—backing things up. "So he didn't yell at you when you couldn't shoot the doe?"

Pilate let out a low chuckle. "My dad? No. He said maybe the world would be a better place if more men failed at pulling triggers. He was a good guy, my dad. A good guy." He then gave me a pointed look. "And if you keep interrupting, we're going to be here all night. Let me finish."

"But what about me? What about Sharlotte being gone and me leading?"

He turned the log so the fire could get to the unscorched side of the wood. "We'll get to that. First, though, back at the Scheutz ranch you asked me about my goddamn faith. I'm going to give you an answer."

"Okay." I strapped on my listening ears.

"So I went to St. Louis and studied at the Kenrick Glennon Seminary. It was so easy for me, Cavvy, especially the celibacy part. I guess I had the same desires as everyone else, but I knew how to turn them off. A switch. Click. I'd read another book or go to another movie and live some more inside my head."

When he switched gears, I kept up.

"The Sino, like all good wars, does a great deal of lying. The war will be over by Christmas. Okay, the war will be over by Groundhog Day. No, no, no, the war will be over by the freakin' Fourth of July. Year after year after year. They needed chaplains. The Father

125

Provincial of my region wanted me specifically to go. 'They need a gentle hand over there, Father,' he told me. I went, even though I was so afraid, even though I'd done everything I could to avoid it. Then again, I'd always liked Father Mulcahy on *MASH*. It's old video about the Korean War, but really, it's about all wars."

I nodded, though I didn't catch any of his references. More prairie dog tunnels twisting to nowhere.

"You can't imagine the Sino, Cavvy. It was a journey into the heart of darkness. *Apocalypse Now*. In the end, it all fell apart. The whole thing. It was years of chaos and bloodshed as the hierarchy and discipline of the troops fell apart. The United States armed forces turned into a killer robot, headless, mindless. Only slaughter mattered. Murder on a scale undreamed of. It made World War I look like a Weller family fight. The generals thought our technology and drones could do the work, but it takes people on the ground to do the actual slaughtering because in the end, people are far cheaper than technology, and we are far better at murdering than machines are." He laughed a little at that. "And there I was, little Father Pilate, anointing the sick, whispering last rites over the dying, hearing confessions that gave me screaming nightmares. God came out of the twentieth century wheeling and ready to fall, and the Sino was that last grand punch. A knockout. God was knocked out of the ring."

He got his stir stick and beat the fire until sparks flew and flames sprang from the mashed corpses of logs. He tossed on more wood and sat back down. "I read about the Khmer Rouge in Cambodia. Back in the 1970s, during the killing fields, the generals found a farm boy, and do you know how they turned that simple farmer into a killer? They made him practice on pigs. The boy slaughtered pigs day after day after day, until killing pigs meant nothing. And then they brought him people. Day after day after day of killing people until killing people meant nothing. That was me in the Sino. A thick, yellow callous grew over my soul. God was dead. My silly words and scriptures didn't matter. But if I helped kill? If there was one less China girl shooting at us? That mattered. Every death brought us closer to home, or that's what I told myself. Couldn't kill a doe, but I could kill people, rather easily, ironically enough."

Pilate let out a long breath. "Petal shares my same story. I pulled her out of the Battle of the Hutongs, and we needed a sniper. I taught her, and she took to it. She knew the anatomy of the enemy, so she could kill more efficiently. And with her medicine, well, it calmed her, so shooting people meant nothing. Just killing pigs. I made her into a killer, and I kept her doped, so she wouldn't crack, so she could shoot. After that, sleeping with her didn't feel like a sin. We needed each other, and war glues people together. Or maybe it's more like chains. Shackles."

That was why he was with Petal. He was shackled to her. The truth slouched sick and slippery in my belly. A hush fell over us. Our people in their tents slept, the cows lowed, and horse hooves shuffled in the dirt. The flames hissed when they found a wet stick, still green.

"My goddamn faith is gone." Pilate smiled sadly. "Has been for years. I don't believe in anything anymore, and I don't believe our souls can heal. Bodies can heal,

I'm living proof. But not souls. I'll never heal from what I've done, from what I continue to do. Unrepentant."

He coughed, cleared his throat several times, then spit off to the side. "Doctors and priests killing right alongside soldiers. That was the Sino. I'm not surprised President Swain sent all the Ladies in Waiting to the Juniper. America likes to march her soldiers far afield but then does a piss-poor job of taking care of them when they get back. I feel for June Mai Angel, but if we were in a gunfight, I'd still do my best to put her down."

He let out a breath, not a sigh but an exhale, like inside it hurt to breathe. "And you know, Cavvy, people think me sleeping with all these women makes me a sinner regardless of my motives. It's not for me, you understand. Even with Petal, it's not for me. I do it as a service, and I know that sounds like the worst pick-up line in history, but it's the truth. I miss celibacy. My head was a whole lot clearer back then."

He paused for a long time, eyes on the fire. I watched him. Kept quiet and waited. My insides stayed sick, listening, and I wasn't sure I could bear to hear more.

"It's just sex," he said finally. "It's crazy to come down against *gillians* when ninety percent of the population is female. Such crapperjack. At times, I think if the Church didn't have sex to talk about, they'd find themselves silent. And the Church can't be silent. Silent churches don't get donations. *Ad meioram Dei gloriam.* All for the greater glory of God. As long as the collection plate is full."

He snorted.

"No," he said, "the sex doesn't matter. But the killing. The hardness that's in me … nursing Petal and watching her crippled soul crawling through this world ... it hurts me. Every time I gave her the medicine, I didn't know if I was treating Petal's sickness or my own despair. In the end, that's what it was. I know it. I gave her the shots because I couldn't handle my own despair.

"Why do you think the minute I got home from the Sino I came to the Juniper? Traded in one war for another. Because if I went back to teaching, if I went back to reading and movies and my quiet life of study, I'd get bored, and then I'd have to drink again, or I'd have to blow my own fucking head off."

He said it ... the f-word ... the worst swear word anyone could say. Not the j-word, but the f-word. It sent a shock through me. Everything he'd said shocked me, but that was the electrical charge that triggered the explosion. I realized I was hearing his confession. And suddenly, the power of it all, my daddy explaining himself, made me cry. Tears fell down my cheeks.

"I forgive you," I said. "I can't give you no penance, Pilate, but I forgive you. Go forth and sin some more."

I didn't hear my own mix-up.

But Pilate did. He laughed and laughed, laughed himself out of his chair and next to that flat fire of coals. All the logs were gone. Burned up.

I kept asking, "What? What? What's so funny?" I was getting vexed as he crawled back into his chair.

Pilate wiped tears of laughter off his face. "You said, 'go forth and sin *some* more.' Not, 'go forth and sin *no* more.' It was perfect, Cavvy. I truly feel God's love. And ..." his voice broke to splinters and new tears, different ones, went down his own cheeks. "And I feel forgiven." He choked on those last words, then got up quick and grabbed his big, black duster. "Thanks, Cavvy, for listening. For hearing my confession. For forgiving me. Petal wants to get clean, and I'm going to do everything I can to help her."

I stood too. "Pilate, I need to know if you think I can lead." I said it quietly so no one would hear.

He turned and stepped up to me. He put out a hand and cupped my chin gently. "You are Cavatica Weller. Between Abigail's genes and my genes, I don't think there is anything you can't do. I give you my blessing. And the nice thing about it, if you screw things up, Wren will just love to tell you all about it."

I felt a grin take over my face. "Yes, she will. Do you think we can get through this? Through the deserts, the Vixxes, the Psycho Princess? I don't see how we're going to get through her territory without facing her."

He nodded at my assessment. Then he shrugged. "I don't do hope well, and I plan on sinning some more, against the Vixx sisters, the Psycho Princess, or whoever else gets in our way. Now that I have your permission."

He swung around and walked back to his tent, leaving me shaking my head. That was Pilate, crying over killing, and then vowing to do it some more.

But I could ponder all that later. I had to get some rest, 'cause like it or not, I was in charge.

I knew I'd helped Pilate with his burdens, and I felt grateful for his blessing, yet the weight of the responsibility of moving our cattle across the wastelands rested squarely on my young shoulders.

**(ii)**

Even before Aunt Bea shuffled her pots and pans to prepare breakfast, I was fully dressed. In the dim light, I got a surprise. Breeze and Keys were sleeping in the same bunk, cuddled together like two pieces of a puzzle. They were scared and taking comfort where they could. I was shocked at first, but their hugs and embraces sure made more sense than Wren's nosedive into her broken-heart bottle of liquor. Or Petal's medicine, the crutch that crippled her.

Was *gillian* love wrong? If there was a genetic component to our sexuality, then it wasn't like they chose to love other women. And sin involves choice. But the New Morality taught that sex wasn't about our desires, but about following the will of God so the world could have babies. Sex was for procreation only.

Then again, if church people didn't talk about sexual morality, what would they talk about? Pilate said quiet churches led to lean collection baskets.

So I didn't know. But still, seeing Breeze and Keys together like that, I had my doubts about the New Morality's stance on *gillian* love. It also made me miss the comfort of Micaiah's arms. I adjusted the bracelet on my wrist and said a prayer for him.

I quietly unzipped the tent to face a spring morning chill.

Bea had breakfast going, sausage gravy on tortillas. We hugged again, and I went to wake people. Crete agreed to take over the remuda, but she wasn't happy about it. I knew she thought it was beneath her, what with all her experience running cattle.

For the rest of that day, it was, "Cavvy, do you think Sharlotte would want us to do this?" "Cavvy, would Sharlotte say we should do it this way?" "Cavvy, we lost a doggie over in a ravine. How long would Sharlotte want us looking for him?"

I found it surprising everyone seemed so helpless. They all knew what to do, but it was like they needed someone to pat 'em on the butt and tell 'em, "Good job." Which I did, even when my hand got sore and my mouth got dry.

And funny, I knew what Sharlotte would say. I could hear her voice echoing through me. It was Sharlotte's voice, also Mama's, 'cause Sharlotte and Mama were so alike.

Maybe Mama had run off when she was Sharlotte's age, to go and work the salvage in the Juniper and get away from her family. Except Mama wouldn't have run off in the middle of a cattle drive when we needed her the most. She'd have stayed on, even if it killed every part of her soul.

Was that a good thing?

Prolly not.

I hit my rack that night exhausted, but we got a few more miles under our belt. Just a few. I wanted to go slow to give Sharlotte time to come to her senses and for Micaiah to contact us.

Petal stayed clean. Wren stayed drunk. Another day, then another. More work. A couple days later, the *Moby Dick* found us with evening in the sky. Under Sketchy's steady hand, the dirigible drifted down to the ground, and we tied her up.

I was there to meet Sketchy, Tech, and Peeperz when they unlocked the back cargo door. It slammed onto the dirt, creating a ramp into the main bay. We used it to wheel big plastic two-hundred-liter barrels of water out onto the plain along with the collapsible plastic troughs we used to water down our headcount.

Sketchy wrapped me up in a hug. Her goggles made her eyes look just as froggy as the rest of her face. She was a huge woman with a wide face and big pink gums and yellow teeth. A wool dress covered her—New Morality all right—though Sketchy cussed like a trooper and claimed to be an atheist. "Couldn't find you girls, searched and searched. That blizzard knocked us back to Sterling. We got more water, got more hay, and we're with you now, to the end. Goddamn Psycho Princess took some shots at us. We are smack dab in the middle of her territory. I get scared and Tech tells me to pray to Jesus, but I don't believe in any of that."

She talked so fast and so much, I had to introduce her to Dolly Day. Of course they knew each other. Of course they tried to talk each other to death. Lots to talk about. June Mai Angel trying to take over the Colorado territory. Micaiah gone. Jenny Bell killed by our new enemy. Sharlotte supposedly scouting around.

Tech, Peeperz, and I worked on unfolding and setting up the collapsible plastic troughs. Tech was a hard woman, but a brilliant engineer, and she wasn't New Morality. Far from it. Tattoos inked up her arms, her neck, everywhere. She was smiley with me, and we both had great mutual respect for the other since we were both engineers.

Peeperz tried to help, but he kept getting distracted. He was their adopted boy, not sure if he was viable or not, but he was little, only ten years old. He played with the dogs, running, chasing, and finally falling down and squealing when Bella, Edward, and Jacob licked his face.

Real nice to see the boy so happy. But I still didn't know why his face was so scarred up.

My curiosity finally got the better of me. While I was tightening down a butterfly nut on the trough, I asked Tech, "I know it's none of my business, but what happened to Peeperz?"

She started with a sigh. "We were delivering a steam combine to a farm not too far from here, actually, on the border of the Psycho Princess' territory. We arrived during an attack. The Psycho Princess and her crazies had already killed Peeperz's father and taken away his mom and his sisters. A small group stayed behind to …" She swallowed hard. "They wore dresses. All these women, in these big, ridiculous dresses and costume jewelry, covered in blood. We stopped them from killing Peeperz. I'd never seen Sketchy so upset. Since he was orphaned, we adopted him."

That was what the Psycho Princess did. Stole the girls. Killed the boys. And we were already inside her territory.

"Horrible." I felt sick and scared.

Tech smiled sadly. "Yeah, but Peeperz still has a good heart. How else could he be so happy playing with your dogs?"

Right on cue, Peeperz giggled. Made me want to giggle, too.

"What do you make of the U.S. government sending the criminals and Ladies in Waiting into the Juniper?" I asked.

Another sigh. "That's how I got here. I had a choice between the Dwight Correctional Center and the Juniper." She smiled at me with white, even teeth.

"Before I got clean and sober, I was a real criminal. Does that surprise you?"

I had to think about that for a bit, and then I shook my head. "No, I guess not. Maybe the Juniper is a prison, but it never felt like it to me growing up. Still doesn't. It's a hard place, but there's goodness here, good people. Like you."

The smile on her face was as joyful as Peeperz's giggles. "I've been accused of a lot of things, but not of being good. Thanks, Cavvy. I try. I really do. I just wish I could be more like Sketchy."

At that, the airship captain spit in the dust and cursed at something Dolly Day said. The whole scene made us both laugh. I'd judged Sketchy harshly the first time I met her, but now I could see through to her heart, which was soft and kind. And she really was the best pilot in the Juniper.

Since the night warmed us with a gentle breeze, and since the *Moby* had found us, I decided to celebrate with baths and a little banquet.

Though it was dangerous to use water for anything other than drinking, I knew getting clean would improve our spirits. The women all took turns splashing themselves with water out of the plastic troughs. We teamed up to comb the snarls out of our hair.

After our washing, it was mealtime. Aunt Bea parted with some of her dried fruit to make cobbler. It was sweet and crumbly—a nice dessert after big, thick steaks sizzled on a campfire. After spending ten hours in the saddle, hips and back aching, untangling cattle from leftover barbwire fences, riding hard to round up strays, such a meal made you feel like a queen instead of a hungry, work-weary cowgirl.

Petal joined us as a shadow. Not even a shadow. The ghost of a shadow.

Wren had run out of liquor and sat at the fire, eyeing us all like she'd rather fight than eat.

Allie sang again, but not a war song, a drunk song. She said it was called *The Fairytale of New York*. Like her best songs, it was as tragic as a funeral.

This time, Wren growled her to a stop. "Goddamn you, Allie Chambers. When you open your mouth, it's like you want to kill us. Sing something happy for once in your dirty, mick life."

Pilate laughed. "Oh, Wren, that song was all about you. Your very own love song. What was the name of that gunslinger you were sweet on? I can never remember his name."

"Only one man I ever loved," Wren said. Her eyes never left Pilate's face, but she wasn't talking about him. I could tell.

Petal couldn't. She jerked herself up and hit Wren like a second Yellowstone Knockout.

It took all of us to yank them apart, but with Petal, it wasn't that simple. She was cracked-up from withdrawals, full of hell, with Satan's talons shredding her heart. She threw Dolly Day to the dirt, karated Keys back, and roundhoused Breeze down.

Wren had the sense to skitter back, wiping at her bloody chin, eyes gleaming happily, 'cause for her booze was just teatime. Fighting was her fix.

It wasn't until Tech and Pilate wrestled Petal down, screaming into her face, "Do no harm! Do no harm!" that Petal went limp and started weeping. The shattered soldier girl, one-time smart doctor, lay like a child in the dirt, crying like the beat of her own heart was a torture far worse than what the Psycho Princess had done to Peeperz.

I knew why Pilate had given her the Skye6 in the first place, how much sense it must've made, 'cause of how agonized she sounded.

Crete wailed, "I can't take no more of you Wellers. I'm sick of all your fightin' and embarrassin' us, and I gotta take care of the remuda when I should be runnin' cattle. And we're all gonna die. Them Vixx women are gonna kill us all, and if they don't, the Psycho Princess, and if she don't, the Wind River people, and if they don't, the Mormons. They steal pretty girls like me and make 'em sleep with old men still viable. I wanna go home!"

Aunt Bea held Crete as the girl wept.

Dolly Day joined in. "Yeah, Cavvy, she's right. Outlaw Warlords are one thing, but them soldier girls and this boy we've gotten mixed up with, well, that's a whole different kind of mess. And your security has fallen to pot. We heard Petal won't shoot no more, and booze has ruined your sister." Dolly dared to let her eyes linger over Wren. "Most likely, the Wind River people will take our scalps. We gotta give up. We can head east now. East and south. Run our headcount to Buzzkill. Maybe prices are better there than Hays."

All eyes fell on me. I didn't know what to say, so I decided to try and quote my sister like I'd been doing for days. "Sharlotte would say that Mavis Meetchum owns Northern Colorado. Just a nicer version of Howerter to deal with. We'll only get pennies for our headcount from her. Yeah, we might make payroll, but we'd lose the ranch and everything Mama and Sharlotte—"

Dolly Day cut me off. "Where is Sharlotte, Cavvy? I signed on to work for her, not you."

I wanted someone to come to my defense, but no one did. Everyone seemed poisoned by Dolly Day and Crete. That got my *shakti* fired up—those girls were trying to kill our spirits. I tried not to sound angry, but I did anyway. "You're wrong, Dolly, you signed on to drive cattle for the Weller family. You all did. I don't know where Sharlotte is. That's the truth. All I know is that I'm a Weller, however young, and these are my beefsteaks. I'm going to lead, unless you want Wren."

My sister brayed laughter. Yeah, Wren wasn't going to be doing any leading any time soon.

"Right, so I'm in charge." I stepped right in the middle of them all. My mama's strength seemed to flow into me as I talked. "Crete says she wants to go home. Well, our home is under fire. Might even be all blown up. But I believe the worst is behind us. We wanted halfway, and after the last couple of days, well, guess what? We got it. We're halfway. Look how far we've come. We made it through June Mai Angel, through a stampede on the highway, a bad blizzard, and through them Vixx sisters. Now is the time to ask for faith and keep on keepin' on. Mama used to say, 'Better to crawl forward than run back.' Let's keep crawling forward."

My heart thumped in my chest, and yeah, I was afraid, but saying Mama's words, sent a shiver down my arms. "You know what I think? I think we'll make it through to Nevada and we'll sell our headcount for a fortune." I smiled and appealed to Dolly Day's pride. "We'll be the first outfit ever to run cattle west. And if you wanna blow through your paycheck, well, you'll be able to get any job you like, saying you can run headcount from Heaven's Gate through the pits of hell and out the backdoor. When all is said and done, people are gonna whisper our names in awe."

Took a minute for my words to sink in, but then a crazy smile lit up Dolly Day's face. "You're right, Cavvy. We do this, people will take us serious. Ran headcount through the worst parts of the Juniper, that's what Dolly Day did with them crazy Weller girls. That's what they'll say."

Kasey Romero spoke up. "Me and Allie been talkin'. We're in this. Don't see how we'll make it, but we're in this to the end."

Allie nodded right along.

Pilate caught my eye, and he smiled at me with such fatherly pride, I had to look away or burst into tears. I'd just saved our cattle drive. Pilate took Petal back into their tent, but his smile continued to warm me.

Dolly Day called over to Crete. "Hey girl, let's not get fearful. Like Cavvy said, maybe we can make it. I just wish Sharlotte was here."

"Well, she's not," I said with some force, "but she'll come back. I know she will."

Dolly shrugged. "Who am I to question the bosses?"

That seemed to settle it for the moment, though I knew hands like Dolly Day loved to talk smack. Well, if she did, she'd find me there to correct her.

With the fighting over, we divided up the night watches, and people drifted off to their tents. I knew I had a victory, but I also knew, halfway or not, we had a long way to go. I couldn't stop thinking about Sharlotte and Micaiah out there and alone. Maybe even picked up by the Vixx sisters or taken by the Psycho Princess. No way to know. No cell phones in the Juniper.

As the leader, I needed to check on Petal and Pilate in their tent, but it was something I didn't want to do. The hell in Petal was hard to witness, and entering her tent would be walking into a dark abyss.

But I was determined to bring a little light in with me.

## (iii)

Praying for help, I unzipped Petal's tent and eased myself in. Cots, guns, and gear littered the floor. Petal still breathed hard, and Pilate held her, only it looked more like a wrestling move.

"She gonna be okay, Pilate?" I asked.

Pilate nodded, but his eyes told me a different story. "Yeah, it gets worse before it gets better before it gets horrible. Petal is okay. She'll apologize."

"I won't." Petal went to struggle, but Pilate held her down.

I crouched to get closer to her. I knew I couldn't do much, but I thought maybe I could heal at least one of her wounds—her jealousy of my sister. "Rosie, I want to talk about my sister Wren. I grew up with her, and she's trouble, yes, but there's something you need to know about her."

Every cell in Petal went still.

I talked softly. "Wren won't show it, but she's hurting like you. And like you, she needs Pilate, but not as a lover. She needs him as a father."

Still nothing from Petal. Only that ferocious light burning in her eyes.

"The only reason why Wren didn't kill herself was because of Pilate. He's my daddy. In some ways, he's a daddy to us all, even Sharlotte, though Shar would slap me for saying that."

Petal softened until she nodded like a toddler. Funny how pain can take us back to being babies. "Yes," she said, "she would slap you. Sharlotte hates Pilate."

"So, Wren's hurting, like you. She thinks her family hates her, and in some ways, we do. Wren's bad. It's hard to love someone who's bad. But Pilate can. You know he can. Pilate can love anyone, whether they deserve it or not."

"Even me," Petal's eyes filled with tears.

Both Pilate and I held her while she wept. It wasn't that awful, tortured sorrow, but a healing sound.

Pilate whispered to me, "She's going to make it. This might be the one chance she has of getting clean, and it's all thanks to you. Thank you."

I laid my head on him, on Petal, and let myself give into the Holy Spirit binding us together.

Yes, it's a hard, old world, and sometimes it feels like God is more of a jailer than a savior, and Jesus is a lie, and death will be our only reward. But all of us together, we can be Jesus to one another. All of us together, that's God. And it's good. Life is good, even for all the trouble.

I had to cling to that idea 'cause out there in the darkness, though we didn't know it, the Psycho Princess was watching us.

# Chapter Nine

*The trauma of our age is unprecedented. A generation of women returned home from the Sino-American war only to face the Sterility Epidemic. The hysteria of the New Morality movement capitalizes upon this trauma as does the marketing campaigns of the ARK. Once again, the souls of women are under siege.*

—Dr. Anna M. Colton, PhD
Professor of Sociology, Princeton University
April 14, 2056, on the First Anniversary of the
landing of the *U.S.S. Exodus*

## (i)

FOR SEVEN DAYS I MOVED US SLOWLY ACROSS THE Wyoming border. Prairie dogs kissed each other on top of their dirt mounds when the coyotes weren't chasing them down. Purple thistle puffballs hung over cacti flowering in meadows of green grass and gray sage. Magpies and turkey vultures owned the sky.

The plains got drier and drier—more sage, less grass—and summer heat threatened to come early. Considering how hot it was, I missed my dress. Nice thing about a dress, you could wave it around your legs and fan your under bits to keep things cool. With jeans? Not so much.

The heat made our cattle thirsty. Lucky for us, the *Moby* brought more water. Sketchy also supplied Aunt Bea's chuck wagon with flour, sugar, beans, and freeze-dried fruits and vegetables. Funny, in order to load up the trailer, we had to move around machine guns, ammo, and grenades—a testament to what our cattle drive had become. In a way, it was far more of a military operation than a cattle drive.

After making sure we were stocked, Sketchy and her crew lifted off to look for more water and to scout. So far, they hadn't seen any sign of the Psycho Princess or the Wind River people. Finally, we had days and nights of just normal cattle driving. No one shot at us. How nice.

My wounds were healing, and I stopped taking the pain meds.

On the afternoon of the ninth day since leaving the Scheutz's ranch, I got called up to the front, where Allie Chambers and Kasey Romero were guiding our cows down a dirt road, narrowed by grasses and time. Didn't take long to see what concerned them.

A two-by-six board had been fixed crosswise to a telephone pole about three meters off the ground. A boy hung on the homemade crucifix—wooly ropes tied his torso to the pole and spikes nailed his wrists and feet to the wood. I spurred Bob D forward, fearing it was Micaiah.

If it was my boy, the sight of his cold body would break me, and I'd wind up like Petal or Wren or even Sharlotte, wandering in the wilderness.

On my horse, I came up even to his chest. I gazed into his face. Even wizened from decay and the elements, I could tell it wasn't Micaiah. His face was too narrow, and his clothes were different. A maroon down jacket covered him to his jeans, and he wore athletic shoes, not the nightclub cowboy boots I hated. I wasn't sure how long the corpse had hung there, but long enough that the stench of dead flesh wasn't stifling. Still, a mist of awful stink hung around him. Dried blood crumbled black against the gray skin. His mouth pulled down into a gray, grim frown. His eye sockets stared empty. Black wounds from bird beaks dotted his brow and cheeks.

The Psycho Princess had made a serial-killer sculpture out of the poor boy, whoever he was. I'd heard stories of boys kidnapped from Mexico, forced to march through the Juniper. In my heart, I prayed extra hard for Micaiah.

"It's that Psycho Princess," Kasey said, sweaty and pale. "This is what she does to boys. Crazy. Makes me think we might try the mountains instead of trying to make it through her territory."

I had to disagree. "Trying to cross the Colorado Rockies this time of year would be just as dangerous. We barely survived the one blizzard that hit us, but up in those hills, spring can bury you in snow. There's a reason the pioneers took the Oregon Trail. Best place to cross the Rockies is in Wyoming." I went on and on. Easier to talk about our route than about the dead boy.

"You're right," Kasey said. "Still, makes me want to run like hell. I won't, though, and I'll fight if it comes to it."

Allie nodded. They were both tough Juniper women. However, I knew if Crete saw the body, she'd go nuts again. For our morale's sake, I made the command decision to hide the body.

Allie made the sign of the cross, then kissed her fingers. I had always liked that quiet, Irish girl. Now I liked her even more since she showed herself to be old-fashioned Catholic.

I forced Bob D up to the telephone pole. He wanted nothing to do with that body and amen to that. But I took hold of my *shakti* and used my Betty knife to saw through the ropes. The corpse wasn't heavy enough on its own to pull through the nails. Grinding my teeth, I touched his cold, leathery flesh. His jacket fell open. Inside, a note was pinned into his skin.

I tore it loose. It was a page from a children's coloring book with a horse galloping across a meadow, colored in with some skill, but words written in heavy black marker ruined the picture. I read it aloud.

Dear Weller Family,

We know what you are doing. We know where you are going. We know Father Pilate is with you. His death will usher in a new age for the Juniper. Women only! We will not cling to men. We will not embrace our oppressors. Women only!

Surrender Pilate to us and we will allow you to continue. Bring him here to this cross at sundown or we will come for you. Defy us and we will kill your cattle. We will kill your horses. We will take you away and you will become Madelines even as we are Madelines.

The choice is yours.

The Women of Magdala.

P.S. We've been watching you. We can see you.

My hands started to shake. I stuffed the note into my pocket.

Allie and Kasey stood in their stirrups, scanning the horizon for any sign of the Psycho Princess and her cracked-crazy soldiers. Even if their snipers were terrible, they could still pick us off at five hundred meters, and we wouldn't see them at all.

We needed to get out of there, get back to our people, but I couldn't leave the boy up on the cross.

I went to throw my lariat around the body but then stopped myself. What if the body was booby-trapped? What if, when we pulled him off, we triggered some kind of tripwire connected to landmines around us?

I'd pray for him, but that was about all I could do. Every flicker of sage seemed malevolent. I wheeled my horse around to run.

An instant later, a gunshot echoed across the plains. Bob D reared. Something wet struck my face. That good horse wouldn't freak from just the noise. Most likely, he'd been hit.

Mad thoughts of running and hiding swept through my mind, but I had to get control of Bob D first, who was bucking as hard as my heart.

I got him quiet and looked for bullet wounds. Couldn't see any blood on him, but my jeans were soaked. Had I been hit and not felt it? I'd heard stories of people shot right through the chest, not feeling a thing, until they pitched forward dead.

Then I saw it. Swinging from a leather strap, my metal canteen had burst open showing ragged metal edges. The sniper hadn't been aiming at me, but at Bob D. The water had splashed my face and drenched my jeans.

I shouted at Kasey and Allie. "You girls find Wren and Pilate. I'll lead them off." I didn't need spurs for Bob D. He was smart enough to know it was time to run and run hard.

Kasey and Allie drove their ponies over the plain back south toward where the chuck wagon would be, and I galloped west, toward a hogback littered with boulders. I had no idea if I was going in the right direction, but the ridge offered the only cover.

I kept low, reins in one hand, a fancy AZ3 assault rifle in the other. I had stuffed three M67 anti-personnel fragmentation grenades into Bob D's saddlebags that morning. I wasn't sure I could use any of the weapons, but I was grateful to be armed.

Bob D's lithe body stretched into a sprint, his hooves throwing dust and dirt and clumps of brush as we thundered away. I didn't know if the sniper took more shots at Bob D and me—couldn't hear anything above the sound of the pounding horse.

At the cluster of boulders, I stepped out of the saddle and rolled across ground coming within millimeters of a prickly-pear cactus that would've gored my hands bloody.

Sunshine cooked the dust, the rocks, everything. Sweat dribbled off my nose and tickled my neck.

Bob shook himself, whinnied, prolly still smarting from the sniper's bullet striking the canteen. He let out his bladder in a stink of yellow spray. I couldn't let him finish and had to pull him by the reins even as he relieved himself. I got us behind the fat, chalky boulders, so we both had cover, then readied my assault rifle. I hoped the sniper recognized me as the leader and let Allie and Kasey get away.

I peeked around the boulder. A bullet tore into the rock—stung my face with pebbles and blinded me with rock dust. I was pinned down. Every one of my heartbeats exploded in my ears.

I didn't have Pilate or Wren to help me. I was alone, hot, near to panicking. But I knew if I allowed the fear to take me, I'd die. So I closed my eyes, couldn't see anything anyway, and let my tears clean my eyeballs. I prayed. I thought of Mama. Took a deep breath, inhaling the smells of dusty rock, gunpowder, and Bob D's sweaty stench.

Rocks shifted in a rattling tumble of shale pieces scratching across hardscrabble. I blinked out the last of the dust. Above me, behind other cream-colored boulders, something pink swept about. It seemed to be a bright pink dress, but who would be walking around in such an outfit?

A woman came into view, staring at me not five meters away. Her bright diamond jewelry sparkled in the noonday sun—necklaces, bracelets, and rings. She was hatless, and her skin had been blasted to the color of autumn leaves long dead. In her hand was an MG21, a Sino assault rifle, like the ones June Mai Angel issued to her troops.

But this woman in the dress wasn't one of June Mai's soldier girls. Far from it.

No, I knew who she was. Tech had told me when we talked about Peeperz's scar. She mentioned the Psycho Princess, or one of her soldiers, might be walking around in a bad bridesmaid's dress from some terrible wedding.

The woman spoke to me. "Hello, my friend. I'm Madeline. From one woman to another, I welcome you to my lands."

She leveled her rifle right, and I found myself staring down the barrel. Not much of a welcome, if you ask me.

## (ii)

Both Bob D and I watched the woman in the pink dress—both of us stood frozen. Bob was close enough that I could've grabbed his reins and put him between me and the woman, but I'd already gotten two horses killed by hiding behind them, poor Mary B and Lambchop. I wouldn't sacrifice another.

The woman, Madeline, might kill my horse, but she wouldn't kill me. She'd take me back to Magdala, where, rumor had it, the Psycho Princess had her headquarters. There, she'd brainwash me into joining her.

"Hi," I said. The AZ3 hung from my shoulder, but I wouldn't have time to bring it around.

"We've been watching you. You found our note. You know." Her hair fell in harsh, brown-colored curls, a shade lighter than her skin. Lord, her hair had been curled recently. In the Juniper, we had Marcel Maxims, pinchers you heated to get yourself curls. Not that I ever used one nor did any of my sisters. That was a monumental waste of time.

"So, you're Madeline. What's your last name?" I asked. Didn't know what else to do but make polite conversation.

"We are all Madeline." Her lips twisted into a smirk. "You probably call us the Psycho Princess, but we are Madeline, women of Magdala. We have transcended individuality, and you will, too. You will be Madeline with us, a sister in our great family. It's good you are young. It will take some time for the balance of the world to be restored, and we need the years you have in front of you."

I listened to her words but couldn't decipher the crazy. I needed a way out and quick. The sniper lay behind me, the woman in pink in front, and every second counted.

She kept the rifle on me, but drew a fancy, sparkly purse from around her back to hold against her middle. "We saw you at the Scheutz ranch. We saw those soldiers. We saw your boy. He escaped us for a time, but we found him. We have him."

My lips went numb. My breath went away. Micaiah. They had Micaiah. All conscious thought swirled away, and I felt my knees buckle.

She noted my reaction and nodded. "Yes. The boy. He's with us, but we want Pilate."

If they had Micaiah, he was surely dead. However, she was using the present tense. It sounded like he was still alive, but how could that be?

She continued. "Pilate has been sinning against the Goddess for years in the Juniper, and we can't evolve if we don't cleanse the world of males. All men must die."

I took in a deep breath and forced myself to calm down. I couldn't get stupid or I'd get dead. I cocked my ears, to listen for any sign of the sniper or any other troops coming from behind. All I heard was the tick of the heat in the brush and the whisper of the dress around the Madeline.

"How does that work exactly?" I asked. "If you kill all the boys, humans can't survive to evolve. You need new generations for natural selection to work. And it'll take a mighty long time to grow new plumbing."

She laughed condescendingly. "Of course you think that. Most people do, but most people are wrong. The world has been dominated by the males for millennia, and what has that brought us? War, rape, the Salem witch trials, hatred, and fear. Without males, the world will know peace, and we will find a way to continue on. We don't need males. We are women. We are the source of life. We must have faith that our cells will change. We will find new ways. You don't believe this now, but you will once you become a Madeline."

Madness. She and all of her kind were insane, clearly, wearing costume jewelry and girly 'strogen costumes as if that made them women who could procreate on their own. For a second, I thought back to science class where we'd studied frogs who could switch gender. Yeah, that was possible, but humans were a little more complex than amphibians. Usually.

The woman dug into the purse and threw bright stainless steel handcuffs into the dirt. "Put those on and come with me. We have you. As for your people, the deal stands. If they take Pilate to the cross, we will let them go. If they don't, we will either do two things: our snipers will either plague them with bullets, day after day, until they beg us to take him; or we will attack them all at once. We've done both over the years. Both have proved effective."

Either guerrilla warfare or a straight-up fight. Sure. That's how the Viet Cong beat us in the Vietnam War.

Behind me, coming closer, I heard horses storming across the plain. It was now or never. Already, it might be too late.

Next to the handcuffs, in the dirt, Bob D's reins slithered like a serpent.

Sweat slipped into my eyes, and in that microsecond, a memory plunked itself into my brain from my days in Cleveland, watching all kinds of video with my best friend Anju Rawat. In all those old westerns videos, when the hero got in a bind, they always did the same thing, and I hoped I could be as fast and my aim as true.

"Guess you got me." I bent down, as if to grab the handcuffs. "But I have to know one thing. Is that boy you grabbed still alive?"

I wanted to wait for an answer, I needed to know, but I was out of time. Instead of the handcuffs, I grabbed a handful of powdery dirt.

The Madeline opened her mouth to answer but instead got a face full of dust. She let out a yell as the fine grains dashed into her eyes, and in that second, I hauled up Bob D's reins and pulled him over. I plucked two grenades out of his saddlebags at the same time I stuck a boot in a stirrup and hauled myself aloft into the saddle. I charged off, going south.

Behind me, I heard her yell, "Deliver Pilate to us by sunset or we'll come for you. At midnight when the

Goddess is the strongest, we will come for you, your women, and for Pilate! Pilate must die!"

Galloping across the plains, Bob D and I were sniper-bait, but I had a plan. I pulled a pin on one of the grenades and threw it as far as I could behind me. Those M67 grenades have a wounding radius of fifteen meters. I didn't throw it to kill, only so the explosion could set them on edge and to blur their vision. The explosion sent a cloud of dust into the air.

I flung another one behind me, trying to get more distance this time, and a second explosion threw up more dirt.

Then everything else was lost in the speed of the horse. I didn't want to chance tumbling off the saddle trying to get the third grenade, and besides, Bob D could gallop at about forty-eight kilometers an hour, which translated to around eight hundred meters a minute.

A minute and a half later I was out of sniper range.

In the end, though, they didn't want to kill me. They wanted me alive so I could become a Madeline.

But did they want Pilate bad enough to kill us all?

The woman's last threat filled my head—they were going to put their guerilla warfare sniper attacks on hold for a full frontal assault.

### (iii)

I didn't stop until I found Pilate and the rest of our crew around the chuck wagon, already planning. Our headcount appreciated the break, but they were restless. Ripples of anxiety washed over them like a bad wind. I spied Bluto butting around another bull, and calves suckled at their mothers a little too vigorously.

Bob D huffed and foamed. Again I stepped from the stirrups, but this time I kept upright and ran into the middle of the group.

"Talked with the Psycho Princess, only they call themselves Madelines, and they're creepy nuts. This woman was in a prom dress or something, all pink and taffeta, and she said if we don't give up Pilate, they'll hit us at midnight. Something about the Goddess, or whatever." Even saying the name of their strange god made my skin crawl. "And they have Micaiah." My voice broke on his name.

"You talked to the Psycho Princess?" Pilate asked in awe.

"No, you don't get it. There ain't no one Psycho Princess. They're all brainwashed to be Madelines."

Wren guffawed. "Vixxes and now Madelines. What the hell? Are these skanks immortal like Micaiah's aunts?"

"Did she tell you they have Micaiah?" Pilate asked.

I nodded. "But before I could find out if he was alive or dead, I threw dirt in her eyes and ran."

"Did that old trick actually work?" Pilate asked.

I nearly screamed in frustration. "Darn it, Pilate, obviously. Tonight they're coming, and I don't know how many girls they have, but it's bound to be a fight."

"Thank God," Wren burst out. "I've been so jackerin' bored!"

The crew collapsed into panic. Crete burst into tears. That girl, always crying.

"They want you, Pilate," I said. "They think if they kill you, it will usher in a new age for the Juniper. They also think they can have babies without men once all the men are gone. Like I said, they ain't right." I pulled the note from my coat and handed it to him.

Pilate read it and smirked. "If only Dr. Anna Colton of Princeton University were here to do a case study. I'm sure she would find this fascinating. You know, the ARK has successfully created an embryo using the eggs from two women. Not that the New Morality people like that very much."

Through sheer force of will, I calmed myself. If I started yelling at Pilate, I would only join the chorus of hysteria around me.

The cows began a low cry, getting louder. We had to get ourselves under control or the noise and consternation would send the cows running. Cattle might be dumb, but they have feelings, and they could sense our fear. I heard Betty Butter caterwaul, getting herself into a tizzy.

"All you, quiet," I said in a low voice. "No need to lose our heads. We have to come up with a plan."

"Easy. Give up Pilate." Wren puckered her lips and made kissing noises at him.

"I do like women in dresses," Pilate said.

I knew they were kidding, but I still had to say, "We are not doing that."

"Cavvy is right," Bea said. "It's not like we're not armed. It's a shame, though, the *Moby* isn't due back until tomorrow. We could really use her for air support."

Ironic that Aunt Bea, this simple rancher and cook, could use military terms so easily. She had no official military training.

155

Pilate shook his head. "Well, if the old dirt-in-the-eye trick can work, maybe we should circle the wagons. Where's Clint Eastwood when you need him?"

"What about the headcount?" I asked. "If we put them in the middle of a gunfight they'll stampede for sure."

"Every cow is cash," Dolly Day added. "And I know you don't want my input, since I'm just hired help, but dammit, I ain't no soldier. I can shoot a gun, sure, but you want us to die for you in a gunfight and all because we got boys with us. Boys are bad luck. We'd have been a whole lot safer if it was just girls."

She sounded like the Madelines, wanting a world of only women. But as she talked, I got an idea; a plan, thank God.

"This is what we're going to do," I said quietly, all eyes firmly fixed on me. People want leadership, even when it comes from an unlikely source.

I told them my plan which confirmed me as a truly unlikely leader. But they listened.

I hadn't seen Petal when I rode up, but she crouched in the shade of the chuck wagon, hunkered down in her blue dress. She paled listening to my plan, and her broken-mirror eyes filled with tears. She knew I needed her to fight, and we both knew what it would take for her to pull a trigger again.

Pilate walked away. Just up and walked away. No sneers, no snorts of dismissal—his despair had silenced him. He wasn't about to say I was too young, or that I needed to be kept safe, or any of that. The reality was, however young and useless in a fight, I was the leader.

Wren liked my plan. Not sure if that was a good thing or not, but she was enough to sway the vote.

The sun crept down the sky as we prepared. The night was going to be moonless, but light didn't matter. Even with a moon, my desperate plan would've made that night dark and dirty.

# Chapter Ten

*We live in the real world. Ethics are fine in theory. In practice, our own sense of morality must be flexible, or we risk being righteous yet ineffectual.*

—Dr. Ravan Singh, PhD
Executive Director of Research and Development of
the American Reproduction Knowledge Initiative
July 2, 2057

## (i)

THE SUNSET CAME AND WENT.

Bonfires threw a flickering light on the little fortress we'd made—a triangle formed by the Chevy Workhorse II, the trailer with only the barest supplies left inside, and the Ford Excelsior. I'd opened the boilers and vents on the Ford and dismantled the piping as if the AIS in the bed had malfunctioned terribly. The steam engine was just fine, but I made a big production of working on it in case anyone was watching.

Pilate stood next to a bonfire to complete the picture.

While I labored, I kept thinking about the first time I saw a killdeer bird. It was on a cattle drive into Hayes. Aunt Bea and Nikki Breeze rode with us, but it was years before Tenisha or Crete joined our operation. I was little, maybe six or seven, and excited about the travel, but scared 'cause even a run into Hayes was fraught with danger.

The weather had turned soggy-wet that spring. Standing puddles shimmered on the remnants of I-70 as we pushed our headcount east. We'd stopped, and I'd gotten off my little pony when I saw a brownish bird, belly bright white, with stick-like legs and a sharp black beak. The bird hopped around on the swampy side of the highway, its wing slightly bent.

"Mama," I remember saying, "we need to save that little bird. He's in trouble."

Mama *tsked*. "That little ol' killdeer is trying to trick us. His nest is around here somewhere, and he thinks we'll go after him instead of his chicks. Don't worry, baby, that bird is just fine."

In school, I read about a variety of other plovers in biology class, but I never forgot that first killdeer. Killdeers are named after the sound of their call, and if those birds could be that smart, well, people could be even smarter.

My plan was simple. Send most of our people with as much gear as they could carry to the east, as if we'd given up on the cattle drive. In the meantime, Pilate, Petal, and I would be the killdeer, acting like we had a broken truck. Pilate, since he was their main target, would waltz around to show he was with us and not the other group. Petal and I would shoot from the triangle of trucks.

Wren rode off with Nikki Breeze and Tenisha Keys. Once the shooting started, they'd gallop in from the flank, and we'd catch the Madelines in a crossfire.

The odds were against us, but then that had always been the case.

My plan had at least three variables that remained a mystery. Were the Vixxes still watching us? Was Micaiah alive? I couldn't think too hard on that or my breath would go feathery. We all agreed that if Micaiah was with the Psycho Madelines, he was prolly dead, which meant the Vixxes were no longer watching us or them.

The third variable—could Petal shoot without her drugs? I was betting she could. Pilate doubted it. Wren didn't care—the less Petal shot, the more skanks for my sister to kill. If we were being watched, Wren would outmaneuver them, so they wouldn't suspect that her, Nikki, and Tenisha were coming back to save the day.

We made stacks of AZ3s inside the fortress. Easier and faster to grab a fresh rifle than to reload. Petal uncased her Mickey Mauser, which is what she called her sniper rifle. Actually, it was a Mauser Trip 6 Redux loaded with .338 Ostrobothnia magnums. On the top was a Zeiss Real 18 scope, but she hardly looked through it. She set it up on its bipod on the bed of the Ford then walked away to sit on the ground and clutch her knees to her chest. She didn't look like a feared sniper—more like a little girl, frightened and in trouble.

Pilate paced back and forth in front of the bonfires, two MG21s, from our June Mai Angel battles, hung on their straps over each shoulder. His black duster, black cowboy hat, and long dark hair inked him in shadows. In chalk-white hands, he gripped his Beijing Homewrecker, a four-barreled snubby weapon that could shoot shotgun shells or lob grenades, depending on

Pilates's mood. He kept track of his ammo using the names of the gospel writers. Four barrels, four books, help us, Lord Jesus.

The stink of the cottonwood bonfires hung in the air around us. All our faces shined with sweat from the heat. Dang Juniper weather decided to go summer on us when we could've used a chill.

I glanced at the glow-in-the-dark dials of my Moto Moto watch. Ten minutes until the attack. We debated if they would wait until midnight, but I knew they would. 'Cause of the Goddess or whatever.

Pilate paced, I paced, and Petal rocked herself back and forth in the dirt. A syringe of Skye6 lumped the front left pocket of my jeans. Wordlessly, Pilate had given it to me. After what he'd told me, he couldn't trust himself to dose her. So if anyone was going to help her relapse, it would be me.

But could I?

Petal whispered rhymes to herself.

> *Mary had a little gun,*
> *And her bullets were full of woe.*
> *And everywhere that Mary went,*
> *Her rifle was sure to go.*
> *It followed her to heaven one day,*
> *but Jesus slammed the door.*
> *She died there at Saint Peter's gates*
> *'Cause God didn't love her no more.*

I'd heard her break apart nursery rhymes before, when she was shooting, and I knew it was the first part of her relapse. I remembered her words. *No more shooting. No more drugs. No more rhymes.* Like they were all tied up together.

She whispered more rhymes, barely moving her thin, chapped lips she'd chewed to bleeding. It was abundantly clear—Petal wouldn't be able to fight if she wasn't on Skye6. If I gave her the drug, it would calm her and make her forget her vows to do no harm. She would kill people as easily as a butcher slaughtering hogs.

If I didn't give her the drug, one less gun might mean defeat. Pilate would be killed, we'd be stolen, and if by some miracle Micaiah was alive, he wouldn't be alive for long.

So I had to choose—Petal's sobriety or our lives. It might've been Petal's one chance to get clean, and if I gave her the drug, it might be the end of her.

My teeth clenched. I couldn't do it, but I had to. I had to.

A few minutes before midnight, I knelt down and showed her the syringe full of Skye6.

She glanced at it, then looked into my eyes. The firelight painted her sweaty face a hellish crimson.

"Give it to me," she whispered. "You're worth more than me. Pilate is, too. I'm a broken Miss Muffet, and I can't tough it, and I deserve the spider's bite."

Was she worth more than me? She'd fought in the Sino so I could be free. What had I ever done? Every battle I'd ever fought, when it came down to the kill shot, I'd chickened out.

What did Petal deserve? She didn't deserve a life of addiction, the spider's bite.

"No." I stood, shaking. I wasn't sure I was doing the right thing, but I wouldn't give Petal the syringe. "You stay there. If you can avoid the fight, do it. If not, do the best you can."

I left to spy through Mickey Mauser's scope, but it didn't have any sort of low-light assistance. I couldn't see a thing. The firelight also messed me up further, but I kept my eyes to the glass until I got dizzy, nauseated from the tension, from the heat of the fire.

Another time-check. It was after midnight. Where were they?

I heard the whistle, like in any war video you ever saw. It was the aerodynamics of a sleek object slicing through the wind and traveling fast enough to cause audible friction.

Some kind of mortar, heading right for us.

No time to run. No time to regret my plan.

When you're a killdeer, sometimes the fox does ignore your chicks. Sometimes the jaws clamp around your throat before you can fly away.

The rocket hit the Ford Excelsior, and that fine piece of American engineering went up in an explosion that seemed to split the earth in two. I was knocked flat. A gash in my forehead flooded my eyes with blood. I wiped away the gore to see what had happened to Petal.

She'd been right there on the ground next to the Ford.

Then … she was gone.

### (ii)

Women on horses came in fast. The riders wore big voluminous gowns from thrift stores or the backs of closets. Costume jewelry gleamed, or maybe the diamonds were the real thing. Didn't matter.

I coughed, dazed, blinked at the blood and sweat stinging my eyes. I stumbled toward the Mauser lying on the ground. My feet tangled under me, and I tripped. A rifle stock swooshed centimeters from my skull, wielded by a Madeline on horseback. She wore a blue dress with puffy short-sleeves, a tiara clinging to her curls.

Pilate yelled, "Matthew!"

The pony shrieked. Caught in the blast radius of the weapon, the horse stumbled and plummeted into the dirt right in front of me. The rider flew from her horse, both dead. The fog of gunpowder, the odor of blood, and the strong stench of the horse all hit my nose. The stink of battle.

I pawed my way over the dead horse and removed the MG21 from the nerveless, ring-laden fingers of the woman Pilate had killed. I heard him scream, "Mark!" This time one of his 20 mm grenades exploded, sending more dust and dirt into the air to mingle with the smoke from our fires, scattered now from the explosions and fighting.

Another Madeline jumped her horse over me, heading straight for Pilate. Her skirts billowed in the wind.

He saw her. "Luke!" A shotgun blast tore her from the saddle.

I listened for any sign of Breeze and Keys, or Wren's pistols and her war cries—nothing but the pounding hooves of horses, Pilate's gospel gun thunder, women hollering, the crackle of the fire, the roaring rattle of machine guns.

"John!"

Pilate's last grenade took out two women and their horses. I gulped, sickened. Those poor animals, they shouldn't have to die just 'cause we humans were always so bloodthirsty and violent.

Pilate had the two MG21s out, one in each hand, throwing lead. The firelight showed him one minute, the smoke hiding him the next. The assault rifles thundered, reaching like extensions of his arms.

"Fall back and regroup!" This from the Madelines. Still no sign of Wren or our other people. Had the Madelines gotten to them? If not, what were they waiting for?

Pilate threw down the MG21s, both empty now, and ran back into our homemade fortress. He grabbed me and threw me toward the chuck wagon. I hit my head against the trailer. He slumped down and snapped open the action of his Beijing Homewrecker. He slid in two shotgun shells and two grenades then snapped it closed.

I wasn't good in a fight, but I could help him arm up. The Madelines would come for us again, and we only had seconds. Or if they used whatever artillery they had, we'd be killed for sure.

I got him two AZ3s, and he frowned. "I hate those new guns. Love me an MG21 almost as much as I love tapioca pudding. Your mom made good pudding."

"I think Petal might be dead." I said it quick, but it still hurt to say.

"I doubt that." Pilate smirked. "She's too much of a pain in the ass to just up and die on me. She's almost as bad as you Wellers. Jesus jackering Christ, is my friend-picker jacked up."

Bad cursing, but I knew he didn't mean it. He was just high on the adrenaline and trying to distance himself from his sorrow so he could reload.

I ignored his outburst and finished what I had to say. Before we were both killed. "If she's dead, she died clean. I didn't give her the Skye6."

165

Pilate laughed out loud. "Well, good for her. Bad for us. Now, are you going to help fight or just sit on your butt? Goddamn. Some people's kids. At least I'm around to see one of your ideas fail. You were batting a thousand there, daughter of mine."

I winced at his words. Winced again when a bullet struck the trailer with a ringing *chang* sound that made my teeth ache. So close. It had been so close.

Pilate stood in a flash, grabbed me again, threw me again, this time into the trailer. I tumbled across the steel bottom until I hit the tents. They'd been too heavy for our people to take them. Neofiber chairs stood stacked against the walls next to twenty-liter jugs of water, and cans of food, sacks of rice, other provisions that had been left behind.

Pilate slammed the door. All light left us. I heard Pilate stacking the tents, the chairs, up against the walls. I knew what he was thinking. The aluminum sides of the trailer wouldn't stop the bullets.

They didn't.

A choking growl of a heavy machine gun ripped holes across the trailer. The metal folded like paper against the onslaught. They weren't hitting us with assault rifles anymore. Now they were using some kind of belt-fed beast of a machine gun.

Holes punched in above us. Firelight flickered in the openings.

A lull. They must've been reloading. "I'm sorry, Cavvy," Pilate said in that last quick moment of quiet. "I'm sorry for all the things I said. I kind of lost it." He paused. "They'll throw in gas grenades to smoke us out."

His face turned red, then yellow, then shadowy, from the little light spilling into the ruined trailer. He smiled and touched my face with a bloody hand. At some point, he'd been shot. How bad, I didn't know. "I love you, Cavvy. If Petal did die clean, it's only because of you and your faith. It's not much, but it's a victory."

He handed me one of the AZ3s. "You ready to go out in a blaze of glory?"

"Yeah," I said, strangely calm now. This was it. I was going to die fighting next to my daddy. There were worse ways to go. "Let's get 'em."

Horses clipped past us, and their riders tossed gas bombs into the trailer.

Pilate threw open the door and leapt out. I was right on his heels. We hit the dirt, back-to-back, guns out.

## (iii)

The swirling smoke puked out of the trailer, and a breeze swept it into my face. I coughed it out, squinting through my tears and the sulfurous stink. The wind changed, and I was ready to shoot. Took long enough I know, but problem was, I had no one to shoot at.

No one.

The women who had charged past to throw in the smoke grenades were gone, prolly shot off their mounts. But by who? Not by Wren's Colts. I'd have recognized their sound. Maybe Breeze and Keys?

After another burst of gunfire in the distance, the night went quiet. Fire crackled, but it had been scattered, the flames going low. A red glow covered the landscape except for where the gas grenade in the trailer billowed black smoke.

A lone horse trotted toward us. I thought it might be Christina Pink and Wren, but it wasn't. One of the

Psycho Madelines sat on the pretty chestnut-colored bay mare, but only for a minute. I expected for her to fire on us, but instead she slid out of the saddle and hit the ground, unmoving. Her yellow dress went over her head to reveal torn white stockings.

The bay mare trotted to me. I checked her over, she was unhurt. Thank God. I'd seen too many horses killed in the last few minutes.

"What the heck, Pilate?" I asked.

Another figure walked through the smoke and fire, drew close. I recognized the gait, her slim form, her mousy, frizzed hair. Petal.

I ran over and pulled her close. Her bones felt sharp and brittle under her skin.

"Are you okay?" I asked.

She nodded. "No spider bite for me. Thanks to you." Pilate climbed up onto the Chevy Workhorse II to scout. He wasn't firing or yelling gospel writers, so we were safe for a minute.

Or so it seemed.

"Did you see what happened?" I asked Petal.

A shake of her head. She wandered over to Pilate and touched his boot.

He glanced down. "Why, Rosie Petal, I heard you were dead."

"Not dead, Pilate, and I didn't have to fight. It was nice."

"Nice for you," Pilate said with a laugh. "I had to fight all those soldiers by myself."

Ouch. Once again, I'd been worthless in a fight.

Pilate jumped down and held her, petting her hair. I let them have their moment and took my gun and the bay mare out past the smoke and fire.

I couldn't understand what had happened. One minute Pilate and I were like Butch and Sundance, going out in a rain of bullets, and the next we found ourselves alone.

From the saddle, I couldn't see anything except for gray plain and night sky. And the bodies of Madelines lying dead in their frou-frou dresses. Who'd killed them?

The darkness seemed to magnify the quiet. Silence. Dead silence. Deeper and more dire after the fighting.

I let the new horse dip her head and pull up some new spring grass, to eat, to get over her nervousness. Then I moved her into the darkness as far as I dared, but still, nothing.

"Wren? Nikki? Tenisha?" Silence answered me. Shapes moved in the gloom, big shadows with long necks and eyes that caught the firelight behind me.

More horses. I maneuvered forward and found five or six horses, all clustered together, still wearing their tack. They must have come together after the fight.

I dismounted and began collecting reins. One of the horses, a big Clydesdale, had a body slung across his saddle. This body wasn't wearing a dress. This one wore jeans. White bare feet glowed. I touched his shirt, and it was silky, expensive. A little whimper escaped me.

I drew back, turned the Clydesdale around, found the boy's neck, scratchy with stubble. Like Micaiah. His hair, longish over his eyes. Like Micaiah.

Couldn't see, could only feel for his pulse, but his neck was still.

The boy across the saddle was dead.

# Chapter Eleven

*I like failure. We failed at the batteries for years on end, and it made me and my team innovate. No way would the Eternas be as good as they are if we hadn't spent years screwing them up.*

—Maggie Jankowski
informal comments
September 1, 2057

## (i)

I PULLED THE HORSES THROUGH THE DARKNESS UNTIL the heat of the fires washed over me. The light was still bad, so I couldn't check the body.

Same hair. Same build. Same silky shirt I'd felt on me even while I wanted to rip it off of him.

One of the bonfires blazed up. Wren stood in the firelight, hands on her hips. Breeze and Keys flanked her, and I counted their three horses. Thank God all had been spared.

*You have to check to see if it's Micaiah.*

I couldn't.

I stepped out of the saddle and threw the reins of all the horses around a torn bit of metal hanging off the trailer. My legs trembled. I forced them steady. If Micaiah was dead, I'd go on. Not sure how, but I would.

First, I had to pet Christina Pink and hug Wren. Got to do one, but not the other. Wren pushed me away. "Yeah, yeah, yeah, glad to see you too, Cavvy, but I'm not about to get sloppy, kissy girly 'strogen. Not when I didn't get to fight."

Breeze and Keys let me hug them, and I did, for a long time.

*You have to check to see if it's Micaiah.*

No. Couldn't.

I turned to Wren. "What happened?"

Wren spit and shook her head. "Goddamn, it was dark out there. But we saw the Psychos come, let them ride past us, and I was fixing to shoot as many as I could, when our old friends, the Regios, showed up. Me, Nikki, Tenisha, we laid low, but they had to have seen us. Those soldier girls were wearing night-vision gear. For real. Had big sniper rifles like Petal only with night-vision scopes as well."

Pilate moved away and kicked over the dead Madeline who had rode up on us. He pointed. "Shot. Right through the throat. Night vision, you say?"

Wren nodded. "Had these masks with goggles, and they wore camo gear, like the high-end bushy stuff."

I hadn't really studied NVDs, or night-vision devices, 'cause all the new stuff was powered with Eterna batteries and wouldn't work in the Juniper. However, I did know the technology went back as far as World War II. You could slice lenses in a certain way to use every bit of light. Cats saw well at night, and they didn't need batteries.

Wren chuckled. "So we sat back and watched. After the initial RPG hit the Ford, the Princesses went after you hard, real hard. Then? One by one, those Regio snipers started taking 'em out. Got real serious after they worked over the trailer with a big ol' machine gun they had on a cart. The Vixx army saved us." She grinned at me. "Your plan sucked, Cavvy. We're alive, so I won't make fun of you too much, but you're slipping."

I gave her the best glare I could muster, then needed to know more. Hope was dawning in me, but I needed more information to embrace it fully. "Then where did the Regios go?"

Wren shrugged. "No idea. Could hardly see a thing. The Psycho Princesses wheeled around and took out some of the Regios, but mostly they just wanted to run. Took their heavy machine gun on its cart, tucked their tails between their legs, and ran. Crazy skanks."

I spun, rushed off, my heart, my breath, strangled 'cause if the Regios had left, they must know, they must know....

At the Clydesdale, I lifted the boy's head up. It wasn't Micaiah. He wore Micaiah's clothes, but it wasn't him.

I dropped to the dirt. The next breath I took was sweet. Not sure where my boy was, but he wasn't dead on the horse above me. And the Madeline had used the present tense. *We have him. He's with us.*

When I found the strength to open my eyes, I looked up into the face of a Regio, but not just any ARK army girl, but Legate Baxter, the woman who'd slapped me three times in the Scheutz's parlor. Charcoal blackened her face—her uniform equally as black. Fake sage bushes covered her shoulders and night-vision goggles hung around her neck.

I only had enough spit to say four words.

"Thanks for saving us."

The Juniper Wars: Machine-Gun Girls

Legate Baxter didn't respond. Instead she held up one of Pilate's shotgun shells—same make and model as the ammo we'd used against June Mai Angel in Strasburg, then against the Regios in Broomfield.

Proof.

## (ii)

The growling sound of internal combustion engines ripped through the night. ATVs sped up, diesel-powered. In minutes, dozens of Regios surrounded us.

Flung over the back of one ATV, I saw a familiar face. Praetor Gianna Edger lay motionless, bungee corded to the back rack of the vehicle. Blood dripped down her gray face and into the dirt. She looked dead.

Legate Baxter pocketed the shotgun shell.

"You going to take us in?" I asked.

"The Praetor is not conscious. We will return and give our report to her superiors. We know where to find you." She walked away. None of the other Regios said one word to us.

Wren shook her head and kind of laughed. "Now, they're going to search what's left of the battlefield, looking for whatever boy they just can't live without. If you girls are so hard up for dates, Pilate here can show you a good time."

Petal hissed at my sister but didn't curse her. Our resident drug addict was improving.

Regios tore the body of the boy off the Clydesdale, searched his pockets, then left him on the ground. They searched the trailer, threw out the tents, the chairs, everything inside. They checked the cab of the

Chevy Workhorse II and walked through the remnants of the Ford Excelsior.

Then they left on their ATVs, Legate Baxter leading the way. The diesel engines disappeared into the night.

No shots fired. No threats. But Edger and the shotgun shell meant they had more reason than ever to suspect we knew something about Micaiah. The whole strange encounter with the Regios took about five minutes. Then they were gone, as if they had never been there in the first place.

"Thank God our mystery boy wasn't with us," Pilate whispered.

Wren squinted, pondering.

"Whatcha thinking," I asked her.

"Them skanks are patient and smart. Instead of murdering us or letting us get killed or taking us in for torture, they're just biding their time. Watching. Waiting. If anything, that makes me nervous. They think they're so tough they own us."

"Or Legate Baxter will take the shotgun shell back to the Vixxes, and then they'll come back to capture us," I said.

"Wouldn't that be fun." Wren spit into the dirt. "Shame I won't get to kill Edger. I've seen dead before, and that girl is coffin meat."

Edger was bad, but the Vixxes were a whole lot worse.

### (iii)

We didn't bury the body of the boy, no time. We needed to rendezvous with our people to make sure our beefsteaks were okay and the Psycho Madelines hadn't attacked them.

Pilate checked the boy's corpse but couldn't find a wound. The boy's ribs showed through his chest, and Pilate figured he'd died of either starvation or dehydration. Maybe he'd even been alive at the start of the fight, maybe not. Still didn't explain why he was wearing Micaiah's wardrobe.

I said a prayer for both boys.

We tossed all of our gear back into the trailer and headed off, but not before putting out the fires. The last thing in the world we needed was a prairie fire, which could kill as quickly and as viciously as any army on Earth.

Wren galloped ahead on Christina Pink, lighting the way with a sapropel lantern. I drove the Chevy, Petal slept in the backseat, and Pilate rode shotgun. Breeze and Keys rode in the bed.

Wren led us onto a dirt road, overgrown, but better than raw plain. The horses I'd collected followed us, tied to the trailer. I'd named the one I'd ridden Maddy after the Madelines. Couldn't quite manage Madeline—the name was ruined for me.

The first cows we came across showed the AW of my mother's brand. Charles Goodnight traipsed over, so intelligent and good-natured. His soft eyes welcomed us back. From his bearing, I knew the night for our people had been quiet. Thank the Lord.

We found the rest of our people at a crossroads where they'd set up a quick camp. Sitting on blankets, they were up drinking coffee and eating cold beans and tortillas.

They let up a whoop when we piled out and into a storm of hugs, kisses, and slaps on the back. We told them the whole story, though I left out the part of me nearly dosing Petal.

We set up a few tents to get at least some sleep and pretend things were normal when they weren't. Aunt Bea fretted over the demolished state of the chuck wagon while Petal cleaned the gash on my forehead. She hooked in three stitches, which hurt, but I didn't bother with pain medication. I asked her about Pilate and the blood I'd seen on his hand.

"He lost the tip of his pinkie finger," she whispered. "They blew off the distal phalanx on his left hand."

That was the extent of the casualties. Sure, we go up against fifty outlaws in prom dresses, and Pilate loses some of his pinkie finger. The man had the luck of the Devil, and prolly the blessing of Jesus as well.

Exhaustion bit at my thoughts, but I couldn't lie down until I checked the camp, brought the new horses into the remuda and made sure everyone played nice, though I knew Puff Daddy wasn't going to like the big Clydesdale. Puff didn't, and I had to separate them. To make things worse, Christina Pink took a liking to the Clydesdale, which of course made Puff Daddy crazy.

I had to smile at that. Another love triangle, as if Sharlotte, Micaiah, and I weren't enough. But we weren't a triangle anymore. We were separate points, no lines connecting anything.

Missing Sharlotte felt like a boot heel on my heart. Micaiah's wire and grass bracelet tickled my wrist. He'd been with the Psycho Madelines, but where was he now? Not with the Vixxes or their Regios. If they'd discovered him during the fight, they wouldn't have searched us like they did.

Once the horses had sniffed and bumped the newcomers, they got sleepy again. I left the temporary corral and started back toward the tents.

Someone grabbed me in the darkness, warm with the scent of the sleeping sage heavy in the air.

I knew who it was. Knew him by his heavy boy smell.

Somehow, Micaiah had found his way back to me. He held me tight, and I let him. But no matter how sweet he felt in my arms, I knew we couldn't go on if he didn't tell me the truth.

I was determined to eat from the Tree of Knowledge and not stop chewing until I'd sucked down every one of his secrets.

## (iv)

I pulled him down into the sagebrush. If those Vixx soldiers were still spying at us, I didn't want to give them anything for their night-vision goggles to see.

"What the heck, Micaiah," I whispered, letting myself be mad at him for a minute. "You just took off."

He nodded. Hunger and rough living had thinned his face and left it dirt-streaked and wan. He rattled around in his new clothes, filthy gray sweatpants two sizes too big and some old *Star Wars* T-shirt, from the later episodes that my friend April insisted were the best in the series. I didn't care much for any of that sci-fi video, and I certainly didn't like his boots, which had somehow survived his adventures. His fancy alligator-skin boots were meant for nightclubs and city streets, worthless when it came time for real work.

He touched the bracelet. "I'm sorry, Cavvy, but if they'd found me with you and your family, they would've killed you all. To keep you quiet. I couldn't let that happen." He faltered for a moment, then said, "I love you."

Those three words made me pause, made me blush, and skyrocketed me into the heavens. "I love you, too." The words burst out of me.

Dang, I just told a boy I loved him—first time in my life I'd done it, and I had to take a minute to savor all the feelings. Then, yeah, I pulled myself back to Earth. "I love you, but I need the truth. All of it."

His breath caught. He turned away. I gently took his chin in my hand and turned him back to me. Couldn't see a thing, but it felt right. "The truth, Micaiah. All of it."

He let out a long breath. "I managed to elude them because they were watching you. Everyone was watching the Wellers on their impossible cattle drive. I found an old Dodge Ram with an AIS, and I got it working. I drove up north, thinking I'd get to Nevada on my own. I found a huge encampment of the Wind River people, but they didn't see me. I was heading west on I-80 when my luck ran out. The Psycho Princess grabbed me. You can't imagine how insane they are."

"I can. I do. I talked to one. But Micaiah …" The dang boy was stalling.

He hardly paused at my intrusion. "They knew Pilate was with you. They were going to kill me and Pilate together, in some big ritual. And this other guy,

Stephen. I, we, I ..." He shut his eyes and covered them with his hands.

"You and Stephen exchanged clothes." I helped him, so we could get to his secrets. "You were afraid the Vixxes would see you, and if you had different clothes, you might somehow outwit them. Stephen is dead. You were with him tonight, weren't you?"

A nod. "He wasn't doing well. They wanted to crucify Pilate, like Jesus, and they needed two thieves, one on his left and one on his right. That's why they kept me alive. Once the fighting started, I managed to get away and hide in the grasses until I saw your chuck wagon. I hopped on board, but I was lucky I wasn't seen. The Regios were everywhere."

I sighed at him. My *shakti* stirred. Was I going to have to beat the truth out of him?

He hurried on. "I was going to run ... but Cavvy, I couldn't stop thinking about you. I know it's stupid ... I'm putting you in such danger, but I had to see you again."

The words heated my face and cooled my anger. I took his hand in mine and held it tight.

"But Cavvy, there's something else I saw when I was north of I-80; south of the Wind River encampment. I think I can help you get to Nevada quickly and safely, but I'm not sure if we can swing it."

How could he help us get to Wendover faster? His words didn't make sense.

I touched his stubbled cheeks, like a blind person might try and read Braille. "All of this is fine, but Micaiah, I was serious when I said we can't go on together until you let me eat from the Tree of Knowledge. It's time for apple pie."

"Can I get some food and water first?" he asked with a quaver in his voice.

It all might be a delay tactic, or it might give him the time to run off again, but I'd have to trust him. He didn't make that easy. I fell into prayers.

"Fine. Don't go anywhere." I backed away, memorizing the dim shapes of the brush and drawing a bead on where he squatted. The slim moon gave me some light, and I was grateful, but it would also help the Regios.

Ten minutes later, I brought back my sleeping bag, a jug of water, and sealed plastic bags full of pemmican and old biscuits. I also carried one of the extra New Morality dresses we'd brought.

Micaiah stayed quiet, even when I moved past him to another dense patch of sagebrush, perfect for hiding us. I hoped it looked like I was making myself a bed next to the remuda to keep an eye on them. I had to assume the Regios or the Madelines were watching.

I found a little space in the brush. Deer or buffalo had widened it into a nest. There, I made a bed for us. Micaiah crept up. I handed him the dress.

He looked at it and I was a little afraid he'd resist, but when he talked I could hear the smile in his voice. "You want me to put on a dress?"

"It's been done before. Just put it on."

Staying low, he took off his T-shirt. In the silvery light of the moon, I could see his flat, muscular belly with a little sprinkle of hair going down.

I got all dry-mouthed.

Beautiful mind, beautiful body.

*Come on, Cavvy, hold it together.*

He put on the dress and then wiggled out of the sweats. Part of me was disappointed he hadn't stripped first so I could get a good look before he put on the dress. It covered him completely, which was the whole purpose of the New Morality dresses.

He lifted the skirt of the dress and flashed his legs. I couldn't help but stare. "How do I look?" he asked.

"Pretty." I said it as a joke, but it wasn't. Even dirty and smelly, he was striking.

He sat, legs crossed, and guzzled the water. The food, he wolfed down. I wanted to hear more about his plan to get us to Nevada, but first things first.

"Okay, Micaiah," I said gently. "Tell me everything."

He nodded and choked down his next swallow. "What do you want to know?"

Sure, he wasn't going to tell me everything right away. I'd have to ask the right questions to bargain the information out of him. Such a clever mind in that boy.

Sure, he was clever, pretty, too, and completely infuriating.

# Chapter Twelve

*I am like most women of our age. I would love to meet a man, fall in love, get married, have children, but so far, like most women, the numbers are against me. Even when 49% of the population was male, meeting that special someone took luck, divine will, and some persistence. Now? It's harder. Not impossible, mind you. I don't believe in the impossible.*

—Sally Browne Burke
Founder of the New Morality Movement
February 14, 2058

## (i)

THE SAGEBRUSH AROUND US SHIVERED IN A WARM wind.

In the Juniper, forever filled the winds. Millions of years ago, the land had been under an ocean. Now it was plains, but still the wind blew. Always and forever.

The horses on the other side of the temporary corral nickered, stepped, munched grass, slept with shut eyes, eyelashes moved by the breeze, manes and tails swished by breezes.

Micaiah and I were negotiating over the truth, and though I didn't want to throw out the first question,

I didn't have a choice. "What about the Vixx sisters? What are they?"

"They are ..." his voice faded. Then a single word. "Engineered."

Engineered. Biogenetic engineering. Not robots, but clones.

Still, I couldn't quite believe it. But I'd seen Renee Vixx survive at least two mortal wounds. Seen it with my own eyes. The Juniper really did have mutants.

I sat there until I could whisper, "So the ARK created super soldiers."

Another nod from Micaiah.

"Why do they want you so bad?" I asked, breathlessly.

He picked up the sweats, dug into the pocket, and pulled out a chalkdrive with the ByteBuild logo on the side. It was top-of-the-line, prolly a hundred ultrabytes on that stick. "This is the Oracle research database for the ARK. I stole it from a secret research facility."

The American Reproduction Knowledge Initiative. The most powerful corporation on earth. Government subsidized to research the Sterility Epidemic and selling Male Product along the way. And apparently brewing up an army as well.

"But the electromagnetic field made it worthless," I said. "That chalkdrive was wiped clean the first second you entered the Juniper."

He shook his head. "No, the ARK developed limited shielding for solid-state memory. It's not perfected, not yet, but it's enough to protect the integrity of the data."

My mouth went slack. "Jesus, help me. You could sell that chalkdrive for a billion dollars. If not for the drive itself, then for the technology of the shielding. You could bring electricity back to the Juniper."

*Just like Mama thought. She hadn't been stupid, Shar. She'd only died too soon to see her prophecies come true.*

I blinked and connected a few more dots in a half-second. "That chalkdrive has the base formula for the Vixx sisters. The science to create an army of them."

"Yeah, I think so." Micaiah sighed. "Not an army of Vixx sisters. There are only four of them, well, three now. Renee is dead, thanks to Wren, but Reb, Ronnie, and Rachel Vixx are still alive. They are better than humans, faster, stronger, bio-engineered to heal almost any wound. The Regios are less perfect, but still strong, fast, modified to follow orders without question."

"Are the Vixxes really your aunts?" I asked.

He winced. "Kind of."

I should've pressed him, but then I realized what could be on the chalkdrive. A chilly sweat broke out across my whole body. "You have it, don't you?"

He didn't respond. He knew what I was asking.

"Tell me." I grabbed his arm. "Do you have the cure for the Sterility Epidemic?"

Blackpoole Biomedical had been a little research company before the Sino, but Hoyt joined it early 'cause he was already in bed with the politicians in Washington, DC. In the early 2030s, when birth rates for boys dropped off, they went to Blackpoole. Hoyt changed the name to the ARK, to market to the Christian element, and made a fortune charging families for Male Product on every continent, in every country, worldwide.

"The cure? Maybe," Micaiah said quickly. "I don't know for sure. And you can't just sell the chalkdrive to the highest bidder. The technology it would take to unencrypt the data is only the first mystery to solve. You'd need a special Oracle plug-in to read it. Only one exists. At the ARK. You'd have to hack Oracle to get another plug-in. And if you could do all of that, you'd need the scientific knowledge to understand the data. Literally, there's only about three people in the world who could unravel the tech and the data. All of whom are on the ARK payroll and closely watched." He pried my hand off his arm and smiled. "Ouch. You're really strong."

I didn't apologize. "You have it. It's crapjack for you to deny it. You have the cure to the Sterility Epidemic. And that's why your daddy is spending millions to find you." Suddenly, his promise of a six-million-dollar reward didn't mean so much.

He dropped his head. And started to cry.

He was raw, emotional, far different than he'd been the last time I'd seen him in the crawlspace above Jenny Bell's attic. Back then he'd been kind and strong, yet distant. Now he seemed fragile.

I took him back into my arms. He'd been on the run, hardly sleeping, then held captive by women who wanted him dead. I couldn't imagine what he'd been through, and he was already such a sensitive soul. I held him like he held me in the crawlspace. I didn't whisper it would be okay, though, 'cause okay was a long way off.

I brushed a hand over his hair to soothe him. "Now, tell me how you can get us to Nevada."

He sniffed at his tears as he got himself together. "There's a train, Cavvy, just a little north of here. And not just any train, a cattle train."

Without meaning to, I grabbed him too hard again. Got another ouch out of him.

## (ii)

The moon climbed higher into the sky, and the smell of sleeping sage perfumed the air.

Micaiah told me about finding the train. He'd driven the Dodge with the AIS steam engine up north, looking for I-80. Somehow, he overshot it, which wasn't that big of a surprise. Salvage monkeys would've melted down the six-lanes of super highway asphalt into road coal for the steam engines of their Cargadors.

By a miracle, he didn't drive right into the Wind River people, but he knew he'd gone too far, so he turned around. Then on the outskirts of what we thought might be Laramie, Wyoming, he saw the train come rumbling into a station not twenty kilometers north of where we were.

He left the truck to creep around, overhearing snips and snatches of conversation to figure out what was going on.

The ARK had purchased a train in Buzzkill, Nebraska to bring reinforcements into the Juniper. More troops to search for Micaiah and the chalkdrive. They hired engineers to fix the tracks all the way to Nevada 'cause the Union Pacific gave up running trains through Wyoming years ago. The Wind River were ruthless when it came to the railroad. The iron horse had stolen their land once, and they weren't going to let that happen again, so they'd attack the Union Pacific trains and sabotage what they could.

He described the train to me: two engines, one in the front, one in the back; and over fifty cattle cars carrying troops, water, food, weapons, and ammunition. Near the back were five flat cars loaded with assault vehicles, jeeps, and extra diesel.

He said the only train they could find was a cattle train, which made sense since a passenger train wouldn't be able to hold as much gear and the big coal trains had stopped running in the West decades ago. Not a lot of coal left in the world.

While he talked, a plan swirled up into my mind to steal the train, but it was desperate. It involved bringing down the wrath of God on those soldiers—wrath we would have to summon without getting murdered ourselves, 'cause a rain of fire will fall on the just and the unjust alike.

Took me a bit 'cause I was thinking so hard, but I realized he'd gone silent. He touched my face, traced my lips. It was a prelude to kissing. He'd told me the truth. We could be together.

My chest tightened.

"Have you told anyone about who I really am? Sharlotte? Wren?"

"No," I whispered. "I never even told them you were in the attic."

"Please, Cavvy, please, try to treat me like any other boy you'd come across in the Juniper, come across, saved, saved again."

I didn't respond. Instead I kissed him, which devolved into a full-on make-out session. Took some effort, but I kept his straying hands from straying too far. Russian hands and Roman fingers, or that's what Mama called it back when there were more boys around.

Eventually, I had to stop completely. I was afraid of what we might do in the sagebrush, within earshot of the horses and the tents. I wasn't ready for that, not a chance, though I knew most every girl in the world would've told me I was crazy for stopping. Boys were rare. Boys you clicked with? Even more so. Impossibly rich, famous, viable boys? The rarest of treasures.

Still, it felt like enough right then. Not for him, I knew that, but enough for me. And I had so much on my mind already. We ended up in the perfect sleeping position. He was on his back, and I was half on the sleeping bag covering the ground, half on him. My head rested on his chest.

I was soothed by the rise and fall of his breathing and the drum of his heart, going from a snappy snare in his excitement to a slow, steady beat once sleep claimed him. I'd grown accustomed to his strong boy smell, mellowed by the sage and the scent of the night.

He slept while my mind roared. Sleep and cute boys don't go together, so I didn't get a lick of rest, and that was a shame 'cause I needed some. In a few short hours I was going to have to convince my people I wasn't crazy, when in truth, I was.

Completely insane.

My last plan had nearly gotten us all killed. Why would this plan be any different?

### (iii)

At first light, I risked escorting Micaiah into the cab of the Chevy Workhorse II. I hoped the New Morality dress would hide him from the spying eyes undoubtedly watching us.

I then swallowed as much of my fear as I could and woke everyone up. I sent Dolly Day and Crete out to secure a perimeter and to get them out of the way 'cause I knew they'd argue against me and I couldn't have that.

Around the morning cookfire, I whispered that Micaiah was back, but told them we had to keep him hidden. We had to assume we were still being watched.

With all eyes on me, I told them about the train.

"Solves everything," I said. "If we can steal that train, we can escape the Vixxes, the Madelines, the Wind River people, even the Mormons. We can get across the deserts and the Great Salt Flats and arrive in Nevada way ahead of schedule."

No one said anything for a long time. I could see they were afraid, tired of fighting, and I was asking them to fight some more.

Pilate laughed abruptly, then coughed. He glanced over at Wren, who smirked and shook her head. "Well, Pilate, her last plan got your pinkie finger blowed off."

He raised the bandage. "Not the whole thing, just the distal phalanx, according to Petal. I never liked that fingernail anyway."

I sighed. "Please, can you be serious? I feel bad about my killdeer plan, okay? Can we drop it?"

"Dropped." Pilate suppressed a cough. "Tell us more."

I kept my voice low for the next part. "Micaiah and I talked a long time last night. I know who he is. I know what he has. That's all I'll say. You'll have to trust him and me, but you'll get the full story once we get to Nevada. Suffice to say, we were right in protecting him. We were doing God's work. Still are."

Aaron Michael Ritchey

Wren gruffed some, but no one else did. She wanted the full story, but I couldn't trust her, not with Micaiah's secrets. She'd wanted to sell him into slavery when she thought he was only a viable. What would she do if she caught wind of what he had in his pocket? Or if she found out who he really was?

Pilate took a different tact. "Did he tell you what his aunties are?"

"Engineered super soldiers," I said. "And yeah, there's only one company rich enough, with enough genetic research to pull that off, and that's the ARK. That's who's gunning for Micaiah. We're prolly the only people in the world who know that the ARK has an actual army and enough weapons for another Sino."

We all fell quiet. I knew it would take a minute for everything I'd said to sink in. It wasn't every day you stumble into what felt like both a supernatural comic book story and an international spy thriller all rolled into one.

After a while, Wren squinted at me. "Why not just leave our headcount and run off with the boy if he's so important."

"Why not take both?" I asked. "Bottom line, if we did suddenly run off, the Vixx sisters would come at us. This way, if we can take their train, we leave half of their assets stranded. And yeah, maybe their Johnny Boy blimps will find the reinforcements, but then they'd have to chase us down. The Juniper is a big place. We go quick, we all get away. Get the reward Micaiah promised as well as the money for the cattle. Set us all up for life."

"What makes you think we'll be safe in Nevada?" Kasey asked. "If the ARK can harass us in the Juniper, they can hunt us down there."

I shrugged. Never really thought about what we'd do once we dropped off the cattle, past paying off the ranch. However, an answer came to me. "I've lived in the World, in Cleveland, for the past four years. Like 'em or not, the Yankees have laws. The ARK won't just be able to gun us down in the streets."

"Oh, Cavatica, that is so naïve," Pilate said, but not unkindly, "but I'll let the world show you that laws and reality rarely go out dancing together. I do want to add a few things to your argument, if I may. Once we sell the headcount, we won't be sneaking around with several thousand cows under our coats. That would help. And I would expect Micaiah would take off. If he's a good sort, he'll make it abundantly clear to the ARK where he is and where he's going. Which would take the heat off us."

"He is a good sort," I said. "I would imagine, with who he is and what he has, he'll make a big stink in the media as well. He just needs to make it out of the Juniper alive." *And with the chalkdrive safely in his pocket.*

Wren chewed on her cheek, gazing at me, trying to guess at what I knew.

"What about Sharlotte?" Aunt Bea asked. She looked pale and aged.

I closed my eyes in a wince. "I don't know about her. Maybe she'll come back. I hope she does. Or maybe the *Moby* can find her."

Another long stretch of silence.

I wanted Sketchy and her zeppelin to find my sister, but I needed the *Moby* first. Couldn't execute my plan without air support. Would she find us in time? If she didn't, all my hopes and plans would be like cottonwood fluff in the wind.

Pilate cleared his throat. "So, Cavvy, you want us to go up against highly-trained, not-quite-human soldiers. We're as outgunned as we are outclassed. I'm sure you've thought that through, though, so what's your plan to steal the train?"

Inside, I was quaking, but I said my next words oh so confidently. "We use the Juniper herself as a weapon."

A rifle report sounded across the plains. A sniper. Kasey Chambers went down. Hard.

# Chapter Thirteen

*For thousands of years before the Yankees stole it away, buffalo and the Wind River people owned the Great Plains. The Sino gave it back to them. I thought if a war could be generous, I could, too. I let loose a thousand head of buffalo onto the open plain above Cheyenne. When I watched those lovely beasts trot across the wind-blown grass, I wept. I cried for Sand Creek. I cried for Wounded Knee. I cried for the brutality of history and the hopelessness of humanity's cruelty. Then I laughed, because through it all there has been the wind. God's embrace. Sometimes gentle, sometimes brutal, but ever present.*

—Mavis Meetchum
*Colorado Courier* Interview
September 7, 2046

## (i)

THE CATTLE AROUND US TOOK OFF IN A RUN, NOT A stampede, but in a fearful push of bodies and horns. Us humans hit the ground. Most of us.

Not Pilate and Wren. Pilate threw Petal's sniper rifle to my sister. "She's north or northwest. That shot was a pass-through, and I saw the bullet hit the dirt." A heartbeat later, Wren was up on the Chevy. She threw

193

open the passenger door, climbed onto the runner, and laid Mickey Mauser on its bipod across the roof the cab. She peered through the Zeiss lens trying to draw a bead on the sniper.

Micaiah stayed hidden inside the cab.

Petal scurried over on her hands and knees to get to Kasey, who had blood running down her neck. My mind flashed to the Madeline's warning—*our snipers will plague you with bullets, day after day, until you beg us to take him.*

Him. Pilate.

Face in the dirt, it was clear to me, if we didn't get on that train, we wouldn't make it. Sniper bullets would fracture our morale and send us scurrying east.

"Petal," I hissed out in a whisper. "Is Kasey going to make it?"

Petal nodded. "Yes, it grazed her ... missed the vertebrae, the jugular, the esophagus. It's a miracle."

Or the sniper was good, too good, 'cause in the end they didn't want us dead, not us girls anyway.

Kasey moaned. I couldn't imagine how much that would hurt.

I still had the syringe of Skye6 in my pocket. I tossed it to Petal, and she stuck Kasey.

"Found you, skanks," Wren said from the top of the Chevy. Mickey Mauser coughed. Wren worked the action, then fired again. More long moments with her at the scope. Then, "Gonna jack you skanks up and right back down. You snipe us, and we'll snipe you right back. I got two of them. Two more are riding off. Too far for a shot and I don't wanna waste the ammo."

Pilate sighed. "Two down, but how many more to go? They won't stop."

Aunt Bea shuffled close to me in the dirt. "We need to steal that train."

"Yes, ma'am," I said. "We do."

## (ii)

Dolly Day and Crete came galloping in on their horses, but thank God, no one shot at them. Wren stayed at the Chevy, scanning the horizon with the Zeiss lens. Micaiah was under her in the cab, using her spotting scope.

I went up to my sister. "You see anything?"

"Yeah," Wren said, her voice strained from squinting. "Those two rode off. A dozen more came back, but I think they know we're on to them. They're hanging back."

Micaiah piped up. "I'd guess they're about twelve-hundred meters away. Just out of range."

Wren grumbled "Out of range for me, prolly, but I'm watching them like they're watching us. *Besharam* skanks."

"For now, that is good news," I said. We needed to be watched for my plan to work.

Pilate and Petal were the first to leave. I'd begged Pilate to take Bob D. He was fast, but more than that, he was smart and calm in a fight. Pilate agreed. Petal took the new horse, Maddy. Together they galloped out of camp, going fast, in a big splash of dust and noise. We needed the Madelines to see Pilate leave. And if God were kind, they would go after him with as many troops as they could muster.

Wren confirmed the Madelines chased after Pilate and Petal the minute they left camp. Good. Scary, but good.

Next, Aunt Bea and Crete saddled up Elvis and Taylor Quick. Aunt Bea shook her head. "This is racist. Just 'cause I'm Mexican doesn't mean those Wind River women will listen to me."

"It's more about your age." I let out a breath. "You and Crete, the old and the young. They might show you some kindness. Be sure to mention you've had dinner with Mavis Meetchum. That might help."

Aunt Bea harrumphed. Crete fought tears. Poor girl.

My stomach churned as I watched them leave. Pilate and Petal had survived the Sino together, and though Petal was done shooting, I knew she still had a whole passel of survival skills.

What Aunt Bea and Crete had to do was far more iffy, their chances not one in a million. Still, we had to try. Had to.

I busied myself packing up for us to move and scanning the skies, always looking up for the *Moby Dick*. Without the zeppelin, my plan didn't stand a chance.

Dolly Day was busy with a limping cow, but the minute that woman saw the bandage on Kasey's neck, she began to gripe, of course. I reminded Dolly that if everything went right, she'd be sipping whiskey in a casino in Nevada in less than a week with a pocketful of cash. That helped. Besides, she was only doing what we had paid her to do. Move cattle.

We couldn't wait for the *Moby*, so we left, on edge and armed, pushing our headcount north. Sketchy would come and find us. I knew she would.

Wren and Micaiah remained in the Chevy with their scopes while I drove. Kasey Chambers rested in the bed. She'd lost a lot of blood, but she fought to stay strong and upright, scanning the skies for the *Moby*.

*Please, God, please bring Sketchy to me.*

For the eyes watching us, it was just another day of our cattle drive. We knew better.

Around noon I heard the chug of the steam engine and, sure enough, the *Moby Dick* came drifting out of the sky and landed. Kasey took over driving the Chevy, even neck-shot.

Wren and I smuggled Micaiah into the *Moby*, still wearing the New Morality dress. We hustled up the back cargo door into the zeppelin, into the sweet smell of hay. Stacked bales reached from floor to ceiling. Blue plastic water barrels lined the walls, fashioned out of NeoFiber. A skin of lightweight, next generation Kevlar covered the infrastructure. Air cells of low-pressure theta-helium, otherwise known as thelium, floated in massive compartments above us.

Tech guided us through aisles in the hay, and we took our places in the cockpit. Sketchy gave Micaiah a wink. "Nice dress, Johnson. Even nicer legs. You like older women?"

Micaiah grinned right back. "Only zeppelin pilots."

Sketchy obviously hadn't expected that answer. She blushed. "Well, yeah, um, well." She shook her head. "Damn, you are familiar to me, boy. Wished I could remember. But hey Tech, can we give the kid some pants? Maybe your jeans might fit him?"

"They might. I'll check." Tech disappeared back to the engine.

"Whatcha all doing on board?" Sketchy asked.

"I'll tell you once we're in the air," I said evenly, though my voice wanted to tremble. If she said no, we'd be sunk.

Tech leaned to speak into a communication tube. "Okay, Peeperz, we're taking off. It's pretty mysterious as to why."

We floated up above the Chevy, our trailer, our cattle and our team on horseback. Despite the tension I felt, I couldn't help but admire the beauty. A blue sky spread over the greening spring plains.

I let out a breath, then told Sketchy I needed her to help us steal a train. She looked dazed for a half-minute, then took to caterwauling. "Cavatica Weller, I ain't risking my beloved zeppelin on some hare-brained scheme. We'd be shot down for sure. Killed and killed again. This ain't Hollywood video, and I won't do it. Don't care that it's illegal, it might even be moral, given you're stealing from such skanks. Still, I couldn't live with myself if I escorted you folks into an early grave."

"I just need you to get us above the train," I said. "Believe me, once the Juniper slaps those ARK soldiers around, they won't care about the *Moby*." If Pilate and Aunt Bea did their jobs. The fear filling my belly threatened to strangle me.

Wren defended my plan. "This'll work. When we get above the train, I'll go first. I got experience from my time in the circus. Once I jump down on the train, I can help catch Cavvy and Micaiah. Do it quick. Cavvy'll hotwire the train while Micaiah helps." She gave him a long look, trying to figure him out.

Tech returned with jeans and a white shirt, kind of blousy.

"If the shirt fits, you'll look like a pirate." I smiled at him.

He smiled back. "I like pirates. Though pirates involve water, right? We'll be stealing a train."

"Stealing a train?" Tech perked up.

I told her the plan while Micaiah changed. She blinked, smiled, shook her head at me. "And I thought I was the only smooth criminal on board."

Micaiah came back dressed in clothes clearly made for a woman. He had to cinch the jeans tight with a belt since he had no hips, and the blouse made him look less like a pirate and more like a crossdresser.

Wren plucked at the sagging chest of the blouse. "It's a good thing you ain't got boobs, Johnson. If you had 'em, you'd never have left home. Am I right?"

Micaiah rolled his eyes.

"Wren, you can't say such things!" I admonished.

"Did say it," my sister returned. "Not only was it funny, but with a boy his age, it was bound to be true."

Micaiah slid back on those dang alligator boots I hated, though they were holding up better than I would've thought. "What do you think about stealing the train, Tech?" Micaiah asked.

Tech shrugged. "I used to steal lots of things back in the day. Nothing this big though. It's bound to violate my parole." She put her finger to her lips. "Oh, that's right. My PO is still back in Illinois. Well, what she don't know can't hurt her."

"I'll do it, but I don't like it," Sketchy said. "Once Peeperz sees the train, we'll go low and tie the *Moby* to the ground and wait. At the first sound of battle, we'll fly you over. Then it's a straight shot. You should leave all the danger behind you except for the Mormons, but a lot of that is rumor. Tech grew up Mormon. They're just your regular Jesus-geek peculiar."

Tech nodded. "Just another sect of Christianity, but so American. Work hard, get a bunch of wives, stay true to God's will, and you get your own planet. Just another way of saying the Kingdom of Heaven is at hand."

Sketchy wiped a hand across her dirty face and adjusted her goggles. "Crazy Weller girls. Won't let nothin' get in their way. Mormon Jesus, or Catholic Jesus, please listen to this old atheist's prayers. Guide us, protect us, love us in our pride and stupidity. But, Cavatica, do you really think Pilate and Aunt Bea can do their part?"

I sighed. "They'll have to is all. Ain't got no choice." *Please, God.*

"What about Sharlotte?"

"I don't know. I just don't know."

We flew north. Micaiah guided Sketchy. It wasn't long before Peeperz's voice sounded through the communication tube. "I see the train, Sketch. Hold up here."

We stopped and staked the *Moby* to the ground and waited. Hours went by. Longest hours of my life.

Then sun was inching toward the western horizon when we heard the first explosion.

Gunfire.

The wrath of God.

Or in this case, the Juniper herself, wielding a hellfire shotgun.

**(iii)**

Tech reeled up the mooring cables, and we soared up and onward toward the train.

"Which group is attacking them?" Micaiah asked.

Sketchy repeated Micaiah's question into the tube.

"Can't tell, Sketch," Peeperz answered. "Too far away."

"We'll know soon enough," Wren growled.

Sketchy let out a long sigh. "Dang Weller girls. Crazy as loons, but who knows, this just might work." She threw every bit of thrust she had into the propellers, and we hurtled across the sky.

In minutes we saw the ghost town. Time, salvage monkeys, and weather had leveled the small city so only the train yard and skeletal buildings remained. Most of the tracks lay rusted or cut, but one set looked new—the tracks the ARK had repaired.

The train itself came into view. Even Sketchy was silenced. I felt like I was staring into a dream, or gazing at one of them big, detailed Renaissance paintings about the life of peasants with every inch of canvas covered with people.

Through the dirty windshield of the *Moby,* we watched a battle being fought on either side of a long cattle train. Aunt Bea and Crete had won the race and found the Wind River people first. Thanks to Micaiah, we knew where to find them. And if the Madelines had gone chasing after Pilate and Petal, they would soon be here, and we'd hit those ARK soldiers with a one-two punch. The Wind River people and the Psycho Madelines.

While the Regios battled the two groups, Wren, Micaiah, and I would steal the train. We'd rendezvous with our headcount and the rest of our people on down the line, west of what remained of Laramie, Wyoming. The *Moby* would fly back to guide them.

I knew if the Wind River people caught wind of a train in their territory they'd come and stop it. Copper-skinned women with long, dark hair flowing behind them rode painted horses alongside the train, firing sleek, black machine guns. Their outfits were a mix of beaded shirts and feathered headdresses and Yankee outdoor gear—North Face jackets, Tough pants, and Wesco boots. ARK soldiers fought back in sagebrush camouflage, armed with top of the line weaponry.

Sketchy wiped a rag across her goggles. "You girls ready?"

I wasn't. I wanted to turn around and run. Too late for that. What if this plan failed? People would lose a lot more than their pinkie fingers.

Wren smirked. "Christ, yes, Sketchy. I missed out on the last fight, and I got a serious case of blue balls."

"Wren!" I gasped.

"Let's do this thing!" Sketchy howled and shoved the yoke forward. The zeppelin shot down toward the ground as we hung on to our seats for dear life. Sketchy shouted into the communication tube, "Peeperz, hang on to your false teeth and chewin' gum. Gonna buzzbomb the Devil." She launched into some old song about buzzbombs.

The adrenaline hit me, sucking away all my fear, and suddenly I was laughing or crying or both. This was crazy. This was life. This was the Juniper.

We staggered back through the swaying airship to the mid-bay hatch where Tech stood, gripping straps anchored into cleats on the floor to keep her balance. The sound of the battle increased. Bullets ricocheted and whined. Explosions blistered the ground. The shriek of horses echoed the dying screams of women.

Through the hatch, the cars flashed underneath us, so fast, faster, a blur. We couldn't make that jump. Sketchy was right. This was something out of Hollywood video.

"Well jacker me down tight," Wren cursed, but I knew it wasn't about the jump down to the train. She'd seen something.

"What?" I asked.

"Praetor Edger is up and running. Along with another of them Vixx skanks." She pointed, and I followed her finger.

Sure enough, Edger and one of the Vixxes raced across the ground to engage the Wind River people. We were too far away to see the nametag, so it might've been Reb or Ronnie, or maybe Rachel, the one Vixx we hadn't met yet.

It seemed like the worst of omens, but how could Edger be fighting? She'd been critically wounded in the battle the night before.

Sketchy's voice erupted from the communication tube next to the hatch in the floor. "Gonna stop for a half second, so you can get down. Up ahead, there's a Little America station, the Laramie one. We'll rendezvous there with you wrong-headed Weller girls. Once I drop you off, I'll fly back and tell your people. Jesus, Mary, and Joseph, ain't this exciting!"

Explosions rocked the *Moby*. I heard the crack of what could only be the windshield shattering. Sketchy yowled laughter. "Ah, a little fresh air. The *Moby* can take your damn missiles. Bring it." Sketchy positioned the zeppelin over the train engine. Its roof was cylindrical, covering the tank and the boiler, with two guardrails across either side.

Smoke tendrils swirled above the engine. Stray bullets sparked off the back. Couldn't tell if they were from the Regios or from the Wind River people.

The *Moby* stuttered to a stop, and Sketchy yelled, "Get off, Wren. Now!"

Arms crossed, Wren dropped through the hatch, fell the three or four meters through the air, and hit the roof of the engine. She rolled to take the impact. Looked as if she'd roll right off the train.

At the last minute, Wren twisted and caught herself on a guardrail.

Sketchy cried out, raw-gut panic in her voice. "Get off, now! Both of you. Gotta get out of here. Gotta …"

Another explosion thrashed the *Moby*. Felt like a Godzilla monster had the airship in his fist.

Micaiah went through the hatch first, and I fell after him, knocking my shoulder against the side.

Then I was falling, falling, falling—felt like a million years.

I landed on the roof of the engine all wrong. My right ankle crumpled under me. I hissed in pain. I looked up in time to see the *Moby* take a missile in her starboard side. Pieces of melting Neofiber rained down. Flames licked around the gaping hole. The *Moby* was hurt but still afloat. The airship struggled away, streaming smoke, losing elevation. I watched until Micaiah and my sister pulled me up.

Wren drew a Colt Terminator. "Okay, Cavvy, let's get this train a-truckin'."

## (iv)

Micaiah and I stayed on top while Wren leaned over to check the engine room. "All clear. Wind River warriors already killed 'em all." She noticed the torment on my face. "You hurt your ankle, Cavvy?"

"Don't matter," I said back. "I can sit to do what needs to be done. We need to get out of here before that Vixx finds us."

Between Micaiah and Wren, they helped me down into the cab of the train engine through the left side door.

Inside lay the bodies of Regios, dead fingers on cold triggers. Micaiah snagged a coat and shouldered it on.

The back of the engine had sliding doors for access to the tender car. Cables and pulleys were rigged to carry fifty-pound blocks of Old Growth from the tender to the firebox. The driver's seat rose up high and to the right. To the left sat the Eterna battery and electronics. Everything else was steam engine. I took a second to familiarize myself with the technology—the firebox at the back, the boiler on the right, at the front, the gauges, breaks, pressure release, whistles. Panels of levers to switch the engine from electric to steam power.

I limped to the control seat which had its own set of gauges. I glanced through the window; the tracks ahead were clear. For now. I had to get us going. Couldn't wait for Pilate to show up.

The instruments showed our temperature and pressure were too low. "Micaiah, load the firebox with the Old Growth."

In seconds, he'd deciphered the mechanics of loading the firebox. He pulled cables until a big brick of Old Growth coal tumbled into the flames while I tried to remember the schematics of the trains I'd pored over back at Jenny Bell's ranch. Yeah, I could do this. Still, worry attacked me. What if the *Moby* crashed and killed Sketchy, Tech, and Peeperz? What if Aunt Bea and Crete were being held captive? What if the Madelines had murdered Pilate and were right then torturing Petal? What if I never saw Sharlotte ever again?

"Quit your 'what iffin'," I hissed at myself. Mama's voice whispered down from heaven. *Cavatica Weller, given half a chance you'd kill yourself with questions. Live, baby, just live.*

Sweating rivers, I watched the temperature increase, which increased the pressure as well. I wanted the engine fit to burst, so once we released the brakes we'd hit it hard.

"Company is coming," Wren hissed. "They get any closer, I'll open up on 'em." She gripped an AZ3. Extra clips were tucked in her belt.

"Cavvy, let's go," Micaiah said.

I released the brake, grabbed the throttle, and hammered that engine down. In train terms, we'd have to wait until the cars stretched out, meaning the slack in the couplers would have to pull tight. We inched forward, and then? The train abruptly slammed to a stop, like a fifty tonne dog on a hundred tonne chain. Hardly moved a meter.

"I bet the brakes are still on in the other engine," I growled. We'd have to go back and unlock it at the very back. Or maybe there was a brake car mid-way. My belly filled with knives.

Micaiah seized Wren. "You get me to the rear engine, and I'll release the brakes." He'd seen me unlock the brakes a minute before, and Micaiah only needed to see things once. He kissed his fingers and touched my check, then dashed out with Wren into the gunfire and explosions.

The howl of the steam whistle made me jump. The train engine had gotten too hot. The automatic release valve must've let loose.

Every soldier within a kilometer would come to investigate. Including Edger, somehow resurrected, and the nearly unstoppable Vixx we'd seen.

I was alone, but I wouldn't be for long.

Dozens of Regios charged across the derelict train yard, heading right toward me.

I didn't even bother with a gun. I was caught.

### (v)

Not a second later, one of the worst horrors in the Juniper saved us all.

The Madelines, at least a hundred of them, thundered in on horseback, dressed in prom dresses, bridesmaid's dresses, all kinds of colorful gowns blurring against the drab landscape. Scarves, veils, and boas flapped in the wind. Sparkling costume jewelry winked in the failing sunlight from the wrists and throats of those battle-broken, serial-killer witches.

The completely demented cavalry hit those Regios coming for me, going through them like a fist through a window—a fist sparkly with Walmart diamonds.

I didn't see Pilate or Petal, but I knew they'd led the Madelines to the train. So far, my plan was working.

Something flashed across the sky in front of me. At first, I thought the *Moby Dick* had returned. But no, this was smaller. I checked one of the mirrors, and yeah, behind me, more slender fliers darted through the sky. Took a minute, but then I realized what they were—single-rider zeppelins, Wind River by the look of them. Deerskin covered air cells, prolly filled with thelium gas, held silvery Neofiber frames, painted with symbols. Smoke drifted from the ultra-light steam engines near the back, spinning propellers. Strings of feathers, bones, and other totems dangled. Underneath the frame, mounted machine guns sparked, spitting lead.

The Wind River people had air support, but like nothing I'd ever seen before. Never even heard rumors of such zeppelins. Lucky us. One more weapon for the Regios to face.

Wren, alone, rode up on some Wind River pony, the saddle decorated like the fliers. My sister leapt off the horse and climbed into the cab. "Brakes are off, Cavvy. We have to go, now!"

"Where's Micaiah?" I screeched.

Wren dropped her eyes. "He got shot off the back of my horse. He went down. If I'd gone back for him, they'd have got me too. I'm sorry, Cavvy, but he's dead."

I found myself yelling at my sister, "How come you didn't go back for him, Wren? What about the reward? I thought you never let your heart get in the way of a paycheck!"

The hurt showed on her face for a quick second before she snarled back at me, "We got the train. We'll get our headcount to Wendover, and then you can be done with me. Okay? I'm sorry, I can't always save everyone. Don't you think I would've tried if I could?"

"I'm going back for him!" I took a step off from the seat and crumbled down on my ankle, the pain seizing me.

Wren came over, put out a hand, but then she was shoved down on top of me.

A square-faced woman stood over us, her fist clenched around a Desert Messiah. The name *Rachel* was embroidered on her uniform.

Once again I was staring down the barrel of a Desert Messiah in the hands of a Vixx.

Only for a moment. Wren kicked out Rachel's legs just as she shot. The bullet screamed off the floor next to my ear to smack around the room like a high-caliber pinball.

The Vixx didn't have time to squeeze off another shot. Wren, back on her feet, grabbed her by the arm, wrestled the big pistol away, and flung her against the firebox, glowing hot. I could smell the fabric of her uniform smoke and burn through to fry her flesh.

The soldier clone hardly flinched. Silent, she smacked the Desert Messiah out of Wren's hand and out the door. She lunged for Wren, who had her Betty knife out, and the two went at each other, Kung-Fu, martial arts, full on.

Rachel Vixx was better trained, but Wren was sneakier and looking to die, taking chances no sane person would take, taking blows on the crown of her head instead of her face.

"Dammit, Cavvy, get the train going. I'll deal with this *kutia*."

I struggled into the driver's seat and tripped the throttle. I'd get us away and then go back for Micaiah. This time when the train lurched forward, we didn't stop. We were moving, gaining speed, then roaring. With the train finally going, I turned to watch as the two warrior women pummeled each other.

Rachel Vixx roundhoused a kick, and Wren went low, punched her right in the groin, and swung a leg around that should've leveled the Vixx, but she leapt over it and, still in the air, drove a foot into Wren's forehead, knocking her back.

"Dirty skank!" Wren was back on Rachel, punching at her face. The Vixx got her arms up to block it and threw a knee. Wren dodged it, only to take a punch on the jaw. That stunned Wren.

The soldier clone didn't seem to care. No smile, no sense of victory, just a machine-like determination to kill us both. She snatched a subcompact pistol out of an ankle holster and stuck it into my sister's face. Wren was quicker. She jammed her palm into the soldier girl's nose, kicked her legs out from under her, and they both went down, but Wren was on top. She stuck her Betty knife into the Vixx's belly, then her chest, again and again.

"Skank! Skank! Skank!" At every stab, Wren spit that word into her face.

"Wren!" I yelled. "The head! Get her head!"

My sister tried to adjust her aim, but before she could, the Vixx chopped Wren in the throat. The soldier clone stood while Wren gagged. Stood right up. Like being gutted and knifed in the heart was nothing.

Wren flashed to her feet and leapt, planted both of her feet into Rachel Vixx's chest and kicked her off the train through the side door. The Vixx hit the ground in a cloud of dust and disappeared behind us. In the distance, the Wind River fliers strafed the remaining ARK soldiers. And the Psycho Madelines as well. It was complete chaos, but we were building up speed, leaving the battle behind.

Other Regios, though, crawled toward the cab, clinging to the sides of the train cars.

"Wren, more are coming."

Wren shook so much she dropped her Betty knife. She huffed in deep breaths, eyes wide. In a gaspy, fearful voice, she asked, "How can I fight them Vixxes if they don't die? How can I do it, Cavvy?"

"Rachel is gone," I said. "But the Regios are coming. You gotta blow 'em away. You gotta." And I had to go back for Micaiah. To see if he was really dead. To save him again if he wasn't. No matter what.

Wren nodded and picked up an AZ3. "Yeah, yeah, I will. I won't chicken out. It's just …"

A soldier jumped down into the back of the engine room from the tender car and Wren machine-gunned her out the door. Then, no time to talk, Wren got set up by the rear door, and she machine gunned more, like a dog ridding itself of fleas.

I limped over to feed her clips from the other AZ3s on the floor. Her shooting, me reloading her, it felt like I was with Mama again. I was so thirsty, so wrung out, and my ankle was licking pain up my leg. Even my shoulder and arm were hurting again.

Deep down I knew Micaiah was still alive, and I would save him. Denial can be a good thing. It allowed me to help my sister wipe out the last of the Regios still aboard the train.

I watched as she shot them, her face focused, and in some ways, serene.

Us Weller girls had demons, bad demons. Wren drank them away when she couldn't use violence to ease the pain.

Mama and Sharlotte had worked them away.

And me?

I had Pilate's love and luck and the Lord Jesus Christ to help me with mine.

So while Wren fought, I prayed. Prayed for the *Moby* to be okay and find Sharlotte and bring her back to us. Prayed for our people, our headcount, to find their way.

I didn't pray to see Micaiah again 'cause I knew I'd find him, with or without God's help. Even if I had to go down to hell and wrestle him away from Satan himself.

# Chapter Fourteen

*Patience in science is critical. Often, scientific advances create a hell first, then a heaven.*

—Dr. Ravan Singh, PhD
Executive Director of Research and Development of
the American Reproduction Knowledge Initiative
July 2, 2043

## (i)

WREN CLIMBED ONTO THE BLOCKS OF OLD Growth coal in the tender to see if any more Regios were coming for us. She smiled.

"What is it?" I asked. "Is it our people?"

"Damn, but your boy is good," Wren said. "Not only is he alive, but he made it on the train."

Minutes later, she helped Micaiah off the Old Growth and into the cab of the engine. I kissed his lips, clutched him to me, and breathed in his smell. No one had ever smelled as sweet as he did right then. I didn't care if Wren was there.

"I knew you weren't dead," I said into his ear. "I knew it. But how did you make it through? They shot you up."

He pulled back. "Me? No, I fell off Wren's horse, but I wasn't shot. I'm okay. I learned how to be tough from you Weller girls. Is there anything you can't do?"

I felt Wren's eyes on us, hard, judging. "Yeah, Johnson, there is. We can't get along, if you hadn't noticed." She shook her head. "I don't get it. You were behind me on the horse, I heard gunfire, then I felt you fall off. I'd have gone back if I hadn't been so certain."

He turned to show us the back of his ARK soldier's coat. "Look, no bullet holes. Sorry to disappoint you, Wren, but I wasn't shot."

My sister still looked troubled. "Yeah, well, then I'm sorry for leaving you. It was crazy, trying to fight our way through them Wind River women and those Regio skanks. I guess I must've lost my head." She smiled. "Now, I better go and see if I can't kill me another Regio or two. They die. Your Vixx aunties on the other hand, well, they sure are engineered well. I stabbed that Rachel a dozen times, and she asked me out for a drink. *Besharam* skank."

Wren slammed a fresh clip into her AZ3 and took off.

I fell back into Micaiah's arms for a few more luscious kisses. He then told me how he'd run for the train, got on the rear engine, and run across the top to get to the forward engine. He counted the cattle cars as he ran, sixty-seven in all. If we could cram forty-four beefsteaks in each car, we'd have enough for all of our headcount.

As an added benefit, we'd stranded the ARK's reinforcements in the middle of the Wyoming desert surrounded by angry Wind River warriors and the

Psycho Madelines. Ha. If only Tibbs Hoyt had been aboard. No such luck.

Still, he and the Vixxes had the four Johnny zeppelins full of soldier girls searching for us. We weren't out of the woods just yet.

We rumbled across the Wyoming plains toward the setting sun. I sat in the engineer's seat with a commanding view of the tracks and the ground flashing by. We were going incredibly fast compared to the slog of moving cattle by foot and horseback.

Micaiah stood next to me. "Cavvy, I don't think we should run the train at night. I'm not sure if the tracks are all repaired. If we drive blindly, we might derail."

"Yeah, I know it," I said. "But before that, we need to get to the rendezvous point, the Little America west of Laramie. Sketchy was going to fly back and tell the rest of our crew, but if she crashed, we might be in trouble. And there is Pilate and Petal, Bea and Crete, to consider. And Sharlotte." I still felt uncomfortable saying my sister's name around Micaiah.

"The ARK soldiers might be ahead of us, too," he said. "They'll know you're heading toward Wendover."

"Yeah, Reb and Ronnie knew all about us," I whispered. It felt like there was a cave inside me, and my fear was a little lone voice calling out. But hope was in there, too, and it rang out loudly.

"This is crazy," Micaiah sighed. "We can't run away on train tracks. It's like trying to sneak around with three thousand cows. Impossible."

I laughed at that. "Thank you, oh voice of doom. I feel like I'm talking with Anju Rawat."

Aaron Michael Ritchey

"Who?" His face was so cute when he was confused. Some girls liked dumb boys. I knew why.

"She was my best friend in Cleveland. Anju was always saying that nothing would ever work out. Well, she was wrong as much as she was right. I think we'll make it. Not sure how, but I have faith. From the beginning, this cattle drive was doomed to fail, but we only ever wanted halfway, but now that halfway is a whole lotta kilometers behind us. And if the *Moby* didn't get blown up ..." I had to take a big breath to make the cave inside me smaller, to make the voice of hope louder. "... our plan might work. Maybe the Vixx sisters won't catch up to us. The Juniper is a big place, and you can't just call ahead to warn people we're coming. Heck, we might even make it to the SLC. I could find a nice Mormon man with fifty wives, and lucky me, I'd be fifty-one." I paused there to add. "And you can get away from your father."

"If my father finds me, I'll give you the chalkdrive, and I'll give myself up. Then you can tell the world about the crimes of Tibbs Hoyt. What he did and didn't do."

"Sins of omission and commission," I said, letting my Catholic show. Then I just had to ask, "How did it feel growing up with Tibbs Hoyt as your daddy? The richest man in the world. You could buy anything, do anything, be anything. How did that feel? Or are you going to tell me more stories about wicked aunts or a mama in Vegas?"

He sighed again, long and hard. "Part of what I said was true. The Vixx sisters really are like my aunts. But I don't know where my mom is. I lost track of her a long time ago."

Even though he was feeling bad, I had to chuckle. "When I asked your name, you were all, muh, muh, muh Micaiah. You didn't even know that was a bible name, did you?"

"No," he said, "but I'm Micaiah now. I don't ever want to be Micah Hoyt again. A cage with bars of gold is still a cage."

I couldn't take his pain seriously at all. "Maybe, but come on. How bad could it have been? I got up before sunrise every day of my life to shovel manure. Nobody in the Juniper is gonna show you much pity."

"You're right about that." He turned sheepish and embarrassed.

I have to say, I liked him like that. I felt uppity, but I knew what he was talking about. A lot of times in elementary school, the poorer folks would avoid me just 'cause I came from the biggest ranch in central Colorado. They assumed I was stuck up when I wasn't. Sometimes when you're rich, you end up alone. Poor folks get to be poor together. There's a joy in that.

"Micaiah," I said, carefully, "we can't let Wren know who you really are. She'd sell you in a minute."

"Maybe, but I don't think so," he said. "Wren is a hard one, but I don't think anyone ever gives her a chance to be soft."

I felt guilty about Wren and Sharlotte for a minute. I should've been nicer to them, more tolerant, tried more—but our family never seemed like a family, more like a foot race, and whoever ran the fastest won all the love.

I changed subjects to talk about something easier than family. "So what is your daddy going to do with his super soldiers? Take over the world?"

"He already owns it," Micaiah said. "Now he just needs to protect it. If the U.S. government demands he give up the cure for the Sterility Epidemic, he has the troops to defend himself. And he's not just going to give it away, not when he can sell Male Product for a fortune. He says he's trying to improve all of humanity, but if that's the case, why clone soldiers? No, he's a greedy egomaniacal jackmaster, and I have to get the truth out."

His words, his rage, surprised me. Calling your father a jackmaster was a far cry from honoring your mother and father, thank you fourth commandment. However, if your father really was a jackass, what did you do then?

"Tell me about Edger." I said. "Last night, she was flat on her back, shot to pieces. And here she is today, up and at 'em. What's that all about?"

Before he could answer, Wren slid from the coal car into the cab. Micaiah and I got quiet—that silence that tells the person who walked into the room that they weren't invited to join in the conversation.

"I checked the train again," she said, "and we're alone. Those poor *kutias*. It's a long walk out of the Juniper."

"Yeah," I said. Could Wren be soft? I didn't know. Micaiah was right. I never gave her much of a chance.

Wren nodded again, knowing me and Micaiah were in the middle of something. "I'm gonna get on top of the train to watch for our people. Any sign of Pilate or the *Moby*?"

I shook my head.

She frowned and left.

Once we were alone again, Micaiah touched my shoulder. "Cavvy, we have to get something straight." The way he said it, it was a break-up start. My questions about Edger went unanswered.

Right then, it didn't seem important. I prepared myself for whatever he had to say; I felt strong. So far, my plan was working. We were on the train, and I had the feeling God held the *Moby* afloat in His great guiding hand. We'd find our people. It would all work out.

"I know, Micaiah, I know, you can't get involved with some young Juniper girl from a crazy family. I getcha."

He touched my hair and ran his fingers through it. I melted.

"No," he said, "I don't care about that. I've met about a million girls in my life, all of them wanting me, but with you it's different. I feel like we're hands laced together."

The image of that felt strong in my head. I wanted to say something, but I had no words, none as nice as his.

He went on. "And I'm stronger for being with you. Being with you, I feel like who I should've been from the beginning. Not Micah Hoyt, heir to an empire, but Micaiah, some lost guy in the Juniper running for his life and taken in by angels."

His words broke through to the very heart of me, and for once, I didn't cry. Pride puffed my heart, swollen with love. Not a weepy, girly 'strogen love, like in a song or a soap opera, but a woman's love, sure, steady, and badger-mean if something or someone got in the way.

"Juniper angels have broken wings," I said. It was a phrase I'd heard all my life. "You didn't want to talk about such sweet things, so let's get it over with. Hit me quick."

"Jenny Bell is dead because of me. And Sharlotte, I manipulated her. With you, I'm not sure I can be the boy you deserve. Now that you know what kind of a person I am, if you want to walk away, I'd understand."

His words rattled me for a second.

"See? You have doubts," he said, mistaking my silence.

"You're on a sacred quest," I said. "You want to cure the Sterility Epidemic. Yeah, you ain't perfect, but you know it. It beats a guy who thinks he walks on water. Only one man who could ever do such a thing. Maybe pray to Him for forgiveness."

"There's going to be more death. More killing. Because of what we are trying to do."

"We," I said the one word and left a quiet behind it.

"We," he echoed. "No matter what."

*No matter what.* Our treasure box of a poem, sealing our love inside.

"As long as you can be honest with me, I'm with you until the end and beyond. Can you be honest with me?" I asked.

I expected a definite answer, a definite yes.

The train clacked down the tracks, the sagebrush a bleary blur from the speed. I couldn't see it, but I could still smell it.

"I'll try." Bad omens and a fearful evil poisoned his whispered words.

My jaw tightened. "You'll have to do better than try." Maybe it was cruel to say, but I couldn't tolerate any more lies or half-truths, not from him. His deceptions already weighed on us.

"I'll go back and start prepping the rear engine," he muttered. "We'll need it once we load in all the cattle."

"Good thinkin'," I said back a little too quickly.

He left. I kept the train thundering down the track, and we hit Little America as the sun touched the horizon.

Little America. Full of ghosts and sorrow.

## (ii)

Little America had been a series of hotels and travel complexes spread about the West. The Laramie one was new, or had been, thirty years prior. A big rambling gas station slumped next to a convenience store, which leaned drunkenly against a hotel. They looked like tombstones plunked down in the middle of the Wyoming plains—sky, sagebrush, coyotes howling out their lonesome, and not much else. Along with gas and trucker music, Little America also sold ice cream cones. A peeling-paint sign welcomed us in, showing a cartoon penguin holding up an ice cream—ninety-nine cents. Cheap.

Only no ice cream for us—hadn't been any for decades. We stopped the train and waited.

Wren climbed into the engine room. She carried a couple of sleeping bags and over her shoulder were two AZ3s. "I saw Micaiah. He looked like he'd lost his best friend. Trouble in paradise, Princess? I figured you and the boy would be all lovey-dovey with Sharlotte out of the picture."

I flashed her a glare. "Keep out of this, Wren. It's none of your business."

She smiled, mouth closed. "Go easy on him, Cavvy. Sometimes life doesn't let us be good, even when we don't have bad in our hearts."

"Wren," I said, "I'm sorry we ain't been close. I know something happened between you and Mama—"

She cut me off. "You don't know jackercrap, so just keep your opinions to yourself. You think I'm evil, like Sharlotte does, and maybe I am. I didn't choose it at first. But then it became habit, and now I am what I am. I'm used to being hated, and you know what? I hate me, too. So if nothing else, we all agree on that."

She turned and threw a sleeping bag at me. That was Wren, always throwing stuff—curses, words, sticks, machine guns. "I brought you some gear and a rifle. It might be a while before the others find us. I'll run recon. Micaiah agreed to keep watch, so you best sleep while you can."

She paused to take in a deep breath, her back to me. She talked over her shoulder just like Sharlotte. Sure, 'cause they were sisters. "Cavvy, I do have a favor. God don't care about my prayers, so you talk to Him. Tell Him that we need Pilate and our people to find us." She took off.

"Wren, wait." I limped out after her, but she was gone. Once again, I'd tried to talk to my sister and it ended in a disaster. I regretted every word I'd said and felt terrible about what I'd heard.

I wasn't tired, and I wanted to keep watch as well. I could see better from on top of the train, so I hopped up the ladder on my left foot and sat on top, with the sleeping bag under me as a cushion. I cradled the AZ3 in my arms.

The moon was nearly full, and the stars swirled milky from horizon to horizon. It was a warm May night, real pretty and gentle, no wind. In the Juniper, that was a rarity.

I thought about Laura Tucker, the little girl back on the train in the Buzzkill, asking her mother all sorts of questions about the Juniper.

Well, yes, Virginia there were mutants in the Juniper, bio-engineered, super-soldier mutants. And Santa Claus? Well, maybe. Maybe not.

My eyes traveled over the gas station, the hotel, the little scatter of derelict businesses, dusty with wind and dirty from time and neglect.

I thought back over the entire cattle drive, from start to finish. I prayed to God for forgiveness, for all the cussing and lusting. I prayed for Wren and for Petal, so they could get to the other side of their pain. Mostly I prayed for Sharlotte, for her to be okay, for her to find us or for the *Moby* to find her, so we could be together again. I liked the new Sharlotte. I remembered her poetic words about the dandelions—Juniper girls, like dandelions, could grow and be pretty wherever you planted us.

I took in a deep breath. I breathed in those miles of sagebrush and smelled the Great Plain with every part of me. Though it was a prison to some, for me it was home, and I loved it. Fear I could feel any old time, but I'd only get to feel love for my troublesome homeland every now and then.

I finally climbed into the sleeping bag and slept on the roof of the train, drifting off, praying and thinking and feeling bad about Micaiah. If honesty was such a chore, he might never get it right, and we could never be together.

Wren's shout woke me.

### (iii)

My heartbeat jumped into high gear until I realized she was yelling, not shooting, so it might be good news.

Pilate, Petal, our hands, and all of our headcount, came riding out of the east in a glow of warm morning sunshine. The *Moby Dick* floated over them. She was scarred, patched together rough, but still flying.

I struggled down the ladder off the train engine and limped into a storm of hugs. I even hugged Crete.

Puff Daddy and Christina Pink knocked each other to get to me, so I could hug 'em. Then I had to push them apart, none too gently. I kissed Bob D and loved the feel of his scratchy hide on my cheek. I petted the rest of my ponies, old and new. Only Prince, Sharlotte's horse, was missing.

Nikki Breeze and Tenisha Keys came along with Dolly Day, Allie, and Kasey. Kasey's wounded throat must've been hurting, 'cause she didn't talk—she rubbed my shoulder to let me know she was glad to see me. Our beefsteaks meandered around us, crying and calling, mad for walking day and night.

Pilate told us his story about the merry chase he gave the Madelines. Those girls really did seem to have one mind 'cause it wasn't long before a hundred were chasing him across the plains. Once they saw the train and all the women, fresh recruits in their minds, they'd jumped into the battle. Pilate said war can be an addiction, and the Madelines were like an addict looking for a fix. And that was what I'd been counting on.

He and Petal hadn't been able to get on the train, but the *Moby* had found them, following the tracks west.

"Aunt Bea, how did it go with you?" I asked.

She shook her head and laughed. "I thought we wouldn't get to say two words to those Wind River people, but your idea of a white flag helped. We told them about the train, and how your mama was friends with Mavis Meetchum, and how I'd even had dinner with Mavis. Thank God they believed me. I think that's what convinced them to let you take the train. At first, they wanted to destroy everything and kill everyone, but they still remember Mavis giving them the buffalo all those years ago. Thank you, *Señora* Meetchum."

She went on to say she and Crete got lost, but the *Moby* also found them, took them aboard, and then they met up with Breeze and Keys and our headcount. We laughed as Sketchy went into excruciating detail about loading the horses into the airship. The ponies had fought them every step of the way, even Bob D.

"Any word on Sharlotte?" I asked.

Everyone suddenly got real interested in their feet.

Aunt Bea cleared her throat. "Headcount is real thirsty. And we have to load them on the trains, and there is a lot of work to be done, Cavvy. Maybe she'll find us before we have to *vamoose*."

"Never thought you'd get us a train, Cavvy," Dolly Day said. "Maybe you aren't such a bad boss after all."

"Thanks, Dolly."

Even though we'd survived my crazy plan, I kept having to swallow the chunk of grief stuck sideways in my throat. Sharlotte gone. It'd kill me to leave her. Petal sat me down in the doorway of the train engine while she looked at my ankle. Her eyes were so clear and sparkly now. "It's not broken, Cavvy, just sprained. Try and stay off it, okay?"

I nodded.

She stood and pushed her cheek against mine. "Thank you for staying strong when I would've used again. Thank you. I'm feeling cleaner than I've felt for a long time."

While I rested my ankle, our people got out the collapsible troughs from the *Moby* and watered down our headcount. Plenty of water. No one had touched the aquifer under Little America for decades.

By mid-afternoon, we had the train loaded with our headcount, from Betty Butter to Bluto to Charles Goodnight. Our water tanks were full, and we had enough Old Growth to get us all the way to San Francisco if need be.

Still no Sharlotte.

We stood around the engine, quiet, eating MREs taken from the ARK's food supply. Sketchy, Tech, and Peeperz ambled up—I could see the trouble on their faces. I knew what was coming.

Sketchy sniffled, then got to it. "Okay, this is gonna hurt to say, but me, Tech, and Peeperz had us a talk. The *Moby* can't take no more fightin'. Her heart is strong, but her arms and legs are busted. We can fix her, but to fix her right we'd have to deflate the damaged air cells, and we don't have the thelium for it. We have supplies in the ZZK"—otherwise known as Buzzkill,

Nebraska—"but that's far away, too far to go and come back. So, this is hard. Oh, Lord, this is hard on me, but we can't go on. We just can't. And about Miss Sharlotte, we looked and looked, but we couldn't find her." The big woman started blubbering, and before long we were all blubbering along with her, well, those of us who were girly 'strogen soft. The rest, like Wren and Tech, looked around uncomfortably.

Sketchy blew her nose into a dirty, red handkerchief, then gestured at Micaiah. "We can take the boy back to the ZZK. That should make y'all safer."

Micaiah stood away from us, quiet, troubled.

We waited until he said something. "I can't go to the ZZK. The ARK has agents in every eastern border town, looking for me. If you can give me a horse and some supplies, I can head off on my own. West."

"No, Skctchy," I said abruptly to her. Couldn't say it to him. "He's coming with us. His fate and ours are entwined." *Like the fingers of two hands, the hands of lovers.* That image hadn't left me, even though I was having trouble with what he'd said.

*I'll try.*

Wren and I glanced at each other. For her, Micaiah meant reward money. For me, it went far deeper.

"Thank you, Sketch, Peeperz, and you too, Tech," I said. "Thanks for everything. We'll make it."

"But how?" Tech asked. "The Vixxes know you're heading for Wendover. They'll be waiting."

"God will provide," I said. Sharlotte was gone. I was the leader, and it was my job to sow hope. I smiled, even with tears in my eyes. "We have a fast train, and we have God's grace, so we'll make it."

We had to. It was our destiny to end the Sterility Epidemic. And save our ranch.

More hugging, more crying, and we all watched as the three climbed on board. Soon the *Moby* was bumping across the sky, dog-tired and done for.

We loaded up one of the train cars with musty-smelling cushions from the motel, so our people would have a place to sit. We'd have to leave the chuck wagon behind, which was sad. I touched the metal of the Chevy Workhorse II one last time, recalling how much time Mama and I had spent working on her.

I took my place in the engine up front. Micaiah manned the rear engine. We spoke through communication tubes, like in the *Moby*.

Our engines were hot, our pressure good. It was time to leave and get a few more kilometers under our belt before dark.

"Are we ready, Cavvy?" he asked.

My grief was still stuck in my throat. Couldn't choke it down. I closed my eyes. *Please, God, take care of Sharlotte.*

"Cavvy, are you there?"

Tears dribbled through my closed eyes. "Yeah, I'm here. Just giving Sharlotte a little more time. You and I both know, if we take off in this train, there ain't no way she'll be able to catch up."

He didn't say anything else. That boy was a genius.

I waited a minute more. Then I released the brake and lowered the throttle lever. Like before, the train stretched out, clanging and squeaking as the couplers pulled tight. We chugged away from Little America, a ghost town once more.

# Chapter Fifteen

*Women in today's world have a unique opportunity to re-invent themselves. Without the yoke of men and traditional gender roles, women can be anything, do anything, and in truth, necessity is forcing this metamorphosis on the willing as well as the resistant. Case in point, Sally Browne Burke. Could she be as active if she were saddled with a husband and four kids? Morning carpool and afternoon soccer practice certainly would get in the way of pushing her misguided, reactionary agenda.*

—Dr. Anna M. Colton, PhD
Professor of Sociology, Princeton University
December 30, 2055

**(i)**

THE NEXT DAY WE HIT THE ROCKY MOUNTAINS, and the train chugged up inclines and past craggy rocks to give us breathtaking vistas of wide valleys green with spring.

I think we all felt a little drunk from the speed. We'd crossed Wyoming in a day. On horseback, it would've taken us weeks. Even though Sharlotte hadn't found us, I was feeling good. I knew we'd outrun the

ARK's army of Regios and Vixxes, and we'd pull into Wendover without a problem.

Pilate, however, preached a different, darker gospel. He climbed into the engine to talk with me. Every so often, a bad cough would rattle him. Frowning and sullen, he chewed his cigar instead of smoking it as he stood next to me.

"How's Petal?" I asked.

"She's clean. She's better. She's even stopped cursing Wren, probably because of what you said in the tent that night." He paused. "Wren's turned bad, though. If you don't have a sufficient substitute for alcohol, sobriety becomes a torture."

"She thinks we hate her and want her dead," I said.

"Do you?" Pilate asked.

"No." Easy word to say. The truth couldn't be boiled down so easily. Wren had told me our mama was dead with a wide smile on her face. Could I ever forgive her for that?

I braked the train around a corner, and the sky painted a dazzling canvass of green trees and sharp red rock cliffs.

"Gorgeous views, right, Pilate?" I asked.

He made a grumbly kind of yes noise, then collapsed into coughing.

"We're so lucky," I said. "Ain't no way those Vixxes can catch us now."

"Don't be too sure. If they get ahead of us, we're in trouble." He spit bits of tobacco on the floor. "I've been thinking about the ARK troopers. I wouldn't be surprised if they bio-engineered the human out of those soldiers. No more PTSD. Just killing machines you unplug when you're done. Maybe that's not so bad. We don't send humans to fight our wars, just clones. Maybe it's better."

He was so down and tired, I couldn't help but ask, "Pilate, don't you feel lucky to be here alive? Don't you feel blessed?"

"I miss my pinkie finger." Pilate laughed. It was a broken-glass kind of sound. "Yes, I'm lucky. I'm just about the luckiest man who ever lived. Blessed by God. Years in the Sino, and I survive. Then more years of combat in the Juniper, and I'm still here. Mostly." He lifted up the bandage on his hand. "To top it all off, you somehow figure out how to steal a train without getting us all killed. Lucky again."

He paused and said something that rang true as a cathedral bell. "It's not luck. It's God. Rarely, Cavatica, do we see God using His evil left hand so clearly. His right hand is easy to understand. We're alive and Petal is getting clean because of God's right hand. I don't believe in the Devil, or hell, but I do believe that a part of this world is completely and insanely evil—God's evil left hand. As a priest of the Holy Roman Catholic Church, I have to explain God's left hand a lot. You would think the Madelines were truly and insanely villainous, yet we've seen how that evil can be used for good. We've seen it with our own eyes."

I nodded. "Like you. Like Petal. Like Wren. Evil, but used for good." I winced. I didn't mean they were wicked exactly, but it'd be a stretch to call them good.

Pilate sighed. "Me, Petal, and Wren. It's kind of hard to hear myself partnered up with them, but I'd be fooling myself if I tried to argue with you. More PTSD to work through."

"So don't argue. Just count yourself lucky. Looks like you found your goddamn faith." I didn't apologize for cursing. It was now a joke between us.

Pilate leaned forward to kiss my cheek. "Yeah, it would seem so. But I'm scared about what's coming up. Not scared for myself, but for you, your sisters, the hands. I can smell the Grim Reaper in the air, that old mothballed jackerdan. I know I'll live. I always live. But the rest of you." He sighed out long and hard, before a cough shook him. "It's hard to feel lucky when everyone around you keeps dying."

Jenny Bell's last words spun through my head. *Dying's easy. It's the living that's hard.*

"I'll pray for you, Pilate," I said.

He laughed. "Please do. God would find such prayers a novelty. He generally only gets complaints."

He gave me another fatherly kiss and left.

I whispered a prayer for Pilate. I could picture Jesus scratching His head. "Did someone really pray for Pilate? Gee, that's a new one."

### (ii)

We stopped the train for the night on the west side of the Rocky Mountains. A nice, warm wind blew down on us. To the right of the train, a precipice dropped down to a river winding through a valley a thousand feet below. On our left lay a field of snow, five feet deep. The ARK had done a good job clearing the tracks. Thank you, Tibbs Hoyt.

I tried to imagine what he was thinking, sitting on a throne somewhere, plotting to get his son and the chalkdrive back. I kept picturing a supervillain from a James Bond video. Prolly had a white cat on his lap.

Our people started melting snow to put in the tanks while I remained in the engine, babying my right ankle and cleaning the coal dust off my face.

Wren wandered over, stuck a boot onto the lip of the cab, folded her arms on her knee, and squinted at me. "I know you're the leader and all, but I gotta plan. You wanna hear it?"

"Sure," I said, though I didn't much like her attitude.

"Sketchy was right. Having the boy with us is too dangerous. Once we get through the mountains, you and Micaiah should leave in one of the jeeps. We'll finish the cattle drive. If we show up in Nevada without the boy, well, the ARK won't have no reason to mess with us."

"Just me and Micaiah alone?"

Wren shrugged. "You said it before. The hands are working for the Weller family. One of us needs to stick around to order 'em around."

"And you'll do it?" I couldn't believe Wren was willing to accept such responsibility.

Wren's face fell into a glare. "Yeah, I'll do it. I'm not worthless. And I want that paycheck. We got beef to sell, and I'd be real surprised if your boy came through on his promise of reward money."

If she only knew. I sat in the conductor's seat, pondering. I did like the plan. It was another killdeer ruse—Wren would stay with our headcount and people to keep up appearances, while the boy and I drove off to civilization.

"Okay, Wren," I said.

Aaron Michael Ritchey

Wren nodded. "Good. And I'd send Pilate with you, but I think we'll need every gun we have if the Vixxes attack. You just be careful."

She whirled and left me alone. Quite a change for her. Maybe Micaiah had been right. Maybe Wren wasn't as bad as we all thought.

But she'd never be easy to handle. Wren would remain as hard and dangerous as the .45 caliber bullet in my pocket, the keepsake she'd given me. I wasn't sure if that bullet was blessed or cursed.

### (iii)

That night, we didn't risk a fire. We sat in the dark on the railroad ties in front of the train and feasted on ARK army rations—Salisbury steak, chicken Marsala, and lamb palak. Hate to say it, but the MREs were a nice break from Aunt Bea's cooking, though she did her best, day after day.

We washed down the food with snowmelt, which had a dirty, earthy taste. A hooded sapropel lantern hissed in the middle of us, our faces lost in the gloom.

Wren had found a bottle of hooch in the ARK supplies, and she said she was taking watch, but I knew it was an excuse to go off and drink alone, a last party before she took over our operation. Everyone else was there—our long-time employees, our new hired hands, and our family. Everyone except Sharlotte.

Petal sat on Pilate's lap, curled up on him. She was actually a person again, not a rhyming harpy with a sniper rifle or a nodding-off ghost. She gave me a secret little smile.

Micaiah sat by himself across from me. I did my best to keep my eyes off him, but I'd fail every other minute. He'd catch me peeking at him, and I'd get all warm inside.

I told them all Wren's plan, and that she'd be taking over. No one really fought me, but no one got excited either. Dolly Day nodded, face stern. She thought boys were bad luck, and she'd be happier with one less male in our group.

Pilate only sighed. He was prolly thinking one more time we'd have to hope God held us in His right hand and didn't slap us around with His left.

After we finished the discussion, Allie murmured in the quiet, "I'd like to sing a song."

"Well, Allie," Pilate said, "you might as well try killing us before the Vixxes do. Take your best shot."

She sang a love song, sweet, determined, and passionate. "Nobody 'Cept You." Nothing mattered, except her boy, and Allie sang it sweet.

Pilate and Petal seemed to get closer as she sang it. Before I knew it, I'd locked eyes with Micaiah. Our connection was as gritty and strong as chains drug through mud. I could feel our words binding us together.

*No matter what.*

I got up and limped off. That darn Allie Chambers, every song she sang had a way of hitting us emotionally below the belt.

Maybe that's why Allie had left Lamar. Howerter kicked her out for singing songs too well.

I shouldn't be mad at Micaiah for telling me the truth—he'd try to be honest. But what did that mean? My love for him felt like a whole world inside of me, beautiful, but fragile.

Another lie, even a small one, would destroy that world in me and I'd be left empty. I was as scared of heartbreak as of dying.

Alone by the train, the darkness and the high-country air chilled me. I turned my eyes to the stars and prayed for guidance.

I didn't see Reb and Ronnie Vixx and their Regios climb aboard our train.

Nobody did. Not even Wren.

We didn't know we'd been infiltrated until it was too late.

# Chapter Sixteen

*Who can forget their first ride in a zeppelin over the Juniper? So old and yet so new.*

—Mavis Meetchum
*Colorado Courier* Interview
September 7, 2046

## (i)

WE DROPPED DOWN OUT OF THE ROCKIES AND roared through Salt Lake City in the morning light. The SLC hadn't been salvaged as much as re-colonized by the Mormon folk. It looked rather pleasant. The Mormon women had torn up the streets to plant crops. Funny to see avenues of green, tilled by women with their hair covered. Mormons in the Juniper had gone back to polygamy, which made sense I guess, given there weren't many men around. I still couldn't imagine sharing my husband with a dozen other women. Both Sally Browne Burke and the Archbishop Corfu hated the Mormons and discounted their religion as heresy.

But what if people were people, doing the best they could? Charlotte had accepted Nikki and Tenisha's *gillian* love. Could I hate them for something that was beyond their control? And some New Morality women talked trash about Catholics, but I was Catholic, and I wasn't evil. So should I hate Mormons? Why? I didn't approve of their lifestyle, but then, I didn't have to partake in it, so what was my opinion worth?

All those thoughts filled my head as we left the SLC behind and chugged past the Great Salt Lake, stinking like hell's own ocean.

We didn't stop until the lake was far behind us and the land flattened into an unbroken white plain. It was like another planet. I kept sniffing the air; didn't smell right, didn't feel right. No life to be seen, no birds, nothing, and the wind blew crazily around in dust devil swirls that smelled like salty rot.

Then it happened.

Micaiah and I'd packed to leave, and I'd given Pilate, Tenisha Keys, and Crete a lesson on the steam engine. We all were walking back toward the jeeps, so I could figure out how to get one off the flat cars—then gunshots.

Time slowed, like sap dripping down a pine.

Tenisha Keys looked down at her chest, clothes full of holes, but no blood for a moment. No blood. And then a lot.

Pilate pushed me down. Crete fled to the train.

All of that took seconds. No time for fear.

Dozens of the ARK's Cuius Regios, armed to the teeth, faces blackened, poured out of train cars near the back. They moved through us, wiping us out with martial arts and bullets. And with them stormed Reb and Ronnie Vixx. That was when I realized they'd climbed on during our last stop in the mountains. That way, they could pick the perfect time to attack. Most likely, they'd sent the Johnny blimps ahead to orchestrate the ambush.

"Matthew!" Pilate's Homewrecker thundered followed by Wren's Colt Terminators. I tried to sprint to the train car where we'd stored the weapons, but my ankle wouldn't let me. I half-skipped, half limped, but went as quickly as I could.

Down from us, the doors of a cattle car rumbled open, followed by the ramp sliding out onto the salt. Horses neighed over the jingle and leather-snap of saddles being cinched. The Regios were stealing our ponies.

Micaiah sped toward me but was knocked to the hard salt ground.

Ronnie Vixx zip tied his hands before yanking him to his feet.

I went for him, hardly feeling my bad ankle. If they wanted to steal him away, they'd have to kill me first. A Regio swiveled her Armalite AZ3 at me. Her finger tightened on the trigger.

At the last minute, Petal darted forward, drove a foot into the soldier's leg, and seized the rifle. Petal ripped the AZ3 away from the soldier girl and aimed it right between the Regio's eyes.

She didn't fire. No. She'd taken an oath. First, do no harm.

"Petal!" Pilate screamed.

Petal's body jerked, slammed by another Regio's bullets, gunning her down. She fell to her knees, then slumped over.

The Regio ran past her, grabbed a horse, and not just any horse, my Bob. Ha, they couldn't take Puff Daddy and Christina Pink. Those two would throw off any Regio who tried to ride them.

Ten soldiers rode away. Micaiah was slung across Bob D's saddle. Reb and Ronnie Vixx led the pack.

From first gunshot to last, it might've been five minutes. Suddenly, we were alone, and the Regios were gone. Took Micaiah with them. An incredible plan, well executed.

The wind paused. The only sound was the hooves of hard-driven horses galloping across the salt flats, and then the wailing started. Heartbroken wailing.

Tenisha Keys. Dead.

Petal. Dying.

## (ii)

My head wouldn't believe what had happened, while my eyes couldn't look away. The stink of gunfire never smelled so foul.

Nikki Breeze hung her head over Tenisha and wept—her sobbing full of love and agony.

Aunt Bea and Crete crouched beside Nikki, petting her and shushing her, and right then, it all became clear to me. Reverend Kip Parson and Sally Browne Burke were fools. To attack homosexuals with nine-tenths of the men gone was worse than stupid. It was evil.

Body parts don't matter. *Gillian* love is love.

Even with our troubles, Micaiah and I had that love, and his bracelet dangled on my wrist.

A gust of wind smacked me with a handful of heat. I took a step toward the jeeps, then stopped, when I heard Pilate whisper, "Petal." He knelt by her on the salt.

No, she couldn't die. She'd gotten off the Skye6, and she was going to find the other side of her pain. She had sworn to do no harm. She shouldn't be punished for it.

Wren joined Pilate, standing over him. I couldn't move to help. All I could do was bear witness.

Petal raised a hand, blood pouring out of her. She cried out and twisted up in pain. "First, do no harm. I didn't, Pilate. I kept my oath."

She wept. She was dying. She knew it. Pilate knew it. God knew it.

She raised a hand and touched Pilate's face. Left blood there. When her hand fell, Pilate grabbed it and put it back in place. "You did no harm, Petal, and I'm glad. You stayed true to yourself, and you beat the Sino. You got clean. You're good, Petal, you're good and wonderful, and it's okay." His voice chopped out the last word. A tear dropped down to mix with the blood.

"Will I get to my other side, Pilate?" Petal asked in a whisper. "You said I couldn't, but maybe, when I'm dead, do you think there's a chance?"

Pilate's jaw muscles jumped. He couldn't answer.

"Is there a chance?" she asked again.

Pilate nodded finally. "Oh, Petal, you've already made it to the other side. I was so wrong before, but this I know for sure: you'll make it right into heaven, right to the other side of it all, and you'll be like you were before the Hutongs, before the Sino."

"But I've hurt so many people. I've done so many horrible things. I'm not good enough to get into heaven." Petal closed her eyes. Never to open them again.

Pilate bent down and kissed her. "Heaven isn't for the good. Heaven is for the broken."

Then she left us to find that other shore. Pilate let loose, and that battle-weary vet, that priest of God, wept with his face pushed down into her hair.

### (iii)

Pilate lost Petal.

Nikki lost Tenisha.

I wasn't going to lose Micaiah.

I skipped in a hurried limp to the jeeps and started undoing the straps and figuring out the ramps. Thank God for my engineering mind. It would take a bit to get a vehicle off the flat car, and that was why the ARK Regios had settled on horses instead of jeeps.

I didn't hear the *Moby* come soaring down, dodging zephyrs and fighting the gales, but I saw the rope ladder strike the hard, salt ground. I knew what Sketchy wanted. She had seen those girls steal Micaiah, and it was time to get him back. Somehow, they had repaired the *Moby* without returning to the ZZK.

The ladder slid across the salt as the *Moby* bounced around in the air currents. I limped over and caught a hold of it.

I had grown so much, had become so strong and fearless since my first trip up that ladder outside of McCook. Even with a hurt ankle, I climbed up the rungs, through the mid-bay hatch, and rolled onto the Neofiber floor. They'd jettisoned most of the hay, but the sweet, dusty smell still drifted from the bales stacked near the back bay doors.

"Move, Cavvy," Tech said. "Wren is coming along."

Of course. Wren wasn't about to miss out on the reward money, and I'd been right to wonder if she really had the moral fiber to follow through on her promise to lead our outfit.

Losing Micaiah, watching two of my friends die, I was enraged. I took it out on Wren. "It's your fault them ARK soldiers snuck aboard the train. If you'd been sober last night, you might have seen them."

I expected her to punch me full in the face. Instead she turned away. "Well, who knows, I might just die today. I bet that'll give you and Sharlotte a tickle."

Tech lost her patience. "This is not the time for your goddamn family drama. We have to get Micaiah back."

"I'm sorry, Wren." It wasn't her fault. We all should've been more careful.

Sketchy caterwauled through the communication tube in the floor. "Up ahead, four Johnny zeppelins. Good Lord, they're big. That's where them Vixx sisters are headed with the boy. And there's a bad storm, worst one I've ever seen in this God-forsaken nothin'. And I can't fight them four Johnny Boys. Not with the *Moby* sick. Gotta get the boy quick or lose him forever. Hit me last night. He's the son of Tibbs Hoyt. Can't believe I didn't recognize him before. Should've flown him out of the Juniper right away, dammit!"

Wren and I stared at each other. "So that's the big secret," she whispered. "And you couldn't tell me 'cause you were scared I'd run away with him. Well, you can go jack yourself, Cavvy. And jacker that damn boy."

It was my turn to look away.

The *Moby*'s cockpit windows had been blown out after the train battle, but Sketchy flew the airship down toward those running horses with her flying goggles strapped across her eyes.

Wren yelled to Sketchy, "Sail the *Moby* over them, Sketch. I aim to use your ladder to fetch Micaiah or Micah or whatever his name is."

"Are you serious, Wren?" Tech asked. "The wind will shake you off."

My sister sneered. "Aw, Tech, I'm circus trained. This'll be too much fun."

Sketchy roared, "You Wellers aren't right in the head, but I'll get you into position." She called into the communication tube. "Hey, Peeperz, you gotta guide me. Wren is going down the ladder to fetch the boy."

"Gosh, Sketch, really?"

I pulled Wren to me. "You'll get him and bring him back, right? You won't take off with him, right?"

A smirk screwed up her face. "You know me, I'm selfish and erratic. Not sure what I'll do, and, God, does it suck to be you 'cause you'll just have to watch and hope. Ha!"

I latched on tighter to her, trying to get a promise out of her, but she shoved me back. She clambered through the mid-bay hatch and down to the bottom of the ladder, clinging to the last rung as we soared ever lower.

My jaws clenched. Yeah, all I could do was watch my sister play out another scene in a Hollywood action video and hope she didn't run off with Micaiah and sell him to the highest bidder.

Peeperz's voice came up from the tube. "Sketch, keep her straight. You're right on them. But there are them Johnnies ahead. And you see the storm?"

"I see it all!" Sketchy yelled.

The sky in the distance boiled with black clouds where the four Johnny Boy blimps waited, ready to spirit my Micaiah away if Wren didn't get to him first.

### (iv)

Tech and I clustered around the hatch, looking down at Wren as she soared over the salt flats toward the ten ARK soldiers riding our own horses in a full gallop—two long lines of soldiers, spread apart like geese on the wing. They were prolly so intent on getting aboard before the storm hit, they weren't looking behind them.

The *Moby* fought the growing wind. Wren was swinging about something awful. I would've been sent flying, but my amazing sister held on. Tech and I weren't breathing. An errant gust of wind would smash Wren to the ground. Or if those riders noticed her, they'd shoot her down easily.

Wren hooked her left arm around a rung. In her right hand was a Colt Terminator. She took down the back two riders. Only the lucky or the damned could have made those shots. Wren Weller was both.

The rest of the riders couldn't hear the gunshots over the noise of those hooves thundering and the wind shrieking like a banshee. One of the Vixx sisters rode Taylor Quick, and she held Bob D's reins, where Micaiah was hogtied. The other Vixx hammered her boots against Beck. Damn Vixxes, hurting my ponies.

Wind bashed the *Moby*, and Wren was flung into a rider. Wren booted her off, and the soldier fell in a cloud of dust and hurt. My sister could've let go to get on the horse, but she didn't.

She turned and kicked another out of the saddle. Four down. Six to go.

Two Regios saw Wren and pulled their guns.

One of the Johnnies drifted down low, prolly to pick up the Vixxes and Micaiah. Tech whispered. "Wren better hurry. We can't fight those Johnnies."

I was wordless. Staring down at my sister, I prolly had a ringside seat to her death. I should've been nicer to her. I should've tried harder. Time and again she had saved us 'cause maybe some part of her loved us, loved me, and if that were true, she'd rescue Micaiah and bring him back to me. But was it true?

Sketchy kept the *Moby* as straight as she could, but the wind slapped Wren about on the ladder, nearly flinging her off. She spun between two riders. The Regios weren't thinking. They killed each other with their own crossfire as Wren whirled around again.

Only four left. Two Regios and two Vixxes on five horses, including the one Micaiah was tied to. Either they were so bent on getting to the airships that they didn't care about Wren, or they hadn't seen her. Who would guess anyone could come storming out of the sky on a rope ladder to deal death so efficiently?

I could almost hear Wren laughing, screaming, calling 'em skanks. Sure. That's what she was doing. With her Colt Terminator backing up every word.

"She just might pull it off," Tech whispered. "How can that be? This isn't happening."

My horses began to slow. Those ARK soldiers drove the ponies like they were motorcycles, but they weren't. Horses can sprint, but not a full-on foamy gallop for all that long. Katy started to hitch her gait, her bad hoof acting up. And Mick's sick eye wept in a sticky stream down his face. He was trying to close it and still run. Those ARK soldiers didn't care about my animals. More importantly, they didn't understand my animals. Wren did.

She waited a moment, and then both Katy and Mick slammed down onto the salt ground, throwing their riders. Poor horses.

All the Regios were gone. Only the Vixx sisters remained.

Wren dropped down onto Bob's saddle, landing right behind Micaiah. I thought she was going to grab him and climb back up. Instead, she let the wind sweep the ladder away, and right then, I knew her plan. She was going to run away with Micaiah and sell him. Of course. I'd been right about her all along. She was too damaged to ever be trusted.

"We have to stop her!" I yelled.

Tech didn't respond. She yelled into the tube, "Sketch, Wren is off the ladder, evasive maneuvers! I'll get to the crow's nest. We're going to have to fight our way out of this one." Tech sprinted toward the doorway and to the ladder which led up to the other machine-gun nest in the canopy above.

Sketchy howled back, "Hello, Johnny Boys! You come to fight? Good. The *Moby* is hurt, and you never wanna fight a hurt animal. Gonna badger the bejesus out of you, as God is my witness. Peeperz, light 'em up with the triple Xs. Light them up!"

The four Johnny Boy blimps blocked out the sky. The ground below me was empty. Had Wren gunned down the Vixxes, or had they turned on her? I didn't know—couldn't see a thing as the *Moby* swerved to the side. I gripped the floor-cleats to keep me from spinning across the floor. From above and below came the dull thud of the triple Xs. Fifty caliber bullets peppered the sides of the Johnny blimps.

Then the full force of the storm hit, blasting us with salt, sand, and debris.

"I gotta get on the ground, Sketch!" I yelled it. If she'd said no, I would've jumped.

But that big woman didn't say anything—too busy flying.

In the swirling sky, the Johnny Boys opened fire on us, tracers, bullets, rockets, and it was the Fourth of July, with us in the middle of the fireworks. Bullet holes punched through the Neofiber all around, letting in light, making a whistling sound from the gale force winds.

The staccato burst of Sketchy laughing vibrated through the tubes. How could she be laughing? "Lotta wind, Johnnies, and I reckon y'all don't like that wind much. But me and the *Moby* don't mind the wind. We're Juniper-born. Now, Cavvy, I'll get you down, but pardon my bump."

We crashed into a zeppelin with a shudder, like rubber balls ricocheting against each other.

The gunners on the Johnnies went quiet, and Sketchy laughed. "Can't stomach the crossfire, huh?" Then, "Hang on, people!"

I couldn't imagine what it was like for Peeperz or Tech in the glass bubbles, staring death in the face. We bounced around some more, so hard I had to close my eyes and grit my teeth, waiting to die from the blimp bumper car madness.

Sketchy's yell made me snap open my eyes. "Cavvy, we only got one chance, and it might kill us all, but here you go."

The ground rushed toward me, coming up too fast, too fast, and we hit with a smash, the Neofiber shaking, snapping, deafening sounds of sheer, mortal destruction.

The *Moby* rose, but not before I rolled down through the mid-bay hatch and onto the crusty salt ground. Hurt my ankle all over again.

Eyes up, I watched as the *Moby* lifted off into the sky. Kevlar shards slapped in the windstorm, whole sections of Neofiber were gone, and the poor airship looked like a colander. Instead of running from the wind, Sketchy headed directly west, directly into the gale.

The four Johnny Boys opened fire again, but the howling wind pushed them backwards. The Johnnies, with their size and structural mass, could only inch along. The *Moby* was far smaller, and it might outrun those beasts.

Watching that brave zeppelin struggle away, I realized it's the little people, the nobodies, who change history, and that's where the power of God rests. In simple people and small things. Like Sketchy. Like the *Moby*. Like me.

## (v)

I slipped on my cattling goggles, put my head down, and started off into the duststorm, or should I say saltstorm? Whatever. Couldn't see a thing.

I growled against the pain of walking on my ankle. But nothing—not pain, not Wren—was going to stop me from getting Micaiah back. I tripped over the body of one of the Regios Wren had killed. I took her AZ3 and snapped the stock to its maximum length. I used it as a crutch, but figured I'd have to use it for real eventually.

Only took a few dozen steps when I saw I wasn't alone in that swirling hell of salt and dust.

Two figures were coming toward me, one on horseback, the other walking with guns spiking out of her body like horns.

Nowhere to hide. I crouched, undid the safety on the rifle, and tried to not throw up.

The soldiers marched forward. Only they weren't soldiers.

From out of the soup walked my sister Wren. Micaiah was upright, but still tied to Bob D. My deepest fears were confirmed.

Wren had said it herself—never let your heart get in the way of a paycheck.

I stood, pressed the AZ3 to my shoulder, and aimed at Wren's chest. It was the worst kind of déjà vu. "Get away from him, Wren!"

The winds dropped for a moment. Emotion washed down Wren's face like rain drizzling down a window. "MTAT," she whispered.

She said it like a word, but it was an acronym, the very basics of gun safety: muzzle, trigger, action, target. Basically, it came down to two things—all guns are loaded, and don't aim at anything you don't want to destroy.

"Second time you done this, Cavvy. Put the gun down or kill me. I can't stand—"

"I won't let you sell him!" Rage boiled in my guts. I would kill her. My eyes showed it.

"I wasn't gonna …" Gunfire stopped her words. Gunfire from behind me. Wren dropped to her knees.

Bob D skittered away carrying Micaiah who watched, wordless.

The world ended. God came down, kissed us, and took off. Gone to Texas.

*Goodbye, God. Goodbye, forever.*

Wren arched backward, and I could see the crimson dashes across her belly. Her intestines and stomach were shot full of holes—a long, hard, awful way to die.

I had to shoot her now. I had to put her out of her misery.

My mind went sluggish. This couldn't be happening. Wren had just swung out of the *Moby* on a ladder to grab Micaiah. She couldn't die. She and Pilate always said that heaven wouldn't take her and hell was afraid she'd take over.

"Wren." I whispered. I turned to see who had shot her. Two soldiers stood in the swirling dust storm, both their faces like squares of emotionless, bio-engineered nothing. Reb and Ronnie Vixx.

They would get me. They would kill me. My feet grew roots into the salt.

Then a deep voice inside of me yelled, *Wren's as good as dead. Now is not the time to jack things up. Now is the time to run.* I don't know if it was Pilate's voice or Mama's or Sharlotte's or Wren's. Sounded like all of them put together.

I threw myself on Bob D, Micaiah behind me, and we galloped away.

Wren's last words plagued me ... *I wasn't gonna ... I wasn't gonna ...*

She wasn't going to run off with Micaiah. She really had gone to rescue him for me, and she'd been killed in the attempt.

I'd left my poor sister behind to die alone.

·

# Chapter Seventeen

*I'll let Sally Browne Burke and Kip Parson talk about morality. I'm here to save our species by any means necessary.*

—Tiberius "Tibbs" Hoyt
Special Congressional Hearing on the Sterility
Epidemic
April 12, 2039

## (i)

MICAIAH AND I GALLOPED ACROSS THE SALT flats, deeper into the storm. No rain, just wind, horrible, terrible wind. The blowing dust and sand blinded us and stung our skins like hordes of fire ants. Surprised me that we didn't start bleeding rivers from windburn. Once we'd put a fair distance between us and the Vixx sisters, I dismounted and cut Micaiah loose.

I could tell west by the smudge of the sun in the muddy sky. I couldn't walk, but Bob D was tired, thirsty, done for. Still, I had to make him carry my weight. That added to my guilt. What kind of a sister was I? I should've bent down, held Wren one last time, apologized, and told her I loved her in such a way that she'd believe me. Then used the AZ3 to end her life quickly.

Every time I felt the lump of the .45 caliber bullet in my pocket, the guilt deepened. Like she'd said, I would keep it in memory of her.

Micaiah, walking next to me, pulled a pair of goggles from out of the saddlebags. The ARK soldiers must've stuffed their gear in there while in the cattle cars.

During a lull in the windstorm, I leaned down. "Micaiah, I'm sorry I've been so distant. I know you'll try to be honest."

The wind swirled back up, and we couldn't talk. He took my hand and squeezed it. We were okay.

When the wind took a break from trying to blow us back to Colorado, we talked a little, enough for me to know I was a horse's ass.

Micaiah had told the Vixx sisters he had the chalkdrive in his pocket so they'd leave us alone, but they hadn't taken it off him. Too busy trying to get to the Johnnies. He also made it clear—Wren had been trying to get back to the train as soon as possible, so she hadn't untied him.

He didn't say I told you so about no one letting Wren be good, but he didn't need to.

Though I had plenty to cry about, my eyes remained dry. My insides were a rocky place where the seeds of sorrow could find no purchase.

I was getting harder, I could feel it. Maybe that's growing up, when the soft parts of ourselves get calloused 'cause the world doesn't care about our tears. All they do is wet our faces and make us thirsty.

And we were thirsty—boy, girl, horse, all of us so thirsty. My canteen laughed every time we cracked it open.

Bob D stayed tough. He licked water out of my hand and gazed at me with those long-lashed eyes, like he was begging me to explain life and its suffering to him. I couldn't. His looks only made me feel harder inside.

But I petted him, especially when Micaiah climbed into the saddle and we'd gallop a short distance to try and stay ahead of the Vixx sisters. I knew they were behind us. It would've been impossible for the Johnny dirigibles to see them in the salt storm, and besides, I figured the Johnnies were chasing after the *Moby*.

I thought about trying to circle around to get back to the train, but it was a long ways away. We were already halfway to Wendover, halfway across a river of blood. Might as well try and trudge to the other side.

I wasn't sure how the Vixxes could track us, but if anyone could, they could. Maybe the ARK spliced bloodhound DNA into their genes. I had a horrid image of them snuffling along the ground on all fours, smelling us out.

I thought that day couldn't get any worse—that long, hard, wind-killed day.

I was wrong.

The Vixx sisters caught us outside of the Silver Mountain Casino, about three miles from Wendover's downtown. On the very edge of the Juniper.

On the very edge of night.

**(ii)**

Micaiah saw the casino first.

Outside of Wendover, on the northern border of the Bonneville Salt Flats State Park, a bunch of jagged rocks rose from the flat, white plain. The Silver Island Mountains. On one slope sat the casino, which had been built before the Yellowstone Knockout, when Utah relaxed a little on their anti-gambling laws. Busloads of people from the SLC used to descend on Wendover to gamble 'cause games of chance were legal in Nevada. Once Utah had their own casino out on the salt flats, well, gambling twenty miles closer to the SLC might've been a good idea, but then the Yellowstone Knockout wiped out the power. Couldn't keep a casino open when the electricity only worked randomly.

When Micaiah and I saw the Silver Island Casino in the hills, we started for it, but Bob froze. He turned his head to look behind us and whinnied as if to say, "Hey, guys, the Vixx sisters are coming for you. They're faster than all of us put together, and I'm sorry I can't run no more."

Sure enough, the Vixxes jogged toward us across the salt.

Quick as a whip crack, Micaiah dragged me off Bob D. "What're you doing?" I asked him, every part of me angry.

He didn't answer. He decked me. A real sucker punch. You go down when you get socked like that, caught unaware. And I did. From the hit. From the betrayal.

I was so dazed and hurt, I didn't fight him when he zip tied my hands behind my back. Prolly got the zip ties out of Bob D's pack. The wire bracelet on my wrist bit into my skin.

"What the hell, Johnson?" I started off mad, then got scared. My voice crumbled as I pleaded with him. "Micaiah, tell me what's going on. How come you're turning on me? Micaiah!"

That one word. Micaiah. It had something to do with false prophets. I knew he was a liar. I just didn't know how much of a Judas he was as well.

He dragged me over to Bob D and pushed me on top. He lashed me to the saddle, pretty good, but then he'd learned all of his knots from me and Sharlotte, and ain't nothing we can't tie down. And Micaiah was so eerie smart.

"Oh, please, please talk to me." I was crying. Babbling. "Please."

Once I was on Bob, Micaiah took the chalkdrive and stuck it into my jean's pocket.

I finally understood and cried harder. "Micaiah, wait, no, we can get away. We can outwit them Vixxes. Micaiah, please. Don't do this."

He fixed those soft eyes on me. Tears tracked down his face through the grit.

He couldn't talk.

"Micaiah, let me go fight 'em while you get away. You're a boy, you're a viable boy, son of the richest man on earth. I'm just some girl. Just some stupid Juniper girl. Oh please, talk to me."

His voice came out low and bitter. "I've spent weeks running, afraid, manipulating you, lying. And you and your people have sacrificed everything for me. I'm done."

"But you're a boy, and I'm just a girl. I'm just a girl, and I ain't worth nothin'."

He touched my hands, looked me in the eye and said, "You're worth more than a hundred of me." He kissed my hand and held it against his cheek. His words tattooed themselves on my soul. "I love you, Cavatica Weller. You've sacrificed enough for me. Now it's time I sacrifice everything for you."

With the AZ3 in one hand, Micaiah took Bob D's reins in his other. He waited until the storm blew dust and salt one last time, hiding us. Then he whipped my poor horse, sending me away, so he could fight the Vixx sisters and die.

I rode off. Screaming his name. Over and over.
*Micaiah!*

Micaiah, 'cause Micah Hoyt was dead and buried. And Micaiah was the name of the boy I loved. The name of the boy who loved me.

No matter what.

# Chapter Eighteen

*We have both Memorial Day and Labor Day for a reason. Sure, you need courage to fight in a war, but do you know what else takes courage? Thursdays. Clocking in at work on any given Thursday—bravest damn thing in the world. Don't only look at wars for heroes, look in the heart of the everyday worker.*

—Former President Jack Kanton
Labor Day, September 4, 2045

## (i)

BOB D SWEPT ME ACROSS THE SALT TOWARD Wendover, Nevada and the setting sun.

I struggled, I wept, but I couldn't get free. The casino was getting farther and farther behind me.

Then Bob went down. Because he loved me. He kept going when I needed him, and he died right when I needed him to do that, too.

When Bob D dropped, I lurched forward. The momentum of the fall put pressure on both my shoulders and the zip ties around my wrist. Either one or the other had to give. My shoulders screamed bloody murder, but I managed to get a hand out of the zip ties. All because of the bracelet. The bracelet hadn't allowed him to secure the zip tie as tightly as it needed, and I was able to pull a hand free. Lucky, but then I was Pilate's daughter, blessed or cursed to survive.

I only had seconds before my poor horse fell on top of me.

Micaiah's knots were good, but not good enough for my fingers. I unraveled them enough so when Bob D rolled over, I leapt forward, landed on my left shoulder, then my face, sliding along the salt.

Blood on my face and salt in the wound, it hurt. The gash from the fight with the Madelines broke open. I didn't care. "Oh, Bob, oh, Bob."

His eyes were blank. He was gone.

Cynics and atheists would say that his heart gave out 'cause Micaiah sent him galloping away and he was already tuckered out. But I knew the truth.

Bob D died to save my life. To save us all. God rest his beautiful soul.

"Thanks, Bob." I petted his mane one last time. "Thank you for dying for me." I stood, eyes dry, jaws clenched against the pain. Oh, the pain. I'd landed on my left shoulder, where I'd been shot only a few weeks before. My right ankle screamed. The gash on my forehead added to the chorus, throbbing away.

Hurt, bleeding, and scared, what could I do against the Vixxes? I scanned the area around the casino, three hundred meters away. The salt flats were clear from horizon to horizon. Micaiah and the Vixx soldiers had to be inside the casino.

How could I fight them? I checked the saddlebags, thinking I might find a gun. But I found something infinitely better.

I found a slate.

On the edge of the Juniper, with the wind blowing, I tried the power. For a minute, it glowed, like it wanted to boot up. Shouldn't have worked. Hard drive should've been wiped clean. Maybe the shielding protecting Micaiah's chalkdrive worked on the slate as well. No time to ponder what that all meant.

I didn't know what I was going to do with that slate—only knew that if there was one weapon I could use, it was a computer.

Back at the academy, I'd ruined Becca Olson with one. Maybe I could take out the Vixx sisters as well.

I limped toward the casino, holding my left arm, gasping at the pain.

Inside, Micaiah and the Vixx sisters were deciding the fate of the world.

Leave it to a Weller to intrude on such a conversation.

## (ii)

Wind squealed through the guts of the Silver Island Casino. Someone must've left an Eterna battery hooked up, 'cause in the dusty twilight the sign flickered on, then off, sounding like a car with a bad starter. *Reer, reer, rumphf.* It reminded me of the video screens in Buzzkill, Nebraska, on the border of the Juniper.

Armed with a dead soldier's slate, I stepped over the broken lock and hobbled through the doors and into gloom. The casino looked like an ancient museum for leftover gambling equipment. Tables and chairs lay piled next to craps tables and slot machines. Roulette wheels rested in dusty stacks. All of the carpet had been rolled up, leaving bare concrete. The place smelled hot, enclosed, musty. The ghosts of stale cigarette smoke haunted every crevice and cranny. I had the idea it might be some kind of warehouse, maybe used to resupply the casinos in Wendover.

Every five or six seconds, or close to it, the place would try and light and then drop back into darkness. *Reer, reer, rumphf.*

A howl sent me scurrying behind a big keno machine painted like a clown's face, colorless from age.

"You will tell us where the chalkdrive is," a voice demanded. Might've been Reb Vixx. Or Ronnie. Or both of them talking at the same time, more like demons than sisters.

Another scream of pain.

I choked back a sob. The way he was screaming, it wouldn't be long before he told them everything. He was such a kind, gentle soul. The pain would kill his heart even if it didn't kill his body.

"Where is it? You had it in your pocket after we secured you at the train. Where is the chalkdrive now?"

"I won't tell you skanks a thing!" Micaiah's voice burst out. He'd picked up some Juniper slang, Wren's favorite word.

How could they be torturing their boss' son? Then I knew. The Vixxes were just following orders, which meant Tibbs Hoyt cared more about his money and power than his own son.

Lights flickered in a stutter. A slot machine *chinged* pathetically. *Reer, reer, rumphf.* Silence and dark again.

To my right was a doorway, and that's where the Vixxes had Micaiah. Prolly where the high stakes poker tables would've been. Ironic. The raw metallic smell of blood struck me, and I knew Micaiah had bet his life, every drop of blood, on me running to the border with the chalkdrive. But I was going to do some gambling of my own. Winner take all.

An empty bar sat across the room next to stairs going up to another level. To my left, the offices. And where there were offices, there was a server room. Sure. Law of nature.

I snuck away from the keno machine, moving slowly and carefully so the broken glass didn't crunch under my boots. The front office had become a technology junkyard—castoff laptops, slates, and a stack of Eterna batteries, boxes the sizes of bread loaves. The batteries weren't Kung Paos, but the older Egg Drop models. I stuck one under my arm and moved deeper into the offices, past broken desks and piles of paper.

Dim lights sparked on, followed by the *reer, reer, rumphf.* In the very back of the office stood a door emblazoned with the words "Server Room" in black. If the door was locked, I would've busted through it with the raw force of my *shakti*. The knob turned and led me into the server room, as dark as a cave. But every so often, a fluorescent light would buzz on weakly, giving me some light.

A Sargasso Sea of cables and wires covered the floor—most of the hardware had been stripped and salvaged out or stacked in the office. But not everything. A busted-up amplifier sat on the floor under looped yellow cables with the ends snipped off.

The amplifier was still plugged into the casino's sound system. If I could create a distraction, I might be able to sneak away with Micaiah. I needed a working slate, and I needed a longer duration of working electricity for the entire casino.

I set the Egg Drop battery down, then thumbed on the slate.

A flicker. The screen glowed, then winked off.

If I could get it to boot up, then I could get it into standby mode and set the auto-launch. I couldn't hear Micaiah, but that didn't mean he wasn't being tortured. *Hurry, Cavvy, hurry.*

For a minute, I focused my troubleshooting skills on the slate. The hard drive hadn't been wiped out, but I figured the battery might not have enough juice to fully boot it up. If I increased the energy input with the Egg Drop, I might prolong the electricity enough to get the slate working. Hopefully the Egg Drop had enough juice to not only light up the slate but the casino as well.

Server rooms had become like utility closets for all electronics. If you had a battery to run your business, you'd keep it in the server room, and a casino that size would have a rack of them. Unless you had a Kung Pao, then you'd need only one.

I found the battery cabinet. A few batteries sat there dead and dusty—only one glowed. Well, I could add to it.

A lot of energy flowed from the batteries. If I touched the wrong lead, the next flicker would fry me.

But I knew what I was doing. The first commandment said not to have any strange gods, but for me, Eterna batteries were idolatry. Growing up in the Juniper, you either hated electricity 'cause you didn't have it, or you worshiped it.

I found the leads, found the plugs, and after the next *reer, reer, rumphf,* I hooked up the new, better Egg

Drop, while doing most of my work in the dark. I pulled the power adaptor cord out of the slate's housing and plugged it into the battery.

And waited, sweating. My heart went from jamming itself down into my belly to flailing up into my throat.

This had to work. More power would give me more time, and the electricity might work for five or six seconds longer and not just a stutter.

Enough time for my plan.

*Please, God, please. You love Pilate enough to keep him alive. Love me enough to save Micaiah and the human race.*

The lights turned full on. I counted to twelve.

The two batteries went a dull yellow-orange and winked out. Twelve seconds. One second for each of the apostles. In computer time, that was forever.

Maybe the Vixx sisters wouldn't notice. I prayed they wouldn't.

Next interval, I turned on the slate, and bang, it booted, and I had enough time to hit the standby mode. Next flicker, I set the auto-launch. Any power now would start the slate.

When things went dark again, I started a Hail Mary. You can say the Hail Mary in eleven seconds. That was my timer.

*Hail Mary, full of grace ...*

Next power interval, I found the pre-loaded media files on the slate—country music and season one of *Lonely Moon*. Sure, 'cause everyone liked country music and Juniper drama.

Another *Hail Mary*. I found the sound recorder. The lights went out. I noticed there wasn't any more *reer,*

*reer, rumphf.* Now there was just a big staticky chunk of sound. Chunk. Silence. Darkness.

*Hail Mary, full of grace ...*

At my amen, the lights came back on.

The slate winked on. I recorded my messages. Set up my batch files. Scheduled them to execute after the auto-launch. In fits, in spurts, waiting in the darkness, I worked in the twelve-second intervals God gave me, saying the *Hail Mary*. Only Saint Francis might've said it more fervently.

I found the amplifier and plugged in the slate. I found the volume and cranked it up.

Lights flickered out. I was ready.

I wasn't crying.

I wasn't even praying.

I was fighting—fighting those Vixx sisters the only way I knew how—with wires, with a slate, with my head.

And a head can outgun a gun any old time.

# Chapter Nineteen

*The Juniper forges women into the hardest steel imaginable.*

—Mavis Meetchum
*Colorado Courier* Interview
September 7, 2046

## (i)

BEFORE I LEFT THE SERVER ROOM, I COILED SOME leftover cabling around my good shoulder. Just in case. It was really nice cable. I was pretty sure some active salvage monkey had stashed it there, prolly stole it from the SLC under the noses of the Mormons.

I limp-skipped through the office. It was so black I banged my left shoulder against a wall, sending shrieking pain through my shoulder. Didn't have time to stop to nurse it or freak out. I made it into the main casino when the lights flickered on.

Over the speakers, my own voice roared like glorious thunder.

"Come out, you dirty skanks! The Weller girls are here, and we have reinforcements. Come out, or we're coming in after you!"

Then darkness, silence.

I inched forward to the doorway. I hid behind a stack of moldering cardboard boxes. The Vixx sisters must've lit a flare 'cause a hellish spitting light washed the walls in crimson. They talked in their robotic voices.

"We must confirm number and resources."

"We can negotiate with the boy's life for intel on the chalkdrive."

"Options."

"Defend, negotiate, terminate with extreme prejudice."

Lights came on. My voice blared over the speakers, playing the next audio file. "We have you surrounded. Come out with your hands up!"

First Vixx. "I will find an exit. The boy is secondary. Primary mission is the chalkdrive."

Second Vixx. "I will confirm assets and risk."

Both of the soldier girls sprinted out of the room. Like I thought, they wanted the chalkdrive. Didn't care too much about the boy.

My plan worked—worked on Becca Olson and worked on the Vixx sisters.

I dashed into the room.

Micaiah hung from the ceiling, ropes tied to beams above the shedding ceiling tiles looped around his armpits. His shirt was unbuttoned. Hands zip tied. Legs zip tied. And bloody. Every inch bloody.

Using my Betty knife, I sliced through the zip ties on his feet. I pulled over a chair and stood on it to cut the rope holding him to the rafters. He came down on top of me, and we rolled to the floor. But only for a second. I picked him up.

"Gotta run, Micaiah. Quietly. Gotta run. We only have …"

Twelve seconds.

When the lights flashed on, so did the theme song of *Lonely Moon*—gunfire and rip-roaring country music. Over the speakers, it sounded like Armageddon.

God willing, we'd be out of there before the Vixxes guessed it was all a trick.

"Cavvy … no … you run …" Micaiah could hardly talk. He was slippery from blood, weak from torture, his face twisted in the flare's fire.

"Shush, now. Shush. My plan worked."

It did, only my exit strategy wasn't too good. Like always.

Ronnie Vixx stood in front of the door leading outside.

At the sound of our footsteps, she turned, her guns up and ready—an AZ3 and a Zeus 2 charge gun. Her face hung expressionless. No thrill of victory for her. Just her mission.

"The chalkdrive? Where is it?" Not sure which was colder, the metal of her gun barrel or the inhuman iron in her eyes.

"I buried it out in the desert." Said it before Micaiah could say a word.

Ronnie Vixx raised her AZ3, and without even aiming, she gunned Micaiah back against slot machines. The sound of that assault rifle thundering shattered me. The flare in the other room had burned out. In total darkness, Micaiah's poor body dropped to the floor.

Lights flickered on, and an old country music song, as mournful as a ghost, whispered through the speakers. Twelve seconds worth.

Then, back into darkness.

"The chalkdrive. Where is it?" Same question. Same toneless voice. Same nothing in her soul.

I ignored her. I went to Micaiah, fell across his body, kissed his face, and touched his bloody chest. My boy. My Micaiah. Gone.

"If you run, you will die," she said.

Couldn't run. Couldn't die. Seeing Micaiah's death had already killed me.

From behind me clattered the footsteps of Reb Vixx. They'd search me and find the chalkdrive, and no one would ever know Tibbs Hoyt had the cure for sterility. He could continue to sell Male Product and get richer and richer and richer.

And he'd killed his own son to do it.

## (ii)

"Stand up." Ronnie Vixx stood in front of me. Reb Vixx was running up from behind.

Lights off. Coffin dark. Me sweating. Micaiah's blood on my fingers. The memory of my lips on his cheek, going cold.

"Goddamn you skanks," I whispered. "Goddamn you, and goddamn that jack-off Tibbs Hoyt."

No answer. They were going to wait for electricity, then they were going to take the chalkdrive, and most likely they'd kill me, too, to cover up their tracks. I was a liability, and I'm sure Hoyt's orders would've been to leave no survivors.

Lights on. Music blasted through the speakers, a pounding rock and roll song with dubstep thumping breaks, and through the doors, like it was her very own theme song, charged Wren Weller.

Her Colt Terminators blazed as shells sprinkled the floor.

Ronnie Vixx turned and then lost her face. Wren was packing .45 hollow points. At that range, it was butchery.

Wren tore past me and the body of Micaiah. She leapt over Ronnie Vixx's corpse and hit Reb Vixx going a million kilometers an hour.

The two warrior women were gonna fight to the death. Blood splattered the floor.

But Wren couldn't be alive. Couldn't. Gut-shot for hours? Suffering as her own bowels poisoned her and her blood gushed. Couldn't be.

But it was. Maybe Wren hadn't been as shot up as I had thought. Or maybe she'd been as contrary with death as she'd been with her family.

With no light, I lost track of Wren and Reb Vixx as they fought with their knives, slicing, cutting, stabbing. Wren was too ferocious to go down; Reb Vixx too well-engineered.

The lights flickered on. More music blared, thundering out a hip-hop song, pounding us with bass and beat. Sharlotte rushed through the door. Impossible.

"Sharlotte!" I tried to yell over the music. "How can you be here?"

Couldn't hear what she said, but I heard Wren screaming, "Kill us both, Shar. Kill us both. I wanna ride this skank down to hell."

I remembered the weapons. I went for the leftovers of Ronnie Vixx, picked up her charge gun and her AZ3, then turned. A second later I had light and Johnny Cash singing.

Wren and the Vixx woman wrestled on the floor. Reb Vixx stuck my sister's own Betty knife into her already torn belly.

I watched her do it. Just like all the other times in my story, I couldn't shoot for fear of killing my own sister. Couldn't 'cause when it came down to it, after all the fighting and tears and arguing, I loved her more than I loved the world.

And I wasn't good with guns. But I had an idea.

In the darkness, I did some emergency engineering with the cable I'd taken from the server room. Maybe I was being stupid. Maybe I should've just killed that Reb Vixx where she stood. But like I told Becca Olson, oh so long ago at the Sally Browne Burke Academy for the Moral and Literate, I'd rather be stupid than heartless.

I stood. The charge gun hung from my shoulder. I emptied the AZ3 into the ceiling to get everyone's attention. "Reb, I'll give you the chalkdrive! Wren, stop fighting!"

Lights came on. Twelve seconds. LeAnna Wright singing about Texas at midnight.

Wren shrieked at me. "Dammit, Cavvy. Kill us! For once in your goddamn life, shoot to kill!"

"*You* stop!" I yelled back. "For once in your own goddamn life, stop fighting and trust me." I dropped the AZ3 and swung the charge gun around. I let the strap fall from my shoulder.

Wren released the demon. Reb stood, robotically, figuring Wren was no longer a threat. She was prolly right.

That soulless Vixx soldier walked over to me, a cobra in combat boots. She reached out a gory glove. "The chalkdrive. Now."

Sharlotte stood breathing hard behind me. "Cavvy, no." Then I figured she saw Micaiah lying dead on the floor, 'cause I heard her gasp his name. I swallowed my sorrow.

"Don't worry, Sharlotte." Then to Reb Vixx, "If I give you the chalkdrive, you'll leave us alone, okay?"

Darkness. Reb didn't answer.

With my heart fluttering, I was about to ask again when the lights came on. More country music. Country Mac Sterling.

Reb ripped the charge gun out of my hand. "The chalkdrive. Now."

I stood unarmed.

"She'll kill us all." Wren hissed the words through her pain.

I dug into my pocket and showed Reb Vixx the chalkdrive, the key that would unlock the future of our world, for Juniper folk and Yankees alike.

Reb snatched it from my hand just as the lights and music went away.

I had to warn her, but I knew it wouldn't do any good. "Let us live, or you'll be sorry. You'll be real sorry."

When the lights shimmered on, she fired that charge gun at me and Shar, point blank, should've roasted us toasty, but it didn't.

I'd looped the cable around the front element of the charge gun and fastened bare wires to the grip.

When she hit the trigger, lightning filled the room.

As bright as the sun.

Long streams of electricity blazed up and down Reb Vixx, electrifying her flesh, sizzling her down. The stench of human flesh burning made me sick.

Twelve seconds worth of hell on earth.

Darkness cut off the electricity, but we could still hear the horrible sizzle of her cooking skin.

When the lights came on, what was left of Reb Vixx, headless and blackened and dead, toppled over. Nothing could've survived that blast.

"Thank you, Maggie," I whispered, "for your very fine batteries."

The chalkdrive clattered out of Reb Vixx's fist and onto the floor. The shielding held. But then, that shielding would have held against a nuclear blast. I'd find that out later, much later.

"Cavvy, what happened?" Sharlotte asked me in the darkness that followed.

Before I could explain my engineering or ask Sharlotte how she'd found us, Wren called out, "Cavvy, you there? You alive still?"

I went to hold her while she died. One last chance to put things right.

### (iii)

Sharlotte and I knelt beside Wren. She was a mess of blood. She latched onto my arm. "Cavvy, you didn't shoot me before, did you? I thought you'd shot me. My own family, killing me. But you didn't. Say you didn't."

"I didn't, Wren. I'd never. It was the Vixx sisters behind me."

Wren shuddered and cried. "Oh, Cavvy, I was scared you did. You know, I petted you as a baby. Like you were my own baby, and I loved you."

My tears fell in a rainstorm. "I love you, too, Wren. Always." In the past weeks, I'd tried to make her believe that. Now I could. "The Vixx sisters are dead, Wren. You killed one, and I tricked the other. But it was you who saved me. You and Sharlotte. And all of us together, we saved the world."

"Cavvy!" Wren cried out again.

I bent and held her close.

"Cavvy, I wasn't gonna steal Micaiah. I was gonna bring him back. I was gonna be good, Cavvy. I wanna be good now."

"I know, Wren. I know."

Wren's body wracked in pain. "Sharlotte, can you forgive me for all I done to you and Mama? Can you love me? I know I'm trouble, but can you love me?"

Sharlotte bent closer and picked up a bloodstained hand. "Yeah, Wren, I can. I'm different now, and I can forgive you. I love you."

We were together, the Weller sisters, a family, at the very end of things.

This time when the lights came back, out of the speakers murmured a quiet girl's voice, singing about redemption and love.

"I petted you, Cavvy. I petted and kissed you and rocked you to sleep and warmed you when it was cold. Like Mama did for me. Like Sharlotte did."

I hugged Wren tighter and kissed her.

We all cried—maybe tears for Wren, maybe tears for Mama, or maybe just tears 'cause the world brings us hurt. But we can get to the other side of it—if not in this life, then the next.

"Go, Wren," I said. "Go and find the other side of your pain. Go and rest."

"Mama!" Wren cried out. It was an old voice in the darkness, an old plea for comfort, for warmth, for love in this hard, cold world.

She let go of the fight and relaxed in my arms. Dead.

"Find your other side," I whispered to her. "I forgive you. I forgive all your trespasses."

"Our Father, who art in heaven," Sharlotte started.

I said it with her. Hallowed be thy name. But God wasn't in heaven right then. He was with us in that room. Crying. God can't stay in heaven. What can He do there?

God is with us, always. When we laugh, He laughs. When we cry, He cries. And when we fight for our lives, He fights along with us.

Until it's time to take that short walk on home.

# Chapter Twenty

*In the 19th century, greed, corruption, and violence built the American West. Maybe now, those strong Juniper women can re-build it using their compassion, kindness, and feminine strength.*

—Sally Browne Burke
Informal Remarks on the Juniper
March 1, 2058

## (i)

A VOICE ASKED IN THE DARKNESS, "ARE YOU ALL okay?" I couldn't believe it. Micaiah.

Sharlotte sucked in a breath—sounded like she was about to curse.

Another song came on with an old, reverb guitar riffing, full of hope, the Wild West, and a pioneering spirit.

And we were about to do some pioneering.

I left Wren and tumbled into Micaiah, holding him, feeling his skin, warm and alive, kissing him. Micaiah was alive! I wanted to sing it to the stars. But how could that be?

"Micaiah, how could you—how come—how can you be alive?"

Then I understood. Micaiah had seemed so lucky to survive the crash, to get away from all of our fights without a bullet touching him, but maybe he wasn't lucky. Maybe he was engineered. I felt the back of his poofy white pirate shirt and found bullet holes from when he'd been shot off the horse with Wren. He must've picked up another Regio's coat to trick us.

"You were shot," I murmured. "Micaiah, can you heal like the Vixxes?"

"Not now," he said. He led me back to Wren. In his hand were two syringes. He bent down, and during another twelve-second interval, he found Wren's vein and slipped that needle in and worked a miracle.

"Micaiah, what are you doing?" I asked.

In the blackness I couldn't see his expression. But his words came out soft and low. "This is the Gulo Delta. The first Gulo serums killed most of the test subjects or twisted them into monsters. But the Gulo Delta, this stuff, just watch."

"What's going on?" Sharlotte asked suspiciously.

Hope sparked in my chest. "Super soldiers. If they could enhance cellular regeneration with the Vixxes, maybe they could do something similar with other folks."

"Not that I understood any of that," Sharlotte said softly.

"It means Wren might heal like a Vixx," Micaiah said, "if we got to her in time. Death is death. My father couldn't fix that part, or at least I don't think he could."

Lights on and we were all there beside Wren. We watched as the skin started to knit together.

Lights off. Breath burst from Wren. A rebirth. *Roll away the stone from the tomb. Why do you look for the living among the dead?*

Sharlotte's voice echoed with awe. "How can this be? How can she still be alive?"

I knew. Micaiah's syringe, the Gulo Delta, had rescued her from death. Inside, I was doing a happy dance. A miracle. *God so loved the world.* I gripped Wren's hand. It all came together in my mind. We'd seen Edger nearly dead, but the next day she'd been healed overnight. Now we knew why.

"The Vixxes gave Edger the same serum, right?" I paused. "Are you a super soldier?"

Micaiah laughed a little. "Hardly. You've seen me in a fight. But yes, Edger must have been dosed with the Gulo Delta. ARK research scientists delved into the deepest mysteries of micro-cellular biology to try and find a cure for the Sterility Epidemic. And they found some amazing things. Only about two percent of our DNA is used. We used to think the remaining ninety-eight percent was junk. But like that old saying, 'God don't make no junk.'"

Wren spoke out in the darkness. "How come I'm not dead?"

We all burst into laughter. More light, more music, and leave it to Sharlotte to say, "Aw, Wren, Pilate always said hell would spit you back out like a bad sunflower seed. Damn that man, but he was right."

Micaiah hit Wren with another syringe, this one for the pain, and she went out again.

We carried her out of that place of death and darkness. That tomb.

I tried to help, but my poor ankle and aching shoulder ganged up on me, nearly bent me over. Almost asked for a little of the Gulo Delta for myself, but Micaiah had used it all on Wren. We had pain medication, but I wanted to save it. God only knew what had happened to our people on the train.

And we still needed to figure out how Sharlotte had found us.

Outside, the night was a painter's palette of blacks, blues, and stars. A big fat moon shone down like a mother gazing on her child. A jeep sat parked in front of the casino. Sharlotte must've grabbed it from the train, picked up Wren, and sped across the salt flats to save us from the Vixxes.

Micaiah helped Sharlotte lay my sister gently into the backseat. Sharlotte gently brushed hair out of Wren's face. She caught me, watching. She nodded, wordless, and came over and held me for a long time. I hugged my big sister back, and time seemed to rewind back to our lives together on the ranch in Burlington. Me. Wren. Sharlotte. Only this time, we weren't arguing or fighting.

We parted. Sharlotte slid behind the wheel of the jeep, and Micaiah rode shotgun. I sat in the back with Wren so I could hold her. We took off into the moonlit landscape.

The electric lights of the jeep worked now, since we were out of the Juniper and back in the World. We headed west, toward Wendover and the end of our impossible cattle drive.

"If you lived, and Wren lived, will them Vixxes?" Sharlotte asked.

Micaiah shook his head. "Severe head trauma, spinal-cord injuries, my father could never fix. Those Vixxes are dead, but there is one left: Rachel. She's bad, but the Severins are worse. And the ARK has a lot more of them. I'm not sure how many. My father kept their identities, and number, hidden."

"If he kept their identities hidden, how do you know about them?" I asked.

"I met one." Micaiah took in a deep breath. "I watched her. I watched her change from a normal woman into something ... else ..."

The way he paused and said that final word jammed fear into my throat. But hopefully, we could avoid them.

Sharlotte still wasn't understanding it all. "So was Wren engineered?"

"No," I said, "She's human, but the Gulo Delta healed her."

"So far, so good," Micaiah murmured. I didn't like the way he said it.

### (ii)

From the back seat of the jeep, I called out to Sharlotte. "Hey Shar, what happened? How did you know where we were?"

"Tracked you." Sharlotte smiled at me in the rearview mirror. She looked so much like Mama right then. "But how come you aren't asking how I got to y'all so fast? Or how I could leave our headcount to chase after you?"

I grinned back. "'Cause you know how to leave when you need to leave. And you know when to stay when you need to stay. You know that family is sometimes more important than responsibility. And that Wren and me are more important than cows."

Sharlotte couldn't talk for a minute. I could see the tears in her eyes. We both knew that maybe Mama had it wrong working so much, leaving Sharlotte to raise Wren, and leaving them both to raise me.

I thought back about how Sharlotte said we were gonna do the cattle drive our own way. Well, we sure did.

"Okay, Sharlotte, how did you get to the train so fast?"

"Flew over the train tracks and found it." A mischievous grin lit her face. "And not in the *Moby* either. You think you're the only one who can do the impossible?"

"No." I sighed, so relieved. "Tell me everything."

Sharlotte told us her story, and it was quite the adventure. She'd come north looking to rejoin our operation, but stumbled into the Wind River people, picking through the bodies of the ARK army they'd helped destroy. The Psycho Madelines had already run off.

Sharlotte tried to run, but the Wind River women rode her down, and my sister thought it was the end of her. Instead, the women welcomed her. They'd already talked to Aunt Bea and Crete. And while Aunt Bea had eaten at Mavis Meetchum's table, Sharlotte had grown up playing with her kids.

The Wind River people still remembered the buffalo Mavis had given them, and so they gave Sharlotte a present back, one of the single-rider zeppelins I'd seen at the train battle. I recalled the insanely clever design, a thelium air cell carrying a NeoFiber frame, powered by an ultra-light steam engine.

Couldn't help it. My mouth fell open.

"That's right," Sharlotte said. "I flew over the train tracks until I found the train, got her stopped, and then grabbed a jeep. Something happened in the landing and busted up the flier, or else I'd have gotten to the casino faster, but I might not have found Wren."

My head whirled. All I'd ever heard were horror stories about the Wind River people, but come to find out they'd helped us not once, but *twice*. And with advanced technology. What other secrets did the Wind River people have?

I'd learn. But later, much later on.

Sharlotte continued with her story. In the jeep, she followed the tracks of the ten horses the Vixxes had stolen. Wasn't long until she found Wren lying in a pool of blood, but Wren said she wouldn't die until she saw me safe. Like I thought, death had come calling and my sister had told him to go jack himself.

She clung to life even though at the time she thought I'd shot her, making her worst fear come true— that family would hate her so much that they'd kill her. But it was a lie.

Most fears are lies at the end of the day.

Sharlotte and I talked more and then fell quiet. I got to thinking about Micaiah. Was he human? Was he really Tibbs Hoyt's son? In the end, it didn't matter. The world saw him as the heir to the ARK throne, and who was I to say anything different? But of course, my curiosity got the best of me.

"Okay, Micaiah," I said, "Sharlotte told us her story, now tell us yours."

"You know everything already," he said, eyes dropping. "What else is there?"

"Try," I said. "This is your chance to try."

Micaiah took in a deep breath. "I'd heard rumors that my father had a cure for the Sterility Epidemic."

Sharlotte hissed. This was all new to her.

"I did some sniffing around, and I found out the rumors were true. I hacked into the ARK's servers, downloaded the Oracle database, along with some samples of the various Gulo serums, mostly the Gulo Gamma, and took off." He paused. "But I lost the samples in the zeppelin crash, so I couldn't have helped you. I found the syringes on Ronnie, just now, in the casino."

"I understand," I said gently.

"I can heal like the Vixxes. In that way, they really were like my aunts, but I'm not immortal. When you found me after my zeppelin crashed, I really did need your help. Starvation, dehydration, exposure, all could've killed me." He stopped talking abruptly.

Everything he wasn't saying shouted at me, but at least he was trying to be honest.

"I wouldn't have given Wren the Gulo Gamma," he said. "The test subjects didn't react well, and most of them had to be isolated and terminated. There were … mutations."

Sharlotte caught my eye in the rearview mirror.

Micaiah hurried on. "But the Gulo Delta seems safe. Hopefully. We'll just have to watch her."

"So, Wren might not be completely human anymore." I shuddered to think what Wren would be like as a mutant. And I prayed for her to be okay. If she had to mutate, maybe she'd mutate her soul a little. It could use it, but then you could say the same thing about all of us.

"The cure," Sharlotte muttered. "The cure for the Sterility Epidemic. And carried around in the pocket of Tibbs Hoyt's son. Dang."

We lapsed back into silence. I had so many more questions, I didn't know where to start, and I didn't have the chance to ask more.

The jeep roared across the salt flats in the moonlight, and it wasn't long until we found our train. Empty. Wendover's electric lights glowed on the horizon.

Had they abandoned the train? Or had Rachel Vixx and her Regios found them?

We followed the cattle tracks, all of us hushed, praying for yet one more miracle.

### (iii)

Micaiah saw our cattle first, wandering in the wilderness.

Still no people. My heart felt sick inside of me. I needed to see Pilate again, to hug Aunt Bea, to see our employees and hired hands who were now family.

The smell of cigar smoke brought a big smile to my face.

Our people on their horses, our family, came into view.

We pulled up in the jeep, and the celebration began. Laughter echoed through the night. I found myself in a big party of hugging, kisses, and tears. Dolly Day howled and gave me a stinky hug. Pilate threw his arms around Micaiah. Aunt Bea and Sharlotte held each other, them strong Juniper women. Allie Chambers laughed. Kasey Romeo told me she was glad to see me in a scratchy voice. For the rest of her life, she'd talk in a scratch 'cause of the sniper's bullet.

Nikki Breeze embraced me and smiled, though she had tearstains on her cheeks for Tenisha.

I even kissed Crete, 'cause I was so happy.

Aunt Bea and Pilate told us how they had to abandon the train after the engine failed and they didn't know how to fix it. Besides, how could we pull into Wendover on a stolen train? Prolly not a good idea. We wouldn't have all the correct paperwork, which outside of the Juniper was very important. Our people thought other ARK assets might come after them, but no one did. No sign of the four Johnny boy blimps that had chased the *Moby Dick* through the storm.

Pilate held me for a long time. "I thought I'd never see you again. I can't believe you're still alive. I wanted to run to help, but Sharlotte …"

I pulled back. "You let Sharlotte leave. I can't believe you didn't go with her."

"Believe me, I argued with your sister, but in the end, you can't argue with a Weller woman for long. She wanted me to take over the drive, and I agreed."

"Dang, Pilate, are you losing your contrariness in your old age?" I asked.

"If so, thank God." The way he said it, bittersweet and wistful, brought new tears to my eyes.

"You reckon we ever run out of tears?" I asked Pilate. "'Cause I've cried oceans in the last few weeks."

"Nope, never, but then the well of laughter runs as deep or deeper," he said. Coughing rattled his lungs, and he had to hock and spit.

"Prolly shouldn't smoke no more," I said.

"Prolly not," he said, echoing my grammar. He then took in a deep breath. "Smell that, Cavvy."

I sniffed the air. "I don't smell nothin' but that foul cigar."

He laughed. "It's life we smell. We're alive. Alive. Even Wren. Even Wren."

I told him how Micaiah gave her the Gulo Delta serum.

"Sounds like a college fraternity ... those damn Gulo Deltas," Pilate said, smirking. And I wanted to kiss that smirk.

More tears for us all. And maybe getting older meant getting more calloused, but maybe the point of maturing isn't not to cry at all. Maybe it's to cry as much as we laugh.

### (iv)

That night, with no food, no water, we let the cows lead us, which they did. They knew the lights of Wendover meant food, water, and rest. A bright moon glowed in the sky over a plain of salt that smelled like the leftovers of an ocean, long gone.

Two horses, Elvis and Prince, carried the bodies of our dead, wrapped in cloth. We didn't want to bury Petal and Tenisha out there in that salty soil. Nope. Like that old song about being buried on the lone prairie. Along with the fallen bodies of our friends, I mourned my eleven lost horses. Poor Katy. Poor Mick. I prayed they'd be strong and follow their noses to water and get to good Mormon people who would take care of them.

I rode and petted Puff Daddy. Sharlotte on Maddy trotted next to us. Sharlotte caught my eye and smiled. I smiled back.

"You okay?" I asked. "I mean, after you left …" Didn't know how to finish the sentence.

Sharlotte knew what I needed to hear. Her words came out velvety. "Yeah, I'm okay. I worked through some things, including how hurt I was that you and Wren got to leave. You went off to school, Wren went to hell, and there's big, reliable Sharlotte with Mama, working on the ranch. Left behind. I thought I'd like leaving, being like Wren, always gone from camp, doing her own thing, but you know, Cavvy? It's lonesome. Without family and work, it can get real lonely."

"And now you're back," I said.

"Yes, I am," Sharlotte said. "And if it's all right by you, I'll take over running things. Is that okay?"

"Be my guest," I said. "You can deal with Dolly Day and her mutinous ways."

She let out a long sigh. "Yeah, it's a lot of work, but it was work I was born to. I prolly won't ever get to leave again, and that's fine." With how she sounded, I knew she didn't think it was fine at all. But then she got a little smiley. "You know what I realized, when I was alone, walking the plains? We did better than Mama would've. You and me, Cavvy, we did better. I heard how well you did leading. I'm proud of you. And I know Mama would've been proud of you, too."

"Shar," I said gently, "you don't hate Mama, do you? She was a hard woman, I know, but she loved us. You felt that right?"

Sharlotte's face fell into stone. "I can't talk about that now, Cavvy. I'm hurt by her dying, and I just can't talk about it." She closed her eyes to settle herself and then opened them, like she opened her heart to me. "I love you, Cavatica. I'm grateful that you're my sister."

"I love you, too." I had to whisper it 'cause emotion clogged my throat.

The silence that followed glued us together.

Some sisters don't automatically love one another. Us Weller girls were examples of that. For some, the love of sisters must be built, brick by brick, minute by minute, out of nothing but tears and blood. If you can build that love, it will outlive the pyramids, and nothing will be able to tear it down, ever.

As we rode, my thoughts turned to Wendover— electricity, money, civilization, but also the end of our journey, where me and Micaiah would split up.

It was early morning, none of us had slept, and the headcount started having trouble. We needed water. Our beefsteaks weren't getting all they needed—more and more were dropping. Great, we'd get to Wendover with half of our headcount gathering flies on the salt flats.

Talk was low, spirits dull, as we counted our wounds and remembered our dead.

Until the *Moby Dick* came floating out of the sky as quiet as a cloud. She was bashed in, shedding Neofiber panels, her skin patched, re-patched, patched again, sagging, drooping, no windshield, flying low.

She landed. Tech slid down the ladder with stakes and a sledgehammer to anchor the zeppelin down. We rode over to them. Peeperz followed. And once Tech got the zeppelin secured, Sketchy climbed to the ground.

And more hugging.

Sketchy kissed my cheeks. Peeperz wrapped himself around my leg and then fell into a pile of dogs as Bella, Edward and Jacob licked his face. Tech smiled warmly at me.

Sketchy talked like machine-gun fire. "So them Johnnies wanted to play rough. Tech and Peeperz on the triple Xs shot two of them out of the air. The other two got blown back, prolly to the SLC, and Lord, did we look for you, but the wind was so bad, and we sprouted leaks, and Peeperz on a rope, patching what he could find, and Tech helping, and oh, it's horrible about Tenisha and Petal, and oh, I'm family now. Like it or not. And we made it. And I got some water and some hay, but we had to jettison most of it...."

And on it went.

I could have listened to her forever. They'd made it, along with the *Moby*, which I loved as much as I'd loved Bob D.

Now the real work of the night began. We bucked the last of bales of hay from the *Moby* and set up the collapsible troughs for water. Before long, our beefsteaks were slurping and eating like it was a discount buffet line.

Aunt Bea started a fire against the cold desert night—wood pallets, cottonwood logs, and some old sagebrush taken from the *Moby*. The smell of the wood burning, so distinct, made me think of Mama starting the stove on cold winter mornings. I thanked her for having daughters, all of my troublesome sisters.

Something made me look for Micaiah, but I couldn't find him. My heart trembled. Would he just leave us without saying goodbye?

No, I found him picking Delia's hooves, like he'd done it all his life. When he was done, I watched from a distance as he combed her, patted her, and walked off, gazing up at the night sky, hands on his hips. Right then, with his cowboy hat on, he looked as Juniper as beans, green chili, and buffalo jerky.

I knew what was coming. Sure I did. He'd go away to the World. I'd take my paycheck and maybe try for Cleveland and get my life back at the Sally Browne Burke Academy for the Moral and Literate, though I'd have to settle the warrants still out for my arrest.

I steeled myself, limped over, and started off with a joke.

"You've gone country," I said to him.

He smiled, a little shyly. "Prolly need new boots." Those awful alligator boots had nearly disintegrated off his feet.

"Prolly? Do you mean probably?" I stressed the b's. "I'm very firm on correct pronunciation."

He looked me in the eyes and smirked, almost as well as Pilate. "Yes, very firm."

He took me in his arms and kissed me like we'd never part. Or maybe he kissed me like he knew he'd never see me again.

Sweet, but oh so sad.

# Chapter Twenty-One

*I've worked my whole life, every day, no vacation. My fondest memories aren't of paychecks or victories, but of my daughters. Back when they were little, I'd check in on my girls before I went to bed. They still don't know it, but I'd look at them while they slept. Sharlotte, Irene, and my little Cavatica. I'm blessed. Not because of my successes, but because of my children. In the end, the Juniper teaches us what's important, but shame on me, it's a lesson I needed to be taught over and over.*

—Abigail Weller
Unpublished Notes from the *Colorado Courier*
Interview
June 6, 2057

## (i)

STANDING UNDER THE MOONLIGHT, IN THE STILL OF the night, Micaiah kissed me one last time, then pulled me close to him. I put my head on his shoulder.

He asked an obvious question. "Do you think we can get the headcount into Wendover tomorrow? Do you think we're close enough?"

"Yeah," I said sleepily. The bloody eternity of the day before, the long night, it was catching up to me. My eyes felt pinched and dry. My ankle and shoulder ached like they'd never heal, but the pain grew distant with my boy holding me.

"It all will change in a few hours," he said. "I figure I'll catch a plane to San Francisco. Well, that is if you'll lend me airfare."

I pulled away so he could see my grin. "Richest kid in the world looking for a handout. Now that is what I call irony."

"My dad will still be looking for me. And Rachel Vixx—the last of the Vixxes—along with the Severins."

"Yeah, but you'll outwit 'em. You're clever like that." I put my cheek back up against him, so warm and comfy.

"Not as clever as you. You saved me, Cavvy. I can never repay you."

"Prolly not," I muttered. Felt like I could drift off to sleep right there.

"I'm still serious about the reward money. I promised you six million dollars, and I'll get it. Somehow."

I had to chuckle. "I suppose you better, but I don't think we're too worried about it. We have all our beefsteaks to sell. To think, in a few hours we'll have ten million dollars. Dang." And I knew Micaiah would get us the money he'd promised. With who he was, with what he had, drumming up cash would be the least of his worries.

"Sharlotte and I talked," he said quietly. "I apologized for playing her. She said she understood. She also said if I hurt you she'd take Tina Machinegun and blow my head off to make sure I stayed dead."

I laughed. Sharlotte would make it. She didn't need to be Mama. And she didn't need a boy to be okay. She was strong and sure in herself.

His body vibrated as he asked me another obvious question. "If I left you, if I rode off into the sunset like in some old cowboy video, well, that would hurt you, wouldn't it?"

I nodded against his warm body. "Yeah, it would."

"Then I won't leave you." He pressed himself against me harder. "I won't leave you. No matter what."

Our words. Our covenant.

"No matter what." I echoed. Emotion filled my throat so I couldn't swallow. I stepped back, to look him full in the face. "Micaiah, you don't mean …"

He nodded. "Let's take the truth to the world together. Come with me. Please, come with me."

"You won't be able to get rid of me," I said, and we kissed again.

This time the kiss went from sweet, to passionate, to more—got dangerously close to complete immorality—but I wasn't ready for that, and I dang sure didn't want to lose my virginity on the Great Salt Flats. Maybe on Juniper dirt, but that was a different story. Whole other book if you want to know the truth.

"Micaiah, I need to know more about your past."

His eyes went down. He pinched his lips together into a line. I waited, watching him struggle to be honest. Trying.

"Are you human?" I asked.

"With you I am."

Right then, that was good enough for me.

## (ii)

Sunday, May 12, 2058, we were less than three miles outside of Wendover. Thanks to some grand larceny on my part, it only took us six weeks to get there. Later, we'd hear everything that happened while we were gone.

Burlington fell. Three days of fighting and our little militia, bolstered by Dob Howerter's people, surrendered right around the time we were trying to sneak through Denver.

Two weeks after that, June Mai Angel marched into Lamar. Worse fighting, but Burlington beef and new conscripts gave June Mai Angel the advantage. She set herself up as Governor of the Colorado territory.

And dared President Amanda Swain to come and take it away.

Dob Howerter escaped to Hays to gather guns and an army.

On the other hand, Mavis Meetchum, like Jenny Bell Scheutz, made June Mai Angel a deal and got to keep her land. Everyone took to cursing Mavis, but she was a tough woman and could take the abuse. She prolly liked the poetry of June Mai Angel's cause.

Even in Nevada, we'd hear rumors of giants and strange things in Denver. Bloodthirsty things. People called them Hogs.

Micaiah had said he'd stolen tanks of the Gulo formula to use as evidence of what his father was doing. He thought that the chemicals had gone up in flames when the zeppelin crashed, but in the end, as we'd learn, that wasn't the case.

In my mind's eye, I could see one of June Mai Angel's girls or a Psycho Madeline coming across the tanks, opening them up, and getting sprayed by gas. They'd change. Mutate. Making all the fairytales and scary stories of the Juniper come true.

For us, that was hundreds of kilometers and many months away, but we'd face them later on; those Hogs and June Mai Angel as well.

## (iii)

Outside of Wendover, we all gathered around the fire, sitting on our saddles. Wren was awake, laughing weakly, open-mouthed, so we could see where Renee Vixx had busted out her teeth.

Kasey Chambers sat next to Nikki Breeze, holding her hand. Nikki didn't smile, since she was missing Tenisha something awful.

Crete kept glaring at me 'cause I was huddled up against Micaiah, who held me close.

Aunt Bea cursed, and Sharlotte shushed her good-naturedly, and it was like old times. We ate protein bars from the *Moby*, drank bottled water, but guess who had some coffee in his pocket? Father Pilate, who would soon be celibate again 'cause me and Micaiah were gonna go back to the World and cure the Sterility Epidemic.

Pilate shared his coffee. We wouldn't be sleeping anyway. We'd push on for Wendover, sell our headcount, and then sleep in hotels with access to the Eternity video library on the Internet, where you could watch *Bonanza*, *Lonesome Dove*, *The Good, the Bad, and the Ugly*, or the *Preacher* movies.

They'd also have vintage *Firefly* 'cause you can't stop the signal. Not ever.

Of course, *Lonely Moon* would be on, but we didn't have to watch it. We'd lived it. Thinking of the Juniper drama, I missed my best friend, Anju Rawat, and said a prayer for her and Billy Finn. What a full life I'd been given, and I was grateful for it—for my time in Cleveland and for the Juniper, my homeland.

We talked about the comforts of the World we loved, and Sketchy bragged about her Kung Pao battery finally working, which made the *Moby* the fastest Jonesy-class zeppelin on the planet.

Civilization called, but that morning, it was the Juniper for us, even though technically we had power. We didn't have electronics anyway. We had something better. The fire sparked, and we laughed and talked.

Dolly Day even passed around her flask, refilled from somewhere.

When the flask went by Wren, she passed it on. "It's the first drink that gets you drunk," she said, quoting Pilate's AA.

Pilate saluted her with his coffee mug. His left hand was still bandaged. We lost everything, but Pilate still had his stainless-steel Starbuck's mug. And a cigar on his lips. His last good one. He was smoking it, even though it made him cough like his lungs were full of mud.

Sketchy took Dolly Day's flask and tipped it back.

Wren grinned good-naturedly. "Hey, Sketch, I heard you wanted to join our family. Well, to be a true Weller, you have to get drunk and make an ass out of yourself. You reckon you can do that?"

Sketchy hopped up, pulled up her skirts, and mooned us. We all howled. Seeing that big white butt prolly gave me a good dose of PTSD if nothing else had.

"How's that for an ass?" Sketchy brayed. "And I'd love to be a Weller. You did it! You brought your headcount west, and you did it." Sketchy looked up at the star-spilled sky, and bawled out, "Abigail Weller! Your daughters did it! Your blood runs true in their veins."

Tech shook her head at her friend and business partner. Then she caught my eye and smiled, then glanced away.

It hit me all at once. Tech was *gillian* and liked me. Well, that was okay. Nothing wrong with being *gillian*. Sally Browne Burke was only human, and the New Morality only knew so much, which was a lot but not everything. You could say the same thing about Archbishop Corfu, or even the Pope in Rome.

Peeperz sat next to Tech, smiling, but not laughing. He reached down to pet Edward, Jacob, and Bella. Those dogs adored him.

Wren raised a cup of coffee. "To my sister, Sharlotte Weller, who led us, even when she wasn't around!"

We hip-hip-hurrayed. Wren then smiled at me. "And to my little sister, Cavatica Weller, who dared to take over and steal that train. To my sisters!"

More whooping and hollering.

"Yes," Pilate said, "to my little brown spider. I love you."

He and I shared a secret moment with a connection that went down to our DNA.

Pilate turned, "And to you, Wren. For your shooting and your wild ways. I love you. And to you, Sharlotte. I love you enough that you can hate me all you want."

Sharlotte frowned. "Aw, Pilate, I'm tired of hating you. It's a full-time job. You go and be you all you want. I'll ignore what I don't like. Which is most of it."

Pilate stood. "Okay, I'll be me for a minute." He cleared his throat, and said, "We are alive. We are alive, but let us remember the fallen." His voice broke. "May they find their other side. Both our friends and our enemies. May we all find the other side of our pain."

He started the *Our Father*, and we all said it together. Even Wren.

Even Micaiah, holding me, who seemed to have learned it overnight. Eerie smart and, I knew, not quite human. Getting the truth out of him would be a hard fight, but I wouldn't let it cool my spirits. I wanted to be happy, though my mind kept going back to the chalkdrive and the slate, both shielded against the effects of the Juniper's EM field. What did that mean?

Allie Chambers stood. "I'd like to sing. For Annabeth. For Jenny Bell. For Tenisha. For Petal. Most of all, I'd like to sing for Abigail."

Pilate grumbled and smirked at the same time. "Dammit, Allie, we survived June Mai Angel, a blizzard, the Psycho Princesses, and cloned super soldiers, but I don't think we can survive another one of your songs. I swear, on our next impossible cattle drive, I'm bringing earplugs."

"No," Allie said, "this song is different. I'll start, but you all know it. Of course you do."

She started singing. Her voice, pretty and haunting, floated over that early morning cold desert landscape. Our fire reached for the sky with fingers of sparks. Our cows lowed around us. Our horses neighed.

The song she sang, well, Mama would sing it to us. It was a song about family. About connections. About ties that transcend our hates and our sorrows.

Allie sang it sweet.

> *I was weeping by my window*
> *On a cold and windy day*
> *Were those angels coming toward me?*
> *Would they carry my mama away?*

That was for Sharlotte, left alone in the house, going through Mama's papers and finding the medical report about our daddy being sterile after Wren was born. And it was for Pilate at Mama's funeral, questioning the love of God, making us all question our faith.

Allie sang the chorus, and we all joined in. Micaiah didn't know it, so he stayed quiet. I loved him a little for not knowing. Not sure why.

> *Will the circle be unbroken,*
> *By and by, Lord, by and by?*
> *Is a better home awaiting*
> *In the sky, Lord, in the sky?*

Allie sang the next part.

> *Well I tried to stop my crying,*
> *Tried to harden and be brave.*
> *But I could not stop the weeping.*
> *Was my mama still in her grave?*

That was me, crying over Mama's body and trying to be like Wren, a tough gunslinger, when I was a girly 'strogen computer tech girl. However, when it came down to it, I'd take my mind over a gun any time.

Again, the chorus. We all sang it with all of our strength. We kept our tears back to keep our voices strong.

Allie sang another verse.

*Oh, my ranch house, it was lonesome*
*Missed my mama, but was she gone?*
*Could we ever stop a-mourning*
*On a farm so sad, so alone?*

That was us, fighting and bickering among ourselves 'cause we were so sad and scared and we felt so alone. Me getting drunk in Burlington and throwing up after Sharlotte told everyone Mama's crazy plan to save our ranch. And Sharlotte at Jenny Bell's. And Wren, always so sad and alone.

We'd taken our headcount through to Wendover, but our home was occupied now. June Mai Angel had it, and she'd prolly stationed troops there. An outlaw was prolly sleeping in my own bed. Didn't that just beat all?

As for the future, our hires would live off their paycheck until they found other work. Getting a job would be easy for them, 'cause they'd soon have a reputation for doing the impossible. Aunt Bea, Nikki Breeze, Crete, they had so much experience, anyone would be happy to have them working for them. But we'd miss them, miss them painfully. Well, maybe not Crete, but Aunt Bea and Nikki for sure.

Wren could go back to Amarillo, though we all knew if she did that, she'd relapse. Maybe she and Sharlotte could find work with Mavis Meetchum, but a Weller working for a Meetchum would be hard to stomach. Knowing my sisters, they'd grab Pilate and

301

prolly team up with Howerter and go after June Mai Angel. Try to get our ranch back, since we'd crossed hell to save it.

Micaiah and I would go off and change the world and love each other until the end of time. Sure we would.

We were all alive. We'd have money soon. And we had hope. If you gave a Weller girl hope and a few dollars, she'd find either work or trouble. Prolly both.

We'd be okay. Our lives would play out as directed by unseen hands. Sometimes pinched by God's evil left hand, but most of the time, He'd carry us in His ever-loving, ever-present right.

Another chorus. And we sang out our hope. That our circle would stay unbroken. That we would be together, if not in this world, then the next.

The last verse Allie changed 'cause she was Irish and smart and good.

> *Do you remember the hymns of*
> *childhood*
> *Songs of faith that spoke of love?*
> *Can you hear the angels singing*
> *With Mother Weller in heaven above?*

Though Abigail Weller taught us the hymns, each of her daughters sang them in her own unique way.

Micaiah held me, Wren and Sharlotte sat close to one another, Pilate, armed with coffee and a cigar, sighed, still sorrowful over Petal, but still breathing in life.

We sang the chorus one last time, my favorite part, 'cause it answered all of the song's questions.

> *Will the circle be unbroken,*
> *By and by, Lord, by and by?*
> *Yes! A better home awaits us*

The Juniper Wars: Machine-Gun Girls

*In the sky, Lord, in the sky!*

# Memorare

*I drove to Reno, but she found me*
*I was hiding in smiles, but she found me*
*Trouble came in with three beers warming*
*And that was family, always family*

*Give me casinos over churches*
*Give me bibles over guns*
*Throw down an ace of hearts,*
*Then run, Mary, run*

—LeAnna Wright
Singer and Songwriter, from *Cash and Jacks*
released by Glitterhouse Records on May 1, 2058

**(i)**

*Remember me, O most gracious Virgin Mary,*
*remember me.*

I WISH MY STORY ENDED AROUND THE CAMPFIRE, OR with Micaiah and me, starting our happily-ever-after the next morning. I wish my adventures stopped there and life allowed me to grow unimpeded into a strong, upright Christian woman, but that didn't happen.

They say God uses our failures and weaknesses to bring us closer to Him, but along the way, we suffer, Lord, how we suffer from our sins.

Dawn threw a crimson light on us and our headcount, stretching out into the horizon, a sea of white-faced, red-coated Herefords, pooling like a bloodstain on the white salt.

Sharlotte, Wren, and I sat on our ponies in front of the ocean of cattle, waiting for Pilate to return. Since he had an American passport, he'd gone into Nevada to run recon.

A fence, like the one I saw in Buzzkill, separated Yankee soil from Juniper dirt. We'd not seen any sign of the Johnnies that had pursued the *Moby Dick*, but that didn't mean we were safe. Sketchy thought the big ARK zeppelins had prolly been blown back to the SLC, but we didn't know for sure.

"You think soldiers will be in Wendover waiting on us?" Sharlotte asked.

Wren slept in the saddle. She didn't answer. She should've been lying flat to heal up from dying, but Wren had insisted she was fine. Of course. Us Wellers were always fine. Chop off one of our legs and we'd shrug and ask for a Band-Aid.

"I hope not," I whispered. "But they can't just grab us now. There are laws in America. There's a whole constitution protecting the rights of her citizens."

"But we aren't her citizens," Sharlotte said.

I tried to swallow the fear creeping up my throat, but it stayed stuck. She was right.

Wren spoke, so unexpected, it made me jump. "I'm hoping Rachel Vixx is there. I hate days when I can't kill skanks."

"That's our Irene," Sharlotte said in an easy voice. "If she don't get her morning coffee, she gets grumpy."

Instead of bristling and demanding Sharlotte call her Wren, my sister grinned. "Y'all would be grumpy too if you'd died last night. And I don't recommend getting gut-shot. It hurts like a jacknasty." Wren winked at me. "I know, I know, gotta watch my language. And yet, sometimes only cussing will do. You still have that lucky bullet I threw at Micaiah?"

I tapped the lump in my pocket. "You want it back? Not sure if it's lucky or not. Almost got us killed. Remember Edger?"

"She was a silly skank," Wren said. "You keep it, Cavvy. And I say it's lucky 'cause we aren't dead, are we?"

"Far from it." Sharlotte raised her head and smiled.

We waited.

Our cattle mooed up a fuss behind us while our people, including Micaiah, kept the perimeters closed as best they could to avoid losing strays. The *Moby* floated in the still air of the morning, hovering over the backs of the cows. The storm of the previous day had blown itself on east.

Pilate galloped back to us on the new Clydesdale we'd taken from the Psycho Madelines. Pilate called him Rocinante, which was quite a name for the big horse. Pilate then started singing some old rock song about a spaceship named the Rocinante. Another reference I was too young to get.

Pilate and the pony drew close, and Rocinante sneezed, flinging snot and water. At least he'd gotten a good drink in town.

"Any sign of the ARK?" Sharlotte asked.

Pilate smiled so broadly his teeth showed and his eyes crinkled. "Not a single sign. I talked with the woman running the stockyards. She literally dropped her slate when I told her that the Wellers were coming in with three thousand cows for her to process."

Sharlotte corrected him. "We lost about five hundred since we started, so it's more like twenty-five hundred."

I was speechless. The mere mention of electronics had me pining for the Hayao slate I'd sold back in Chicago. Well, soon, I'd buy another one. Even though we'd lost a fair portion of our herd, we'd still get around 8.3 million dollars at $5.56 per kilo, enough to pay off Howerter and save the ranch.

Sharlotte stood up in her stirrups and whistled loud enough to ring my ears. She reined Maddy around. "I'll be right back. I have to go check with Aunt Bea on something."

Lucky she did. Or, with what happened later, we might've all been killed. Or, at the very least, I'd have been blinded.

Sharlotte moved back through the cows as Pilate, Wren, and I rode forward.

The sun's fire rose higher into the sky as we trotted triumphantly through the razor wire topped chain-link of the border, opened to allow us and our cows through.

I didn't see American guards, and a little seed of anxiety grew roots in my belly. Something wasn't right.

Aaron Michael Ritchey

I turned to Pilate, looked at Wren, but I didn't say anything.

I should've. I should've warned them.

'Cause the ARK was in Wendover. We just didn't know it then.

Dang, but I wish my story had ended happily around the fire, singing old school songs with Micaiah's arm around me, but it didn't.

Rachel Vixx had beat us to Nevada, and there she waited like death on a pale horse.

And hell followed with her.

**To be continued …**

Cavatica Weller will return in *Inferno Girls*, Book Three of the Juniper Wars series

# Glossary of Historical Figures, Slang, and Technology

**Angel, June Mai**—The most powerful of the outlaw warlords and the most organized. Her past is a mystery, but her soldiers are fierce. She controls the Denver area, from Colorado Springs to Fort Collins.

**ASI Attachment**—A steam engine that can interface with the drive trains of larger vehicles, such as trucks or minivans. Manufactured by the American Steam Ingenuity Company.

**ARK**—The American Reproduction Knowledge Initiative; A publicly funded corporation researching the Sterility Epidemic and running insemination clinics across the world.

**AZ3**—The next generation of assault rifle manufactured by Armalite Industries. Includes self-correcting laser targeting, tactical readout/ammunition count, and water-cooled barrels.

**Beefsteaks**—Cattle

**Besharam**—Shameless (from the Hindi word)

**Besiya**—Prostitute (from the Hindi word)

**Burke, Sally Browne**—Co-founder of the New Morality movement

**Chalkdrive**—Removable computer storage device

**Cargador**—A large steam-powered vehicle used in the Juniper for salvaging operations and later as military vehicles.

**Colton, Anna**—Professor of Sociology, Princeton University, and a firm supporter of women's rights outside of religious or domestic roles.

**Corfu, Archbishop Jeremy**—An archbishop of the Roman Catholic Church in the U.S. and highly critical of the ARK and any artificial insemination outside of marriage.

**CTRA**—The Colorado Territory Ranching Association—An organization created by Robert "Dob" Howerter, presumably to ensure high quality beef and ethical ranching practices, but in reality was used to fix prices and drive other ranchers out of business.

**EMAT**—Emergency Medication Absorption Tape; A delivery system for medication during combat situations.

**Eterna Batteries**—A perfectly clean power source created by General Electric. Named after Chinese food, the most powerful and efficient is the Kung Pao. A weaker version is the Egg Drop.
**Frictionless Automobiles**—The next generation in

automotive engineering, frictionless cars float thirty centimeters off the ground.

**Gillian**—Lesbian (from the Mandarin phrase *tong xing lian*)

**Girly 'strogen**—Excessively feminine ('strogen is short for estrogen)

**Headcount**—The number of cattle owned by a ranch.

**Howerter, Robert "Dob"**—Founder of the Colorado Territory Ranching Association and the largest cattle baron in the Juniper.

**Hoyt, Tiberius "Tibbs"**—President and CEO of the American Reproduction Knowledge Initiative.

**Jankowski, Maggie**—Lead engineer on the Eterna battery project funded by General Electric.

**Johnson**—A derogatory term for a male.

**Jones, Calvin "Crush"**—Founder of the Old Glory Salvage and Renewal Company and the first to become what was later known as the Juniper Millionaires.

**Juniper**—1,438,577 square kilometers in the middle of the United States of America comprising what once was Colorado, New Mexico, Utah, Wyoming, Montana, and sections of surrounding states. Due to the Yellowstone Knockout and the subsequent flood basalt, electrical current does not function in this area.

**Kanton, Jack Anthony**—48th President of the United States of America and the second president to hold four terms in office.

**Kutia**—Female dog (from the Hindi word)

**MG21**—Standard issue assault rifle in the Sino-American War.

**Male Product**—The male reproductive cell

**Masterson-Wayne Act**—Signed into law by President Jack Kanton in 2033, this act of Congress relegated the five states affected by the Yellowstone Knockout back to being territories.

**Meetchum, Mavis**—Second largest cattle operator in the Colorado territory. Located in Sterling, she has established treaties with the Wind River people and is a strong advocate for Native American rights. She introduced buffalo back into Wyoming in the mid-2030s during a critical time for the Wind River people.

**MRE**—Meal, Ready-to-Eat

**Neofiber**—A variant of carbon fiber but stronger and lighter.

**New Morality**—A religious movement with socio-political connections that encouraged women to remain chaste, dress appropriately, and behave in a conservative manner.

**New Morality Dress**—A dress of a neutral color (usually gray, brown, or cream-colored) that covers as much of a woman's body as possible to comply with New Morality etiquette.

**Old Growth**—A synthetic coal created from wood taken from old-growth forests.

**Parson, Reverend Kip**—Co-founder of the New Morality movement.

**RSD**—Reality Simulator Displays; Video screens with near-perfect resolution

**Sapropel**—A weak fuel used for heating and lighting in the Juniper. Chemically manufactured by using remnants of oil shale.

**Shakti**—Raw female power (from the Hindi word)

**SISBI**—The Security, Identity, and Special Borders Injunction (SISBI) is a set of laws enacted by a special executive order that requires all U.S. citizens to register eye-scans with the government. It also allows for border fences around the Juniper and military units to secure the perimeter of the territories.

**Skye6**—Diacetylmorphinesextus (a synthetic morphine)

**Slate**—Tablet computer

**Sterility Epidemic**—First cases discovered in January

of 2030. One in ten births are male. Of males born, 90% are sterile.

**Thelium**—Theta-helium—Synthetic helium manufactured to give zeppelins greater lift.

**Thor Stunner**—Eterna-powered electrical non-lethal weapon

**Viable**—Non-sterile (refers to males)

**Weller, Abigail**—Growing up in the family business (The Buckeye Urban Recycling and Reclamation Company), Abigail Weller chose to enter the Juniper to run salvage for Crush Jones. After the Salvage Era, she operated the third largest ranch in the Colorado territory until her death in the winter of 2058. She had three daughters: Sharlotte, Wren, and Cavatica.

**Wind River People**—The general term for all Native American tribes living in the Wyoming and Montana territories.

**Yellowstone Knockout**—A term used to describe China's missile attack on the Yellowstone caldera and the subsequent flood basalt.

**Zeppelins**—Four classes of airships: Jonesies, Jimmies, Johnnies, and Bobbies. All manufactured by Boeing for use in the Juniper. Jimmies are engineered for maximum speed and Johnnies for maximum cargo hold. Bobbies are a mid-size zeppelin. Lastly, Jonesies are the most customizable. Also known as dirigibles or blimps, the airships have rigid skeletons of Neofiber covered with next-generation lightweight Kevlar. The superstructure contains air cells filled with thelium.

**Zeus 2 Charge Gun**—Eterna-powered electric rifle for short-range lethal combat and area-of-attack demolition.

# Books, Mailing List, and Reviews

If you enjoyed reading about Cavatica and the rest of the gang in The Juniper Wars and want to stay in the loop about the latest book releases, awesome promotional deals, and upcoming book giveaways be sure to subscribe to our email list at:

www.ShadowAlleyPress.com

Word-of-mouth and book reviews are crazy helpful for the success of any writer. If you *really* enjoyed reading *Machine-Gun Girls*, please consider leaving a short, honest review—just a couple of lines about your overall reading experience. Thank you in advance!

# Books by Shadow Alley Press

If you enjoyed *Machine-Gun Girls*, you might also enjoy other awesome stories from Shadow Alley Press, such as Viridian Gate Online, Rogue Dungeon, the Yancy Lazarus Series, War God's Mantle, American Dragons, Dungeon Bringer, Full Frontal Galaxy, or the Jubal Van Zandt Series. You can find all of our books listed at www.ShadowAlleyPress.com.

## James A. Hunter

Viridian Gate Online: Cataclysm (Book 1)
Viridian Gate Online: Crimson Alliance (Book 2)
Viridian Gate Online: The Jade Lord (Book 3)
Viridian Gate Online: The Imperial Legion (Book 4)
Viridian Gate Online: The Lich Priest (Book 5)
Viridian Gate Online: Doom Forge (Book 6)

Viridian Gate Online: The Artificer (Imperial Initiative)
Viridian Gate Online: Nomad Soul (Illusionist 1)
Viridian Gate Online: Dead Man's Tide (Illusionist 2)
Viridian Gate Online: Inquisitor's Foil (Illusionist 3)
Viridian Gate Online: Firebrand (Firebrand 1)
Viridian Gate Online: Embers of Rebellion (Firebrand 2)
Viridian Gate Online: Path of the Blood Phoenix (Firebrand 3)

Aaron Michael Ritchey

Viridian Gate Online: Vindication (The Alchemic
Weaponeer 1)
Viridian Gate Online: Absolution (The Alchemic
Weaponeer 2)

⏊

Rogue Dungeon (Book 1)
Rogue Dungeon: Civil War (Book 2)
Rogue Dungeon: Troll Nation (Book 3)

⏊

Strange Magic: Yancy Lazarus Episode One
Cold Heatred: Yancy Lazarus Episode Two
Flashback: Siren Song (Episode 2.5)
Wendigo Rising: Yancy Lazarus Episode Three
Flashback: The Morrigan (Episode 3.5)
Savage Prophet: Yancy Lazarus Episode Four
Brimstone Blues: Yancy Lazarus Episode Five

⏊

MudMan: A Lazarus World Novel

⏊

Two Faced: Legend of the Treesinger (Book 1)
Soul Game: Legend of the Treesinger (Book 2)

⏊

**Eden Hudson**

Revenge of the Bloodslinger: A Jubal Van Zandt Novel

The Juniper Wars: Machine-Gun Girls

Beautiful Corpse: A Jubal Van Zandt Novel
Soul Jar: A Jubal Van Zandt Novel
Garden of Time: A Jubal Van Zandt Novel
Wasteside: A Jubal Van Zandt Novel

⊥

Darkening Skies (Path of the Thunderbird 1)
Stone Soul (Path of the Thunderbird 2)

**Aaron Crash**

War God's Mantle: Ascension (Book 1)
War God's Mantle: Descent (Book 2)
War God's Mantle: Underworld (Book 3)

American Dragons: Denver Fury (Book 1)
American Dragons: Cheyenne Magic (Book 2)
American Dragons: Montana Firestorm (Book 3)
American Dragons: Texas Showdown (Book 4)
American Dragons: California Imperium (Book 5)
American Dragons: Dodge City Knights (Book 6)
American Dragons: Leadville Crucible (Book 7)

⊥

**Nick Harrow**

Dungeon Bringer 1
Dungeon Bringer 2
Dungeon Bringer 3

Aaron Michael Ritchey

Witch King 1

**Aaron Ritchey**

Armageddon Girls (The Juniper Wars 1)
Machine-Gun Girls (The Juniper Wars 2)
Inferno Girls (The Juniper Wars 3)

# About the Author

Aaron Michael Ritchey is the author of *The Never Prayer*, *Long Live the Suicide King*, and *Elizabeth's Midnight*. He was born on a cold and snowy September day in Denver, Colorado, and while he's lived and traveled all over the world, he's a child of the American West. Sagebrush makes him homesick. While he pines for Paris, he still lives in Colorado with his cactus flower of a wife and two stormy daughters.

# A Note from the Author

I hoped you enjoyed reading *Machine-Gun Girls*. The third book, *Inferno Girls*, will be available in the coming months.

A prequel novella based in the world of The Juniper Wars series is available now. *Armageddon Dimes* takes place five years before the events of *Armageddon Girls* and follows the adventures of a returning Sino-American War veteran, Mariposa Hernandez. Bored of civilian life, haunted by the war, Mariposa is invited by a long lost friend on a treasure hunt into the wastelands of Denver. Can Mariposa reclaim a fortune in abandoned dimes before the ghosts of her past consume her?

For more about me, my books, and The Juniper Wars, visit my website at www.aaronmritchey.com.